M000014071

FULFILL MY DESIRES
SEBASTIAN & LOLA PART I

STEELE INTERNATIONAL, INC. A BILLIONAIRES
ROMANCE SERIES BOOK 1

CHARMAINE LOUISE SHELTON

Fulfill My Desires Sebastian & Lola Part I
Copyright © 2020 by Charmaine Louise Shelton

All rights reserved. No part of this book may be reproduced or
transmitted in any form or by any means, electronic or mechanical,
including but not limited to photocopying, recording, or by any
information storage and retrieval system without written permission
from the author.

ISBN: 978-1-7352917-1-0 (Paperback)
ISBN: 978-1-7352917-0-3 (eBook)
Published by CharmaineLouise New York, Inc.
Sexy Fantasies Fulfill Your Desires Publications

Fulfill My Desires Sebastian & Lola Part I is a work of fiction. Names,
characters, businesses, places, events, and incidents are either the product
of the author's imagination or used in a fictitious manner. Any
resemblance to actual persons, living or dead, or actual events is purely
coincidental.

CONTENTS

FREE BOOK

Get the start of the STEELE International, Inc. A Billionaires Romance Series with *Discover My Desires Sebastian & Lola Prequel* **FREE!**

Click Cover Below or visit **bit.ly/CLBooksNewsletter** to subscribe to my newsletter and start reading the steamy billionaire romance short story of Sebastian Steele and Lola Lewis.

Their stories. Their discovery of unknown desires...

FREE BOOK!

EXCLUSIVE FOR SUBSCRIBERS!

ALSO BY CHARMAINE LOUISE SHELTON

STEELE INTERNATIONAL, INC.
A BILLIONAIRES ROMANCE SERIES

Discover My Desires Sebastian & Lola Prequel
(Available Exclusively to Subscribers)

Fulfill My Desires Sebastian & Lola Part I

Heighten My Desires Sebastian & Lola Part II

Ignite My Desires Roger & Leonie Part I

Stoke My Desires Roger & Leonie Part II

Justify My Desires Roger & Leonie Part III

Deepen My Desires Sebastian & Lola Part III

Capture My Desires Malcolm & Starr Part I

Embrace My Desires Malcolm & Starr Part II

Cherish My Desires Malcolm & Starr Part III

A Trilogy of Desires Sebastian & Lola Parts I-III

ABOUT STEELE INTERNATIONAL, INC. A BILLIONAIRES ROMANCE SERIES

Welcome to the titillating world of the multibillion-dollar global company and the love affairs of the family that controls it.

STEELE International, Inc. is a series of interconnecting Billionaire romance. Follow the Steele family as they fly around the world chasing the women they love and their happily ever afters. Get ready for glitz, glamour, and steamy romance books. What's better than that? The Jet-set Lifestyle has never been hotter...

The Desires Series is not for the tea set; it's for the top-shelf vodka straight up in a pretty crystal glass coterie!

Don't miss any of the sizzling romance books in the STEELE International, Inc. A Billionaires Romance Series:

Discover My Desires Sebastian & Lola Prequel
(Available Exclusively to Subscribers)

Fulfill My Desires Sebastian & Lola Part I

Heighten My Desires Sebastian & Lola Part II

Ignite My Desires Roger & Leonie Part I

Stoke My Desires Roger & Leonie Part II

Justify My Desires Roger & Leonie Part III

Deepen My Desires Sebastian & Lola Part III

Capture My Desires Malcolm & Starr Part I

Embrace My Desires Malcolm & Starr Part II

Cherish My Desires Malcolm & Starr Part III

A Trilogy of Desires Sebastian & Lola Parts I-III

A Trilogy of Desires Roger & Leonie Parts I-III

Series Extras

Series Playlist

ABOUT FULFILL MY DESIRES
SEBASTIAN & LOLA PART I

Lola Lewis is feisty, business driven, and focused on her luxury lingerie company—she has no time for relationships. Battles her desire for punishment at LEVELS New York... Wait, what?

Sebastian Steele is heir apparent to his family's luxury real estate empire; a playboy who's never with the same woman twice—a string of steamy encounters at LEVELS. Until his latest hookup, who just happens to be the owner of the company he's meeting with the next morning...

Can they overcome the taboo: never mix business with pleasure?

Travel with Sebastian and Lola from New York City to Monte Carlo to St. Barth's as their love affair sparks in this soul mate romance story.

Sebastian and Lola's love story is a standalone trilogy in the series. Get a glimpse of their dynamism in other books.

Anthem: "Erotica" Madonna
https://www.youtube.com/watch?v=WyhdvRWEWRw

Playlist:
https://www.youtube.com/playlist?
list=PLXwYvn0e218Bfsk5rVIJamWHOMjuDvWCv

Visit CharmaineLouiseBooks.com

"Good evening, Mr. Steele," one of the two stunning greeters purrs as I step into the lobby for LEVELS New York.

This is the flagship location of the global, luxury, members-only BDSM/dance clubs in Manhattan's Meatpacking District. They chose the historic location as a play on the area's name. Put a club where men pack their meat into willing women and willing men allow women to pack them with their toys. The theme for the lobby is minimal and industrial. The fixtures and furniture that appear well worn are high-end, modern replicas used to add authenticity without the grime of old pieces. The two sides have coordinating greeter stations that allow access to the separate Dine & Dance levels and the BDSM levels. The other greeter turns her head in my direction and briefly smiles at me before she returns her attention to a couple entering the BDSM side.

My cousin Lucien Jackson cooked up the idea and roped my younger brother Malcolm into it. Lucien literally cooked it up since he thought of it as he finished his hospitality and culinary training at Le Cordon Bleu in Paris.

Who the hell goes through that prestigious training to come up with a titty bar? Well, five years later his idea proves it's bigger than that and has a high profit margin with more locations in Paris and London. That's all that concerns me: will it add to STEELE International's bottom line? Yes, well, it's a go. No, then no go.

LEVELS is one of many business partnerships that STEELE has with Jackson Corporation. World-renown for their award-winning eateries, choice cigars, and distinguished liquors and wines, their products pair well within STEELE's casinos, hotels, resorts, and residential and retail properties.

On the personal side, my mother is best friends with the Jackson Matriarch. They spent most of their adult lives together forming a closer bond than they have with their blood siblings and relatives. Not sharing DNA doesn't keep our families from being a close-knit group.

"Good evening," I respond as I make my way to the D&D elevator.

Once inside, I place my keycard against the panel to select the third floor for the Level 4 Restaurant. I'm a Global All-Access member. I can choose from any of the seven levels: 7th Sky Lounge that offers a stunning, 360-degree view of Manhattan and across the Hudson River to New Jersey's shoreline, a bar, restaurant by day dance club by night, a coverable pool that's open during the warmer months, and a glass-retractable roof; 6th and 5th multilevel dance club with two bars and a lounge for food and drinks; 4th Level 4 Restaurant and bar open for breakfast, lunch, and dinner; 3rd has twelve private suites for members to continue their pleasure apart from the BDSM levels; 2nd Peepshow for BDSM with seating alcoves, primary stage, mini-stages, performance rooms, and a bar that serves non-alcoholic mocktails; below ground the Cellar a BDSM dungeon with mocktails bar. The Dine/Dance members only have access to the party levels—Sky Lounge, Dance Club, and Level 4 Restaurant.

Tonight, I need to eat and fuck hard in that order. I'm bound to find a female at the restaurant or bar who's willing to be my pet for the evening. One night only, maybe two if she's not clingy or a gold digger, but two fucks is my maximum. I'm not looking for a relationship and damn sure not marriage, just enough time to satisfy my Dom needs and my physical release for the moment. A short-term encounter to balance out my business-focused life.

As president of the Retail Properties Division of STEELE, I bust my ass fourteen hours a day to make it super profitable and to prove that I deserve my future role as CEO of the entire luxury real estate development and management company when my father retires next year. It's not just my last name getting me into the head position. I'm damn capable since I've worked my way up the ranks to learn our multigenerational, multibillion-dollar business combined with my Harvard undergrad and MBA degrees.

My father, Morgan, trusts me to carry the legacy into the future and my younger brothers and sister respect me and accept my leadership. Each sibling works at STEELE: Malcolm president of the Entertainment Properties Division; Roger, president of the Residential Properties Division; Harris and Haley, fraternal twins, co-founders of the subsidiary STEELE Technology and Cyber Security. At 35, I take my role as the eldest seriously, so I don't have time for nor care to get involved in a relationship. Thanks to Lucien and Malcolm, LEVELS provides exactly what I need.

As I step off of the elevator, I take in my surroundings. The bar is bustling as usual with the crème de la crème of society. They hobnob with top-shelf drinks. Seating ranges from the leather and black metal stools at the long, reclaimed-wood-covered bar to the dozen high-top tables styled to match. The bar along the right wall features a floor-to-ceiling mirrored wall of shelves of only the best spirits and wines—most are from the Jackson labels. The bartenders serve signature cocktails. Tables on the left complete the layout of the open-plan room. A path between the two areas leads to the LEVEL 4 Restaurant's maître d' station. There, the patrons eat delicious meals prepared by chefs trained by Lucien. My destination awaits.

As I stride towards the maître d', my gaze alights on several recognizable faces enjoying nightcaps at the bar area's high-top tables. Tonight, the U.S. Attorney for the Southern District of New York, the former governor of California, and a high-powered female CFO of a Wall Street investment bank are present. The club caters to the most wealthy and influential in society. They prefer the relative safety that one can expect from the ironclad nondisclosure agreement that LEVELS requires every member and their guests to sign.

I smile and nod in greeting—every Steele is instantly recognizable—but keep it moving as I'm not here tonight for small talk. As I approach the hostess at the dining area's maître d' podium, I also notice several pairs of lust-filled eyes including those of a few men track my movement as I walk past them. Sadly for the men, I'm strictly a female to a male individual. As I approach the station, the maître d' on duty tonight looks up with an alluring smile on her pretty face.

"Good evening, Mr. Steele," says Susan, as her name tag denotes. She angles her chin down to allow her to peek up at me from beneath her long eyelashes without direct eye contact.

"Your usual table, Sir?"

I don't miss her emphasis on Sir as a sub innuendo. Susan is one of many LEVELS employees who want to have my marks on them and my dick in every one of their holes. Disappointingly for the staff though, I don't mix business with pleasure. That can only end in a messy situation and unnecessarily complicate matters—doesn't fit with my trajectory.

"Good evening, Susan. That's good, thank you," I reply.

Susan's full lips curl up into a dazzling smile as she visibly preens. Her reaction as though I petted her head for a job well done after I fucked her throat and she didn't spill a single drop of my copious amount of cum. Susan seductively sways her hips, long legs stressed by stilettos and her form-fitted, black mini dress molded to her curvy body. She leads me to my table in the center of the room with an unobstructed view of the large dining area and of the bar. A spot from which I can easily observe all the patrons to cherry-pick my companion for tonight. However, the sight before me has me second-guessing my no business/pleasure rule. Susan deliberately bends over the table to straighten the napkin, giving me a visual of her cuffed to my pommel horse and a cane in my hand. Damn if my cock didn't just twitch from looking at her plump bottom and grip-worthy hips. Fortunately, I hadn't unbuttoned my suit jacket, or my piqued dick would be on full display.

I give the heads, on my neck and at my groin, firm, shakes to clear the vision. Then, without making eye contact, I thank Susan, take my seat, and pick up the menu discouraging further attention.

With an audible sigh, Susan bids me, "Enjoy your dinner, Mr. Steele," and walks away. Then on second thought she turns and offers, "Should you need anything at all, please let me know."

Keeping my gaze on the menu, I nod, and Susan dejectedly walks away with less sway to her hips, albeit still an eye-catching vision. Sorry, sweetheart.

If I'm not entertaining business associates or attending social gatherings like charity functions, I frequently dine at Level 4. I prefer that then eating takeout at home or hiring a personal chef to cook for only one person. Both are extravagances that I can afford, but why waste resources with my mutable schedule that changes as often as I change boxers.

Dinner out at whatever time is convenient in a city with thousands of excellent restaurants suits my lifestyle. Level 4 is one of them with a menu that offers the expected fare typical of Continental cuisine of pastas, meat, and steaks with favorable sauces. Lucien complements the usual dishes with appealing specials that change daily to keep the choices fresh and habitual guests like me from getting bored.

The client care is impeccable. So, I don't flinch when the server quietly appears at my side and places a napkin-covered basket with an assortment of warm, fresh-baked breads on the table. I glance up to see a youthful man who is model-perfect and well-groomed with a clean-shaven jaw, slicked-back ebony hair, and intelligent brown eyes. His all-black uniform of a long-sleeved shirt, pants, butcher apron, and shiny Oxford shoes is spotless—the de rigueur fashion for LEVELS employees.

"Welcome to Level 4, sir. My name is Andrew and I'll be your server this evening. May I take your drink order?"

"Thank you, Andrew. I'll have a bottle of Pellegrino," I respond with a pleasant smile.

"Very good, sir. We have some lovely specials tonight. May I share them with you?"

Since I plan to play tonight, I select a light meal comprising the tossed salad to start and the grilled langoustines with white wine sauce entrée. A clear head is best for my evening plan of play.

As Andrew heads to the kitchen to submit my order, my gaze wanders around the room admiring the decor. Just as with the lobby and the bar, Lucien and Malcolm stayed true to the original use of the warehouse. Clean lines and antique pieces for the decor: floor-to-ceiling mullion windows allow natural light to filter through to the room during the day, now dimly lit for dinner; light fixtures hang from the ceiling where the dark metal duct work and copper pipes are visible; exposed brick walls; the floor poured concrete; the well-heeled patrons sit on antique leather chairs at wooden tables. The guys really did a hell of a job with their enterprise. Few can pull off and maintain a high-end, respectable establishment, especially one that's a combo BDSM/dance club with a restaurant.

Perfectly situated for visibility by those at the bar and within the dining room, sit two lovely beauties laughing and tossing their long, glossy hair over their shoulders. Their eyes roam the vicinity hoping to connect with potential partners. The duo is more focused on attracting company for the evening, then on eating the salads that they absentmindedly move around on their plates.

The blonde spots me watching them, and a grin appears on her face lighting up her baby blues. As she nods her head to show her friend she's spotted a potential hookup, her little pink tongue pokes out to dampen her glossy, lush lips.

I wonder if her pussy is as shiny and wet as that mouth.

Her friend shifts slightly in her seat to adjust her position casually. As she runs her red-manicured hand through her sable-colored, shoulder-length hair, she spies me. The green darkens with lust when I wink at her. With a smirk, I turn my attention to Andrew as he places my salad in front of me. Now that I have the attention of both women, I nod and eat. I know they're interested, so no need to rush my meal. They'll be a double order of tonight's dessert special.

I spend the next thirty-five minutes purposely ignoring them. I only allow my gaze to shift occasionally in their direction, never direct eye contact. That dominant behavior—and who I am—will keep them intrigued. As they cross and uncross their legs, the movement affords me a better view higher up their toned thighs. Green Eyes has on a clingy, silk wrap dress that showcases her ample cleavage, the red color complementing her bronze skin. The blue of Luscious' eyes, enhanced by the cobalt color of her strapless, stretch-jersey dress, make them as prominent as her pebbled nipples. Delightful.

First item on tonight's agenda is complete—dinner eaten, now it's time to fuck.

They automatically place the bill on my membership account, so no need to waste time signing the check. I stand and take my time to button my suit jacket, drawing the attention of my pets. Once our eyes lock, I walk past their table to head to one of the high-tops at the bar.

Susan gives me a wistful stare and bids me, "Good night, Mr. Steele. We look forward to seeing you again soon."

"It was a pleasure as always, Susan. Good night," I offer her in consolation.

Moments after I settle at the closest available table, I feel one hand caress my back and another hand lands on my forearm.

I glance to my left and am greeted with a sultry, "Hello." Green eyes glitter in the candlelight like vivid emeralds.

A squeeze to my forearm draws my attention to my right to see freshly glossed lips beaming, "Hello. There aren't any other tables available, would you mind it if my friend and I share with you?"

"Would your friend and you mind sharing me for a fuck?"

Without missing a beat, Green Eyes responds breathlessly, "Absolutely."

SEBASTIAN

$\mathcal{N}$ot one to waste a second on a prime opportunity whether business or pleasure, I turn on my heel and lead them through the bar. Again, I smile and nod at more members. This time among them is the CEO of a high-end, privately owned retailer whose stores serve as the anchor in several of STEELE's malls. He's with a breathtaking model who's not his wife, whom I've seen on his arm at functions we've attended in the past. Well, to each his own as long as it's consenting adults. Just another reminder of why I'm not in a relationship. Right now I'm loyal to STEELE spending the vast majority of my time on our company leaving no room to split my loyalty with a woman. In no way am I a cheater.

Before reaching the elevator, a petite figure suddenly steps in front of me causing me to stop in my tracks. I glance down and recognize the pretty face of a fling from two weeks ago, but can't recall her name.

"Baz, I've been trying to reach you!"

With a frown, her arched eyebrows scrunch and her full lips pout. "Taylor insists that he gives you my messages, but I haven't heard a peep from you!"

Suddenly, I'm flanked by Green Eyes and Glossy Lips who possessively link their arms through mine while imposingly towering over my petite fling.

She takes a step back. Her brown eyes shoot venomous daggers at them. Then she turns her glare to me, tilting her head back to look me directly in the eye.

"Well, now I see what's kept you busy, Sebastian," she accuses.

Her lips no longer turned up in a coy smile. Rather turned down scornfully.

With the realization I need to diffuse this situation posthaste and not allow it to derail my evening plans, I gently detach my pets. Then, I offer my petite agitator an ingenuous look, taking her lightly by the elbow to move us away from their ears.

"I did not intend to ignore you nor to cause you any hurt," I tell her in a sincere, but no-room-for-debate tone. "We had a lovely evening together, but as I explained to you in advance, it was a onetime situation for us to achieve mutual satisfaction. Nothing beyond that night."

I cock an eyebrow at her and smirk, "I believe that I was a man of my word."

She blushes prettily from the exposed café au lait skin of her bosom to her curly hairline. Then, she looks up at me from beneath her eyelashes.

Demurely she replies, "Yes, you most certainly are a man of many... words."

Her lust-filled gaze travels from my eyes to my broad chest before it rests on my crotch. She smiles coyly when she notices the large bulge straining against the zipper of my custom-tailored trousers.

She flicks her little pink tongue across her lips. With a sultry smile, she returns her simmering gaze to my face.

"It appears that you require some help. Would you like me to ease your need? I know how much you enjoyed me on my knees."

I sense tonight's pets impatiently shifting behind me and needing to wrap this conversation up now.

"Sweetheart..."

"Kimberly. My name is Kimberly, Baz."

"Kimberly," I sigh, "as tempting as your offer may be, I set my plans for the night. Please excuse me. Good night."

The once hopeful expression on her face drops. Her almost forgotten pride replaces hope as she pivots in her strappy sandals with her head held high to make her way to the bar.

Damn. I'll have a word with Taylor as the head of membership to let him know not to accept any messages for me. Particularly since he never told me about Kimberly's efforts to communicate with me. I'll also have the concierge send flowers and a pleasant note to her home in the morning. I find pleasure in many women who willingly let me fuck them, but I'm not a cad. No one deserves to feel hurt, even unintentionally.

After shooting quick texts to Taylor and to the concierge, I turn to my pets who as expected did not move from where I left them.

"Pardon me ladies," I say when I rejoin them, "you have my undivided attention for the rest of the night. Shall we?"

We reach the elevator as the doors open to more members coming for dinner at Level 4 or to have cocktails at the bar.

The three of us are alone on the ride down to Level 3, where my personal suite is always ready for me. In the reflective doors, I spy the women appraising me and eyeing each other, relishing the catch they know I am.

I stand at least seven inches taller than them at six feet four inches. My thick, black hair styled slicked back highlights my gray eyes and sharp cheekbones. It's late, so my five o'clock shadow covers my firm jaw. The cut of my bespoke Saville Row double-breasted vest suit emphasizes my fit physique.

They notice my Patek Phillipe as I adjust the cuffs of my custom shirt. Turning in my A. Testoni Oxfords, I ask their names—can't keep referring to them as Green Eyes and Glossy Lips.

"I'm Emma," says the blonde in a low, sultry voice, "and this is Natalie."

Emma is the leader in this duo.

The elevator doors ping as they open. The foyer sparsely decorated and dimly lit sets the mood for carnality. The hypnotic thrumming of sensuous music piped in through hidden speakers add to the intensity and expectation of the sexual activities that happen behind the twelve closed doors. On this level, they carpet the floor to mask the sounds of footsteps.

Politely gesturing them out of the elevator ahead of me, I say, "Nice to meet you, Emma and Natalie. I am Sebastian."

They smile and move aside to allow me to lead them down the quiet, dimly lit hallway to my corner suite. At the door, I place my palm on the plaque to disengage the lock. No need to dig for keys, Lucien and Malcolm thought of every convenience, and Harris and Haley implemented the best technology for security.

Once again, I wave Emma and Natalie ahead of me. Their eyes dance in delight once they see how my decked-out suite compares to others. As members, they would have access to the private suites, but none are as elaborate as mine. One of many investor perks.

I look at the suite through their eyes: set in the middle of the room is an impressive, handmade to my specifications mahogany wood, king-size bed with four thick carved posters and a brass lattice canopy with rings strategically attached; the mattress covered in matching deep-blue silk sheets, velvet duvet, and velvet accent pillows, a deep red cashmere blanket draped over the foot; from the mahogany coffered ceiling, along with the Swarovski crystal chandelier and recessed lights, hang various hooks; the walls and ceiling panels covered in blue silk damask; the floor carpeted in almost black-blue, silk on silk; a large, double-door armoire has drawers filled with anal plugs, clamps, cords, cuffs, vibrators, and a plethora of other toys; a St. Andrew's Cross and pommel horse take prime spots on the wall opposite the armoire; below windows treated to not allow visibility from the outside sits a chaise with brass rings; on either side of the entry door hang an assortment of canes, crops, feathers, paddles, and whips; one door next to the armoire leads to the all white, Carrara marble bathroom that has a walk-in shower big enough to hold four, an extra-large claw-foot tub, double vanities, and a separate water closet for the bidet and toilet; the other door is my dressing room filled with suits, casual wear, and footwear.

The opulently decorated suite perfectly reflects my tastes for elegance and experience as a BDSM Dom. The other suites are just as resplendent in their sumptuous decor. They vary based on their individual color schemes and BDSM fixtures.

Returning my gaze to Emma and Natalie, I notice them staring toward the St. Andrew's Cross and pommel horse. They shift from foot to foot as though just the mere sight of those items has their cores dripping honey.

"Emma, Natalie, we need to discuss a few things."

Their heads swivel to me, their eyes bright with lust.

"First, you are lovely and beautiful," I start and they visibly preen pushing their ample bosoms out and swishing their curvy hips. "I want to be clear that tonight will be all about your pleasure, but will only be for this one night. I do not commit to relationships of any kind. This is purely fucking. Do you understand?"

I let that statement settle in their minds. Particularly after the Kimberly encounter, I want to be extra clear in my intentions.

Emma glances at Natalie to gauge her response. Then through some unspoken agreement, Emma turns to me and they nod simultaneously.

"Words please, ladies."

Again in unison, they affirm, "Yes, Sir."

"Second, I know that you are members and have signed the nondisclosure agreement and consent form, but I want to further emphasize that what we do is confidential and consensual." I pause again and wait for their verbal assent.

"Last, tell me your experience level with BDSM such as your hard limits and safewords."

At that, the passion reignites in their eyes and their faces flush with excitement. They all but bounce on the balls of their feet as they gush over their preferences.

Emma's lush tits almost spill over the top of her strapless dress. The dark pink of her areoles is as visible as the taut tips of her nipples.

Natalie runs her fingers up and down the opening of her wrap dress practically pulling it off revealing the bountiful curve of her under boob.

Now that the details are complete, I can get some relief for my aching cock that at this point has the imprint from the zipper teeth of my trousers.

"Natalie, come here," I command.

Immediately, Natalie sashays her way to stand in front of me.

"Ah ah… crawl to me on your hands and knees with that plump ass high and your head low."

The flush of her face and chest increases as she gracefully drops to her knees and lowers to her hands, keeping her ass high as I commanded. Her eyes don't rise from the floor as she makes her way to me.

"Obedient girl," I cajole—a natural sub.

I turn my attention to Emma, issuing the command for her to remove her dress in a slow striptease.

With a coy smirk, she faces away from me, raises her arms overhead, and begins a well-practiced shimmy of her body. Her round ass and curvy hips move to their own beat in a sensuous display of enticement.

My balls grow heavy.

Pressure on the top of my right shoe draws my attention away from the blonde vixen and to the top of Natalie's glossy, sable-haired head. Her lips press to the top of my left shoe, and my dick twitches. Yup, a natural sub.

I squat before Natalie and lift her chin with the tip of my index finger to bring her eyes in line with mine.

"Oh, Pet, so far you are a delightful little girl. Make me proud and give my cock some attention."

As I rise to my full height, my fingertip guides her to her knees.

"Unwrap that pretty dress, I want to see your tits bounce as I fuck your face," I smirk down at her.

With a blink, Natalie unties the bow of her dress. Like a present at Christmas, her tits bounce free. My mouth salivates at the lush beauty of her ample, natural breasts and taut nipples that beg to be suckled and clamped.

As the dress falls to the floor, Natalie reaches for the fly of my trousers. A whimper falls from her lips when my massive length at last springs free from the constraint of my pants. Her enormous eyes fly to mine and she swallows thickly.

"Yes, Pet. You will take all of me everywhere before the night is over, starting with your mouth... Now!" I growl at her as she visibly shivers at the thought of my colossal dick in each of her holes.

An indistinct murmur from across the room distracts me from watching Natalie's full lips part to take my length into her mouth.

Emma, not wanting to be out of our play, has her dress off. Her long legs for days ending in stilettos on display. She strokes her fingers over her bare mound, her eyes locked on Natalie who's deep throating me with gusto.

"Come," I command, trying to keep my voice from shaking with the intense jolts zinging through me.

Instantly, Emma drops to her hands and knees with her ass high to emulate Natalie's crawl. As she reaches Natalie's rear, I raise my hand to signal Emma to stop.

My cock has now reached the back of Natalie's throat. She's humming in delight while cradling my balls in one of her little hands, making the tingle start at the base of my spine. Shit, at this rate, I'll blow my load before we even get started.

I withdraw my dick from Natalie's hot, wet mouth with

a pop, as I gently push between her shoulder blades to return her to all fours. I turn to Emma with a smirk, "Eat Natalie like you want me to eat you, Pet."

The gleam in Emma's eyes sparkles as she eyes her friend's plump ass and glistening pussy dripping wet from sucking me off. Unconsciously, Emma licks her lips in anticipation.

I step back to remove my clothes and watch as Emma grips Natalie's hips and plants her face between Natalie's butt cheeks, a moan spilling from her lips.

The sight and sounds of Natalie mewling and trembling in ecstasy has my hand reaching to stroke my thick cock and smearing the pre-cum across the tip with my thumb. I walk to the armoire to get a strip of condoms, clamps, red silk cords, and an enormous dildo. Then, place the treats on the tray table next to the bed. I call to my pets to join me.

Natalie gives a sharp cry and jumps as Emma must have nipped her clit. Damn, that one needs to learn that I'm the Alpha here.

"Pets, here, now," I command.

Emma reluctantly stops her ministrations on Natalie's pussy and they crawl over to kneel at my feet beside the bed. Emma's lips and chin are shiny from her friend's juices while Natalie has a dazed look on her reddened, damp face.

"On the bed, Emma, on your back, arms and legs spread. Natalie, stand above Emma, feet on either side of her hips, arms overhead."

I attach the red, suede-lined cuffs to Emma's wrists and ankles, ensuring that the fit is snug, yet comfortable. I suckle on her left nipple as she moans, then place the clamp on the tight bud. I repeat the process on her right nipple, smirking at her discomfort.

Once I have Emma situated, I turn my attention to Natalie. I stand behind her to tie her arms with the cords above her head to one of the brass rings on the lattice canopy. Then, tug on the cords to make sure that her arms have room and not stretched too tight. I give her ass two resounding slaps that makes her lift to her toes and squeal. Her flesh jiggles at the impact and immediately turns bright pink.

I have to taste her pussy; the scent is potent from Emma's feasting.

On my knees behind her, I raise her right leg, holding under her thigh. Then, I spread her pussy lips with the fingers on my other hand, revealing her engorged clit and slippery core. A deep inhale of her tantalizing aroma makes my dick jump. I eat her with relish, her moans and cries spurring me on.

The sight is too much for Emma and she twists beneath us as she whimpers her dissatisfaction at being ignored. I reach down and spank her pussy three times. The sound of my fingers hitting the wetness of her labia is loud in the room. Oh, Pet, you will wait your turn patiently or get reprimanded.

I feel Natalie's inner walls quiver as her orgasm nears. I

pull away to growl, "Do not cum until I tell you or I will punish you."

Her eyes squeeze shut as she tries to push the orgasm away despite my unending onslaught. I lave, lick, and lap at her core, drinking her ambrosia. Her hips move and I grip her tighter to keep her in place. Then using her pussy juices for lube, I press my thumb against her back hole, applying enough pressure to pass the tight ring of muscle. Natalie nearly jumps in the air and wails in anguish from keeping her orgasm at bay.

Another few licks and a few thumb thrusts and I pull back enough to command, "Cum for me, Pet. Cum now!"

Natalie lets go, screaming my name as a gush of her honey pours down my throat. I don't relent. Instead continue to nip and to suck her pussy, drawing three more orgasms from her until she's limp, dangling heavily on the cords.

I stand and kiss her deeply, letting her taste her sweetness on my tongue as I hold her close to my chest and release the knots. As her breathing returns to normal, I lower her to the bed to lie beside Emma who's red faced and moaning pitifully.

"Your turn, Pet," I remark to her.

I position my cock at her mouth and my lips at her weeping pussy. We'll get some mutual satisfaction before I fuck them both.

Emma's fiery mouth closes around my thick dick in pure bliss. The suction of her cheeks is intense and draws my balls up tight. The moans she makes as I fuck her face and eat her pussy reverberate up and down my spine. My hips buck and I begin to piston, timing my movements to my tongue fucking her pussy. Emma lets off a keening moan and I feel tremors from her pussy on my tongue. I pull out and give her wet pussy lips three quick spanks as a reminder not to cum until I allow her release.

A whimper escapes from her mouth around my dick. I return to my ministrations, adding the dildo to increase her sense of fullness. I continue to eat her and edge her for at least ten more minutes—she'll blow when I blow.

Soon, I can't hold back my load and I work her even harder with the dildo in her pussy and my mouth on her clit. I reach between us and remove the clamps, knowing the return of the blood to the sensitive areas will set her off. She wails and I feel her pussy clench down hard on the dildo, I tell her, "Cum, Pet, cum now!"

Her sweat-glistening body stiffens, her back arches off of the bed, and a resounding scream of my name wrenches from her lips, as she convulses in unending waves of ecstasy.

My cock falls from her mouth and my seed spills on her face, neck, and breasts as I roar my release. A release so strong that my toes curl and I see a white flash in front of my eyes. The pleasure makes me collapse to Emma's side opposite Natalie. I catch my breath, then uncuff Emma, tenderly rubbing her wrists and ankles. Her face is now serene with her eyes closed as a languid smile plays on her swollen lips.

Damn, that was good.

The intense pleasure of multiple climaxes forced from them wore my pets out, so I go to the bathroom to get warm, wet washcloths to clean them gently. When I return to the room, Natalie is kneeling on the bed with her hands clasped behind her head. Her large breasts jutting towards me, her knees spread wide revealing her distended clit, and her eyes downcast in a classic sub position. My dick twitches to life at the sight.

"I'd like to satisfy you, Sir," Natalie purrs.

"Oh, would you, now," I ask as I gently clean a still passed out Emma, but who breathes steadily.

"Yes, Sir, if I may," Natalie replies.

I place the washcloth on the tray table by the bed, pick up the strip of condoms, and turn to Natalie, my cock standing proud.

"Well, Pet, I see we will use these after all."

LOLA

*R*upaul's 1993 hit song blares from the surround-sound speakers of the photography studio. My best friend and muse Leonie Beaulieu—*The Lion* as she's known in the modeling world because her name means brave as a lion and her long, mahogany hair looks like a mane—strikes alluring poses in a piece from the new collections for my eponymous luxury lingerie company Lola's Coterie.

These collections are extra special since I designed them specifically as exclusives for my New York City and Las Vegas boutiques. No, they're not open yet, but my goal is to have them open by my thirtieth birthday that's four months away. Ambitious, yes, but I never back down from my goals nor from a challenge.

* * *

"LOLA, sweetie, come give your father and me a kiss good night," my mom yells down the hall from the front door to our apartment.

While my parents go to dinner with their friends from out of town, I'm staying at my childhood apartment on Manhattan's Upper Eastside for the weekend. I need to take a break from my studies at FIT, the prestigious Fashion Institute of Technology in Chelsea.

I fell in love with lingerie when I saw Elizabeth Taylor wearing a silk lace-trimmed slip in the classic movie Butterfield 8. The bombshell leaning against the wall in nothing but her slip and high-heel shoes sipping liquor from a crystal glass. Her image remained forever etched into my thirteen-year-old brain. From that day onward, I knew that I wanted to give women an air of sultriness in sexy lingerie.

The specialized high school that I attended allows students to graduate at seventeen. So, I applied and attained acceptance to FIT, the internationally recognized hotbed for talented designers, this past fall. I love my studies in design and business and take extra courses so I can finish in three years instead of four—hence the need for a break.

So instead of hitting the books—as I have each weekend over these last two semesters—my mom and I spent the day planning my eighteenth birthday party that's in two months. As their only child, my parents dote on me and I adore them. We are close since it's just the three of us—no extended family—and mean everything to each other.

Now, my parents head out. They offered to stay in and order Thai my favorite food, but I told them to go have fun. Especially since they had plans with their friends before I came home unexpectedly.

"Have fun and tell Mr. and Mrs. Shaw hi for me," I say as I kiss and hug my parents.

The landline ringtone for the apartment intercom wakes me and I almost roll off of the sofa where I fell asleep binge-watching GOT. I sit up to reach for the handset to answer it, as I wonder the time.

"Hello," I clear my voice.

"Ms. Lewis, the police are here to see you," responds the doorman.

My heart palpitates, and I glance around for the clock on the television. It's 12:15 a.m. I jump and drop the handset as the front doorbell chimes.

The two uniform police officers appear grim when I open the door. Tears fill my eyes and my vision blurs.

"May we come in, Ms. Lewis?"

With a nod, my throat too tight to respond vocally, I step back and they enter the foyer.

"We're sorry to inform you, your parents died in a car accident..."

* * *

"Shantay, shantay, shanty," shouts Leonie singing her personal anthem as she twirls for the camera, her infectious laugh brings me out of my reverie. My eyes glisten with unshed tears and my face is flush with emotion.

I change my focus to peer around the room, taking in

the sight of my success: the studio bustles with activity; the famous fashion photographer known for his glamorous shots of women who appear sexy and not slutty even in the skimpiest of lingerie like the cream, lace teddy and matching barely there thong that Leonie prances in; his assistants moving back and forth swapping lenses and adjusting the lighting; the makeup artist who has a wait list of six months touches up Leonie's full lips; meanwhile, the hair stylist that *Vogue* named the *Best of the Decade* adjusts Leonie's bed-head updo, their assistants eagerly standing to the side holding brushes and pins; my assistant Blair Thomas animatedly talking on her mobile while typing on her tablet; a table of food and beverages overseen by the caterer.

Lola's Coterie is in dedication to my parents. I envision each success as a kiss and a hug from them; each setback I hear my father whispering his favorite saying in my ear, "Lola, are you a wolf or super wolf? Because there are no sheep in this family." As I harness the super wolf that they raised me to be, it pushes me to work harder to turn each setback around. At their funeral, I promised them I would never forget how much they loved and believed in me and that I would make them proud. In my heart, I know that they're pleased with all that I've accomplished in such a scant time—graduated FIT at twenty; completed an apprenticeship here in Paris at twenty-four; opened my first boutique on the Champs-Élysées at twenty-five; the second location on London's Bond Street at twenty-eight; expansion back home in

New York City and another in Las Vegas in a few months…

"Chérie, stop thinking so hard!"

A glance to my left shows Leonie strutting in my direction, her wavy hair now loosely flowing down her back, a predatory stare sets her amber eyes glittering. Long, toned legs make quick work of the distance between us. I raise my hazel eyes to glance up at her standing at six feet, four inches in her five-inch mules reminds me of the difference between our body types. My petite, five-foot-five-inch, curvy body so opposite to her tall, voluptuous frame.

The Parisian-born, feline beauty is the perfect spokesmodel for Lola's Coterie. Her sensuous, statuesque figure reminds me of the bombshells of yesteryear and the '90s supermodels, full bust, small waist, shapely. Her golden, caramel skin that looks great with any color or material reflects her biracial heritage—her mother is Tunisian and her father is French.

And, yes, everything looks good on her. Rupaul would be proud.

"Lola, you didn't hear a word that we said to you," Leonie accuses tossing her head and pursing her lips.

"Sorry, what did you say," I ask abashed for being caught not paying attention to this important photoshoot.

Leonie flutters her eyes and blows out a lengthy breath in mock annoyance, then laughs, "Yes, you are as they say, busted!"

Looping her arm through mine, Leonie walks us to the racks of lingerie to select the next pieces.

"Seriously, are you okay," Leonie asks with concern on her face.

I turn to her with a bright smile and respond, "Definitely. I was thinking about how far Lola's Coterie has come since we met six years ago."

Leonie's amber eyes glow as she laughs, "Oh, *Chérie*, you've done so well!"

With an exaggerated roll of her eyes, she continues, "I remember Luc insisting that I meet a new lingerie designer and I thought, *mon Dieu*, really?"

At twenty-five, Leonie was at the height of her career with well-established designers and cosmetics companies pleading with her agents to book her for shows and exclusive contracts. So, an up-and-coming designer like myself was far from her radar. Luckily, my guardian angel and mentor, Luc Montaigne, knew her and insisted that she meet with me.

"Ah, persistent Luc... very handsome and sexy. How could I say, no? But really, I knew that if he said you were worth it, you must be special."

As we reach the racks, Leonie stops to hug me before she continues, "*C'était fait accompli!*"

Yes, it was a done deal.

Leonie and I hit it off right from that first meeting. Two years apart, only children, driven, and confident, we complement each other well. Leonie's fun-loving personality balances my serious demeanor and my feistiness balances her easy-going behavior, particularly when men try to paw all over her when we're dancing at clubs. Yes, this native New Yorker will rail on someone in a minute, even in fluent French. We're sisters in every aspect except DNA.

"Ooh la la c'est magnifique!"

The beige, satin-trimmed, embroidered tulle chemise with matching bra and thong is extraordinary with the gold thread of the lace covering only the soft cups and along the hem leaving the center sheer tulle. The front of the panties matches the lace and has bands of satin along the hips connecting in the rear for the thong. A matching bra is available, worn with the panties not under the chemise. The delicate set is my favorite in the collection for the New York boutique.

"I absolutely must model this next. It's divine," Leonie croons as she carries it to the dressing room.

Soon, Leonie emerges looking like a goddess. Her hair is curled in ringlets cascading around her face and down her back, the shiny mahogany shines beneath the lights. Her makeup is soft with a touch of nude gloss on her lips. The cups of the chemise barely contain her breasts, a hint of the dark nipples peek through. Her toned torso framed by the sheer core of the chemise, while the dainty embroidered hem grazes the tops of her thighs. A slight glimmer of gold body makeup adds sparkle to her caramel skin. As she pads over to the set, Leonie is the epitome of feline feminine grace.

"Gorgeous, darling, absolutely marvelous," gushes Henri as his cameras click in rapid succession taking frame after frame of Leonie as she turns to the left, then turns to the right.

I glance up to heaven and smile.

Luc Montaigne

"*Bon soir, Monsieur Montaigne,*" greets the maître d' at Arpège. "*Comment ça va ce soir?*"

"*Bon soir. C'est bien, je vous remercie,*" I reply with a smile I'm fine this evening.

The three Michelin star restaurant is buzzing with the sounds of patrons chatting while they dine on the award-winning food.

This is Lola's favorite restaurant in Paris. I first brought her for dinner almost five years ago to celebrate the opening of her flagship boutique on the Champs-Élysées. A year later we returned for the anniversary of our initial meeting.

I have to smile to myself when I think back on her literally falling at my feet one evening as I was leaving Banque Montaigne's headquarters. The parcels in her arms flew in the air and landed on the sidewalk when she tripped over a trail of fabric from a bolt of lace. Fortunately, I caught her before she too landed on the asphalt. The curses in English and in French that rushed from her mouth were explicit enough to redden even a sailor's face.

After she regained her footing, the words worsened when Lola realized that she broke the heel on her shoe. I heard her mumble the expletives under her breath as we collected her packages and bolts of material.

"Mademoiselle, let me help you. You can sit inside to situate your shoe," I said, hands full of packages as I showed with a tilt of my chin the front doors of my bank's headquarters.

Mesmerizing, hazel eyes gave me the once over. With a nod the petite beauty, apparently I didn't seem threatening, allowed me to guide her into the lobby.

"Monsieur Montaigne!" Called one of the security staff, "*Laissez-moi vous aider.*"

I handed the packages to him and to the other guard before I took her by the elbow and led her to one of the lobby sofas. The scent of her alluring perfume stirred my once-lifeless loins.

"*Merci*, Monsieur Montaigne," she said, holding out her hand.

"You're very welcome, mademoiselle," I responded, surprised that she caught my name. As I took her small hand in my large one, she surprised me once again with a firm shake.

"Once I fix my shoe, I'll be on my way."

"My dear, your shoe is beyond fixing," I laughed and she joined in holding the two pieces of her shoe in both hands.

The sound of her laughter was like a breath of fresh air that I hadn't experienced in over a year. Before allowing my mind to drift as it so easily did in those days, I asked her where she planned to go with such an assemblage of goods.

"I'm an apprentice for a lace maker and was returning to his atelier with supplies," she responded, her eyes shining with exuberance.

It was then that I noticed how much younger than me Lola was, at least eighteen, maybe twenty years.

"I see, your dedication is admirable to carry so much so late in the evening."

"Yes, well, his work inspires me... Anyhow, I must go, thank you, again."

She stood and made to lift her packages.

My gut told me to not let her go so quickly. Her apprenticeship, dedication, even her tempestuous little mouth, noticeably a lush and kissable one, intrigued me. My reaction shocked me, but not enough to stop myself from offering to give her a ride.

"My car and driver are out front, please allow me to take you to the atelier. Your shoe and those packages are not a pleasant combination."

I paused and held my breath for her reaction.

Again, she appraised me, then nodded. With a perfectly arched eyebrow raised she responded, "Well, I know who you are. I'll text Monsieur Thibault to let him know that you're bringing me to his studio now."

"Sorry I'm late!"

With a blink, I look up and see Lola leaning down to double kiss my cheeks in greeting. I didn't notice the time pass as I reminisced.

Her pretty, heart-shaped face flushed from rushing to the restaurant is even more appealing. Her wavy, black hair flowing down her back is in stark contrast to the cream silk blouse tucked into a black leather pencil skirt. I laugh to myself when I notice that she's wearing shoes similar to the ones she had on that long-ago evening, this time paired with black fishnets.

Still a temptress for this older, yet fit, man.

"Oh, *petite chérie*, no need to apologize. No doubt Leonie took longer than expected," I joke. Leonie is the utmost professional who never displays a diva attitude.

"Of course," Lola winks, going along with my jest. "She's infatuated with the new collections and coerced me into giving her most of the samples!"

The server arrives to take our order and Lola requests her favorite dishes.

Once we're alone, I sit back. With a stern tone I ask, "And if Leonie has all the samples, how do you presume to present them to the president of STEELE International's Retail Properties Division the day after tomorrow?"

Lola nearly chokes on her sip of wine as her gaze flies to mine, eyebrows hitting her hairline.

"What?" She sputters, delicately wiping her lips with the linen napkin.

"Mmhmmm," I respond, pulling on the cuffs of my custom-tailored dress shirt.

"What do you mean... What are you saying, Luc, tell me!" Lola demands, mouth agape.

A minor part of my mind wonders what my thick length would feel like filling her inviting mouth—six years and I still barely restrain myself. As usual, dispersing the thought with a quick shake of my head, I smile at my unsuspecting little protégée. Despite occasional tangents, I make every effort to maintain the father-figure role with Lola serving as her benefactor to guide her in her business endeavors.

"A business associate of mine has a partnership for his stores with STEELE. He told me word was out that they're looking to make up for a poor deal and need to move fast with one that will offset the loss."

Intrigued, Lola leans forward and my eyes briefly drift to the gap in her blouse created by the movement.

"So, what does that mean?" She insists, eyebrows scrunched.

"It means, *petite chérie*, that now is an excellent time to negotiate boutiques in New York and Las Vegas where STEELE has several properties. Rents on Fifth Avenue, on Prince Street, and in their premier Vegas shopping mall are not inexpensive. Lola's Coterie can benefit from long-term leases set now when STEELE is not in the best position to play hardball," I finish with a relish.

"Oh, Luc"—Lola jumps from her chair and pulls me into her warm embrace—"you are *incroyable!*"

Again seated, Lola is all business, the smart, feisty woman I met six years ago resurfaces.

"When do we leave?" Her hazel eyes twinkle with glee.

LOLA

*L*uc Montaigne

What else is new? I ask myself as I sit on my G650 waiting on the tarmac at Le Bourget Airport for Lola and Leonie—Double L Trouble I nicknamed them.

Not only did Lola reinvigorate my desire to live a year after I tragically lost my wife and unborn son and only heir. But my relationship with Leonie developed from mere acquaintances introduced at one or another society gala to another young woman whom I've taken under my wing.

Both have blossomed into confident, business-savvy women determined to achieve their goals. Lola's set on her luxury lingerie company going global. Leonie starting a new career in upscale residential interior design. Developed over the years from her appreciation of staying in remarkable properties as a highly sought-after supermodel who travels the world.

The vibration from my mobile alerts me to an incoming text.

We're 10 minutes away! :)

It wasn't foresight that made me ask my pilot team to schedule the flight plan for five and not four this afternoon.

Ça va

"Monsieur Montaigne, Ms. Lewis just sent a text that she and Ms. Beaulieu are ten minutes away," Blair informs me.

I glance up and smile, "*Merci*, Blair."

Lola's assistant is the daughter of a friend who three years ago mentioned that the attractive brunette was interested in fashion and not their family's manufacturing business. Lola was trying to handle all aspects of her company despite my advice to focus on the creative design side and let an assistant handle the day-to-day tasks. After a one-month trial period, Blair proved herself to be efficient, dependable, and clever when balancing the activities that didn't need Lola's constant or immediate attention.

"You're welcome, Monsieur Montaigne," Blair replies, a blush forming on her cheeks.

What I find amusing is how flustered she gets around me. Leonie lasciviously teases that Blair wouldn't mind handling personal calls for *Le Renard Argenté*.

Silver Fox, I chuckle to myself. Yes, my black hair now has some gray sprinkled in it and I do workout regularly and eat healthily, so the nickname is appropriate for an attractive, fifty-year-old man. Obviously, Blair agrees.

"I have the latest copy of the *Financial Times* if you would like to read it. There's an interesting article on the banking industry and additional security measures to protect clients' personal information," Blair says to engage me in conversation to extend our interaction.

Not wanting to hurt her feelings since I read the advance copy yesterday afternoon, I tell her that would be interesting.

With a flash of her bright smile at me, she turns on her heels to retrieve the newspaper.

"*Pardonnez-moi*, Monsieur Montaigne, Monsieur Richard confirms we are ready to depart when the rest of your guests arrive."

"*Merci*, Daphne," I respond to my head flight attendant.

"Here's the article," Blair says as she bustles past Daphne giving her a face and sitting beside me holding the newspaper in my direction.

"We're here!"

"Arrivé, arrivé!"

A chorus from the private jet's door brings our attention to Lola entering the plane, followed by Leonie.

I stand and make my way to them, thankful that the spacious cabin has the headroom to accommodate my six-foot-four-inch frame.

"*Bonjour, Chères*," I greet L&L with double kisses and hugs.

"*Bonjour, Renard Argenté*," winks Leonie peering over my shoulder at Blair and Daphne.

"*Bonjour*, Luc," Lola adds, "so sorry! The traffic was ghastly!"

"I can imagine… That's why I left earlier," I tease her with a quirk of my eyebrow.

Turning to Daphne, I ask her to inform the pilots we're ready to depart.

Daphne scurries past me with a side-long stare before she hurries to the cockpit to deliver my message to the crew. Leonie and Lola titter in amusement while they seat themselves—Lola across from me and Leonie stretches out in the adjacent four-seat cluster.

"Ms. Lewis," Blair clears her throat, "do you need anything at the moment?"

Lola shifts in her seat to address Blair. "I'm fine, thank you. You can get settled now," Lola nods her head to the rear of the jet where the other assistants and two members of my staff sit buckled into their seats.

With a nod to Lola and a coquettish glance at me, Blair heads down the aisle. Her plump *derriere* encased in a form-fitting dress and lifted by the high heels that adorn her feet. The sight makes my cock twitch. Discreetly adjusting my bulge, I stride to my seat and buckle up just as the twin Rolls-Royce engines roar to life.

Lola

The level of luxury that Luc's multibillionaire status affords him always astounds me, even after experiencing it vicariously for over six years. The finer things in life were not new to me since my mother was a high-powered medical attorney and my father was one of the world's top cardiologists. But millions and billions are very different, rich and über-wealthy have two different meanings and degrees in access. The rich fly first class or perhaps charter; the wealthy own private jets like Luc's G650. The best money can buy and customized to suit his every whim. With a base price that starts at sixty-five million dollars, you should be able to have whatever you want. The atmosphere at eight thousand feet tires you out? Poor baby…. Gulfstream structures its gold-standard of private aviation to simulate the pressure of three thousand or four thousand feet, so you're well rested and comfy when you arrive at Teterboro. A tidbit I picked up from the pilots when they proudly gave me a tour. Eye roll sure, but it damn sure beats commercial and rental.

That fateful night I fell into Luc's arms changed the course of my life.

"*OH, HELL… DAMMIT… MOTHERFUCKER!*"

"*Merde!*"

I knew I should have taken a taxi instead of walking with all of this stuff.

"*Oof, putain!*"

"*Mademoiselle, let me help you. You can sit inside to situate your shoe.*"

I peer up at my savior to see the hottest, older man, ever.

Dark blue eyes ringed with black thick lashes; short, jet black hair the kind that you want to run your fingers through; an aristocratic nose; cleft chin to run your tongue over. The face of a god loomed close to mine as he held my arms to prevent a spectacular fall.

His stunning visage rendered me speechless, so I could only nod in response.

As he led me to an impressive old-world bank, I noticed the cut of his immaculate, custom three-piece suit. My designer eye caught the perfect stitching and the alignment of the stripes, not an easy feat. His sturdy arms easily carried my parcels while I carried the offending bolt of lace that almost caused my demise.

Immediately upon entering the plush lobby, security rushes to take the offending items out of his arms. Okay, so this guy was the owner of this bank, hhhmmm. Actually, I later learned, not only the owner, but the CEO & Chairman of the Board of his family's multigenerational, multibazzillion banking empire.

Once inside, I quickly situate myself. I need to get going or Monsieur Thibault will have to stay later than expected.

"Merci, Monsieur Montaigne," I say as I shake his enormous hand firmly. You can always tell the character of a person by their handshake, my father's voice pops into my head.

"Once I fix my shoe, I'll be on my way."

Monsieur Montaigne looks at me as if I have two heads—how could I blame him after our comical encounter—and offers to give me a ride. I sense that he is trustworthy, but to be safe, I send a text to Monsieur T. to let him know that I'm getting a ride to his atelier.

. . .

THAT WAS, as they say, the start of a beautiful friendship. Luc became my advisor, benefactor, and confidante. As we became more acquainted, my original attraction to him developed into a mentee to a mentor, or my guardian angel as I tell him. He can never replace my father, but he fills in as a father figure over the years.

The banker in Luc added the role of financial manager. His wise investments turned my inheritance into a multi-million-dollar cache. So, yes, I can afford luxuries, but I still revel in Luc's wonderful fortune.

"Let's go over your presentation."

Aside from being my mentor, Luc is the Vice Chair of Lola's Coterie and a major investor. My company's success is as ingrained in him as it is in me.

"The presentation must not leave room for questions and predispose any concerns so that by the end of it we can focus on the negotiations," Luc continues.

We spend the next couple of hours making revisions and rehearsing until it's memorized and flows naturally.

"That pretty much sums it up and the numbers are tight," Luc beams at me.

The pride that he shows makes my heart swell. He's tough and demands the best, not allowing me to slide or to cut corners. Luc's keen business sense combined with my creativity and vision have led to the successful growth of Lola's Coterie in only five years.

The expansion to New York City and Las Vegas is not out of reach. I'll definitely make my goal of the two boutique openings by my thirtieth birthday. I'm super excited. STEELE International, Inc. here we come.

I glance to my left and notice that Leonie has her head buried in one of her schoolbooks. I'm so proud that's she successfully made it to her last year at the Paris American Academy for her bachelor's degree in interior design. She's so nervous about her ultimate project where she must design an entire house. I'm sure that she'll find someone who will let her redo their home.

"Hey, Bookworm," I call to her, "ready for some dinner?"

Leonie peers at me over the top of her reading glasses. Her amber eyes glint in the light; her wavy mane pulled atop her head in a messy bun with a pen holding it in place; her ample bosom peeking from the slightly unzipped jacket of her velour tracksuit. Even dressed casually with books and binders piled around her, Leonie effortlessly looks like a sex kitten, a little nerdy kitty.

Leonie smirks, "Bookworm, huh, okay *Ms. Are My Numbers Right?*"

I laugh and stand to stretch my arms overhead, rolling my shoulders to get the kinks out after sitting for so long.

"I'm not the only nerd," I retort as I head to the bar to get a bottle of water.

"Do you guys want anything?" I ask.

"Let Daphne or Stephanie get that for you," Luc admonishes me with a frown.

When I do mundane tasks that a member of the staff

should handle for me, Luc twinges. Raised in the French nobility, he's the last *duc* in his aristocratic family's line. I tease him relentlessly and call him a snob. He always gives me that arrogant Gallic shrug: sticks out his lush lower lip; raises his thick eyebrows and broad shoulders simultaneously; followed by a patronizing, "*Bof.*"

I roll my eyes and purposely lob a bottle to him he catches effortlessly. As I return to my seat, I hand one to Leonie who promptly uncaps it, curls her lips into a smirk, and drinks straight from the bottle.

"*Pardonnez-moi, Monsieur,* I didn't mean to offend you," I jest.

With a gleam in his beautiful, blue eyes, Luc also uncaps his water and drinks from the bottle.

"How are your studies, Leonie? It must please you that this is your last year," asks Luc. He's just as concerned with Leonie's success as he is with mine.

"*Tres bien!*" Leonie declares with an ecstatic grin. "I just have to find a house for my last project. It's a hands-on redo from consultation to plans to placing the last flower in the vase."

She playfully bites her fingernails and trembles nervously.

"Let me ask around. I'm sure we can persuade someone to proffer their home," Luc nods sagely.

After eating a delicious six-course meal served on the finest Bernardaud china and vintage wine in Lalique crystal glasses, we drift into separate areas of the jet. Luc moves to the bedroom after Leonie and I decline the use of it. Instead, Leonie reclines her chair into a bed to sleep and I remain upright, my nerves not allowing me to rest for the rest of the flight.

An hour or so later, five o'clock in the evening New York time, we land at Meridian Teterboro the deluxe FBO at the private jet airport. We don't linger as the ten of us hop onto one of Luc's Sikorsky S-92 Executive luxury helicopters. Designated to take us the seven miles from New Jersey to Manhattan's West 30th Street Heliport in less than fifteen minutes. Yup, the billionaire level is fierce. A thirty-minute drive in excellent traffic conditions is an inconvenience for someone like Luc.

Somehow, Blair finagles a seat next to him and periodically brushes her thigh against his. I laugh to myself when I notice him shift in his seat. I guess her touches are getting to Luc. Leonie nudges me and winks, then both of us burst into giggles, drawing Luc's attention our way, his face reddening in embarrassment. Blair looks uncomfortable, too, and turns her gaze to the scenery outside of the window, a flush creeping up from her chest to her hairline.

Soon we disembark and stride to the awaiting vehicles. Two Mercedes-Benz Sprinters for the larger luggage and trunks for the collections. Two Escalades with drivers for the staff. Luc's Black Badge Rolls-Royce Cullinan for the three of us—the most gorgeous SUV ever crafted. His New York driver greets us as he holds the door open.

"Let's have breakfast at the Astor Court at 7:30

tomorrow morning. That will leave us plenty of time to review the presentation once more and to arrive at The STEELE Tower for the ten o'clock meeting," Luc tells Leonie and me.

I frown, "I'm so nervous. I probably won't eat anything, but I'll have some tea and possibly toast."

"Oh, *Chérie*," Leonie croons. "You'll be *formidable!*"

Ever my cheerleader, I smile at Leonie and nod my thanks.

"*Bon*," Luc injects. "Get some rest and don't worry. You're ready."

He drops Leonie and me off at the St. Regis New York where we'll stay in the Presidential Suite. Luc continues to his palatial Fifth Avenue penthouse overlooking Central Park.

A smartly dressed doorman opens the door as the Cullinan pulls up to the hotel's entrance on Fifty-fifth Street around the corner from Fifth Avenue.

"Good evening, welcome to the St. Regis New York."

"Thank you."

"*Merci.*"

"Enjoy your stay," he enthuses.

Two bellmen swiftly appear to take our carry-ons and to usher Leonie and me up the red-carpeted stairs. Another doorman greets us with a flourish, "Good evening ladies, welcome to the St. Regis New York."

"Thank you."

"*Merci.*"

Luc's driver called ahead to inform the concierge of our imminent arrival, so he greets us at the entrance and takes us directly to our suite. Suite is an understatement for what's more like a grand apartment. It features a large foyer that leads to the formal dining room, living room, exquisite wood-paneled library, three bedrooms, four bathrooms, powder room, and a complete kitchen. The floor-to-ceiling windows open onto large balconies with spectacular views of Central Park, Fifth Avenue, and Fifty-fifth Street. A personal butler is on call to oversee our every need. With a five-figure per night rate, it has every luxury imaginable for a home away from home.

I spend most of my time in Paris, so I don't have a residence in the city. I sold my childhood apartment years ago. If, or rather when I lease my New York and Las Vegas boutiques, I'll purchase an apartment here to have a base in the United States. I'll split my time between here and Paris.

"… will you require any further help this evening, *mademoiselles?*"

I catch the tail end of the concierge's comments, so I wait for Leonie to answer him and the butler.

"We're fine for now, *merci,*" she responds.

"Very well. We'll take our leave," they bow slightly and exit the suite.

Leonie twirls and flops onto a silk-covered, pillow back sofa, placing her long legs up on the armrest with a sigh.

"It's only after six. What should we do?"

I anxiously wring my hands and flop onto the twin sofa opposite her.

"I can't sleep and besides, we need to adjust to New York time to avoid jet lag," I answer hesitantly.

"Okaaay, so what should we do?" Leonie persists.

I sit up, face Leonie, and with a neutral face tell her, "Let's go to LEVELS New York."

Her eyebrows almost fly off of her face as she raises them in surprise and straightens on the sofa.

"LEVELS... really? Didn't Simon want to take you to the Paris location, but you chickened out?" She asks shocked, her amber eyes wide.

I think back to last year when I had my third date with Simon Blanchet—the second man with whom I'd had sex—during which he spanked me. The punishment gave me the most intense feelings ever. Sure, it was only my second time having sex in my entire life, but the feelings were incomparable. After Simon fell asleep, I slipped out of his apartment. Embarrassment flooded me that I—an independent woman who owns a company—would reach such intense satisfaction from being spanked by an Alpha male. No way!

To avoid thinking about it, I redoubled my efforts on the success of Lola's Coterie and I haven't been in a relationship since that night.

Part of the reason I want to go is it's in New York. Plus, I won't risk bumping into Simon, especially since I refused all of his calls and texts. The other reason is that I need to get my nerves in check and the release that I felt after Simon's spanking was mind-blowing.

"Yes, but now we're in New York and not in Paris. Plus,

you'll be with me. Let's go," I declare, standing and heading to one of the three bedrooms to get ready before I wimp out.

Leonie lets out a wolfish whistle and prances to one of the other bedrooms.

LOLA

*F*or three hours, we soak in the oversize bathtubs to loosen our travel-weary muscles, wash and style our hair, then artfully apply makeup to our faces. Our heels click on the hotel lobby's marble floors. Leonie and I strut arm-in-arm from the elevators to the front doors. We pass well-dressed guests on their way to dinner or to one of the city's happening night spots. Several do a double take when they recognize *The Lion* with her glossy, mahogany hair flowing behind her like a mane. The supermodel whose stunning visage graces magazine covers on the newsstands and on the billboards in Times Square impresses even the most jaded New Yorker. With her signature predatory smile on her face, amber eyes twinkling, Leonie prances past the gawkers and nods at the doorman as he smiles sheepishly at her. We glide down the stairs and sweep into the chauffeured Bentley Bentayga that I hired for our seven-day stay.

"Good evening, Ms. Lewis and Ms. Beaulieu," the driver greets us as we settle into the plush leather seats. "My name is Stan, and it is a pleasure to be your driver while you are in New York. Your requested beverages are in the center console."

"Good evening, Stan. Please take us to LEVELS New York in the Meatpacking District, thank you," I reply confidently.

As the quintessential professional, Stan's face remains neutral even though I'm sure that he knows LEVELS is a hedonistic establishment and responds, "Yes, Ms. Lewis, right away."

While Leonie's mobile commands her attention, I gaze out of the window, ever amazed by the constant activity on the city's streets. Tourists gaping at the store windows of the pricey retailers; vendors with pretzel carts on the corners; natives bustling past everyone else as they hurriedly make their way to their destinations.

I open the window and close my eyes to take in a whiff of my former home. The various smells fill my nostrils, reminding me of the marvelous times. As a child, ice skating with my dad at Rockefeller Center. Lunch with my teenage friends at Serendipity's. Going to the boutiques on Madison Avenue with my mom to shop for my high school graduation dress and shoes.

Although the pain is still fresh, I truly miss the place of my childhood. A boutique here will be the impetus for me to return, especially since I'll be so busy that I won't have time to dwell on my anguish. The boutique will provide fresh experiences and better memories, reestablishing my presence here.

A squeal from Leonie breaks my reverie.

"Gio invited me to Monaco for the Grand Prix next month!"

She does a shimmy in her seat and taps her toes on the SUV's floorboard. Her exuberance makes me laugh.

"I thought you were over *Mr. Thinks He's God Gift to Women*," I taunt her.

Giovanni Mattei is a wealthy nobleman from an aristocratic family dating back to the Middle Ages and her on-again-off-again paramour.

"*Bof*," Leonie scoffs. "He's angling to get off of my shit list. Two weeks ago, he sent that oil painting from his Paris gallery that I had my eye on. I promptly returned it. Last week it was a beautiful pair of yellow diamond earrings with a note. 'They remind me of your eyes right after you cum screaming on my cock'... Returned to sender!"

I'll give it to him, Giovanni—that handsome devil—definitely has the confidence of a man used to getting whatever he wants in life. He doesn't give a damn about how others view his arrogance.

"Then, why are you going on and on about the Grand Prix," I ask with my eyebrow raised.

With that infamous Gallic shrug—Leonie is as bad as Luc—she responds, "I always have fun! It's the best time in Monte Carlo. You know that you enjoy it as much as I do. The thrill of the tight turns. The roar of the engines. The glamorous crowd losing themselves cheering on their favorite team..."

"Oh, like you're not one of the glamorous crowd," I tease her.

"*Mais oui!*" She retorts. "It's just such a thrill to watch. Heart pounding!"

"Or is Giovanni 'a thrill to watch. Heart pounding!'" I laugh.

The Bentayga stops in front of a renovated warehouse in a prime spot of the Meatpacking District that offers unobstructed views of the Hudson River and of the New Jersey coastline. The building is six stories and has a brick facade with oversized windows treated to block outsiders from seeing through the panes of glass since the interior is not visible.

Two men in custom-tailored black suits stand outside. A queue that extends around the corner of people in expensive attire patiently await admittance to the club. Not surprising given LEVELS is for the über-wealthy and influential, too refined to behave boorishly. The hopeful patrons are not rambunctious as one would ordinarily see waiting outside a Manhattan nightclub.

One doorman opens the Bentley's door while Stan opens the other.

"Welcome to LEVELS New York, ladies. May I have your names?"

When Leonie and I emerge, he pulls out a mobile device from the breast pocket of his jacket.

"Lola Lewis and Leonie Beaulieu," I respond.

After a quick perusal of the screen, he ushers us through the front doors to the lobby.

"Taylor is waiting for you at the greeter station to your right. Enjoy your evening."

While still in Paris this morning, I spoke with Taylor as the head of membership and purchased two seven-day, all access passes for Leonie and for me. I knew if I waited until I arrived that I may have chickened out, again. Plus, the cost wasn't a trifle to waste.

"Good evening, Ms. Lewis, Ms. Beaulieu. I'm Taylor Hunt. Welcome to LEVELS New York," he greets us as we approach. "Please allow me to give you a tour. Would you like to check your coats?"

Leonie and I decline since we have on outfits more suitable for a lover's tryst than for a tour of the entire club.

Taylor then introduces us to Chester the greeter for the BDSM levels—just like the doorman, the two men are very attractive and impeccably dressed. Next, Taylor leads us to the other greeter for, as he explains, the Dine/Dance levels. He guides Leonie and me onto the elevator that quickly whisks us to the Sky Lounge on the 7th Level. As I suspected the view is spectacular. A few boats bobbing on the river and lights from properties on the New Jersey coast shining in the night sky. From there, we go down to the Dance Club on levels 6 and 5. The deejay is pumping some booty-shaking songs. Partiers are definitely shaking their things on the dance floors. The bartenders are busy serving drinks. Taylor explains that this is where the queue out front hopes to gain entry. He notes that it's an excellent way to vet more members and keep things fresh for existing ones. As we head to the elevator, he says that the restaurant also allows outsiders on certain days for the same reason. The Level 4 Restaurant and bar are in contrast to the club with soft jazz music playing and well-heeled patrons dining on delicious-smelling food and sipping tasty cocktails. The D&D side is on my list as a place that I would frequent regularly.

We return to the main level and take the BDSM elevator to Level 3 to view the twelve private suites. As we exit the elevator, a devastatingly handsome man towers over us. My vision locks on his magnetic gray eyes and a thrill rushes through me as if a jolt of electricity shocked me. I suck in a breath and my step falters.

Leonie reaches for me, but his powerful hands catch me by the forearms and hold me in place.

His eyes darken to a slate gray and he inhales sharply as if he experienced the unexpected jolt, too.

"Pardon us, sir," Taylor says to the sizable man and reaches for my elbow.

The man gives him a glare with what I must have imagined was a low, feral snarl.

I regain my composure and extricate myself from the man's tight grip.

"Excuse me," I assert and move around him only for his imposing form to block my path. A bit of a dance ensues as I sidestep him and he blocks my path, again. His intoxicating musky scent, a mix of bergamot, patchouli, and vanilla wafts into my nose and beckons to me, making my pussy clench.

Leonie senses my frustration and takes me by the arm to elbow our way past him, muttering, "*Âne.*"

He definitely is an ass. But, I can't help but to peek over my shoulder at him as he speaks animatedly with Taylor, the man's eyes darting between Taylor and me. Resigned to ignore him, I turn away to take in the dimly lit foyer. I note the minimal style of the decor and the silence only broken by the soft hum of sensuous music. The alluring atmosphere prepares you for the carnal activities just inside the doors of the suites that line the hallway.

"I apologize, Ms. Lewis, Ms. Beaulieu. Please right this way," Taylor approaches and gestures down the hallways. I peer beyond him to find that the gray-eyed stranger left the floor. My disappointment is palpable.

After the brief encounter, I find it hard to concentrate on Taylor's commentary as he shows us some suites that are unoccupied. My mind is back with the handsome stranger.

Did he really snarl possessively? He couldn't have. The thought he could have makes my nipples tighten and my pussy throb—what a caveman.

Leonie takes my arm once again since I failed to notice her and Taylor walking to exit the suite.

"Are you all right?" Leonie inquires with a frown. "He was such a brute. Did he really snarl?"

I snort and cover my mouth, laughing. I didn't imagine a thing!

"Now, we'll go to Peepshow on the 2nd level. It's the perfect spot to give in to your voyeurism…"

Once again, my mind drifts this time to a scene with Captain Caveman…

"MINE!"

Comes his snarl as he roughly yanks me from the arms of my would-be playmate for the evening. I nearly topple over in my mules as the gray-eyed stranger pulls me close, my back to his hard chest. I tense as his enormous cock hardens and lengthens against my plump bottom. He ignites a flame deep in my core, my juices immediately pour from my seam and trickle down my thighs.

I peek up and over my shoulder at him. His upper lip curls, his nostrils flare, his eyes the color of molten platinum shoot poisonous darts at the Dom who was preparing me for a scene.

My unknown cockblocker wants to take me as his very own.

As I decide whether I want this to happen, the Dom puts his hands up and beats a hasty retreat—even he couldn't best this caveman.

Suddenly, I'm hoisted onto the stranger's shoulder as though I weigh nothing. He swiftly strides to one of the darker areas of the dungeon. I kick my legs and pummel his back—my small fists ineffectively hit a wall of steel and earns me three swift smacks on my rear. A zing shoots through my core, pumping more of my juices between my thighs.

Curses pour from my mouth as he sits on a red velvet sofa in the alcove and drapes me over his hard, muscular thighs. My

58

belly presses against his thick dick that promptly pulses when our bodies collide.

He makes quick work of lifting my chemise and snatching my thong down my thighs. The skimpy material keeps my legs bound above my knees. My bare ass and pussy exposed to his view. He gently runs his hands over my lush curves—quite a contrast to his previous brutish behavior. I shiver under his delicate touch, his rough hands caress my supple skin...

"Owweee," I yell as the first smack of his palm against my soft tush shocks me from the gentle lull. I reach back to shield myself with my hands, only to have him grab both of my wrists in one gigantic hand and hold them against my lower back. His other hand never misses a beat and continues to spank me—left, right, left, crease of my ass and thigh, right, left. I dance on his lap.

"You are mine. No one else will ever touch you again."

He growls as he punctuates each word with a hard spank, drawing heat and pumping blood to the surface of my bare, jiggling ass.

A sudden shift in his movements brings two of his thick fingers to my seam—I'm sopping wet for him.

"Is this all for me?"

His voice deepens with lust as he slides his fingers in and out of my pussy, fucking me, the wet sounds loud in my ears. As if I were a puppet on a string, I widen my legs to allow him more access to my slippery core, but don't respond.

My lack of a verbal answer results in another volley of spanks—left, right, left, crease of my ass and thigh, right, left.

"Yes!" I scream as I squirm on his lap attempting to get out of his reach and to close my legs.

"Open!" He commands, and my thighs instantly part again, my traitorous body taking over from my brain.

"So, sweet."

The sound of the caveman licking his fingers clean of my essence makes me gush even more than before.

A dark chuckle falls from his mouth. He bends to press his lips against my ear to whisper, "You like being mine and receiving the sting of my palm on your luscious ass, don't you, Pet? How would you like to have my colossal dick in your little ass?"

I whimper and tremble, aching to have his thick cock in all three of my holes. I can't deny that I want this beast to take me harshly in every single one of my holes, bent over and fucked by him like a feral animal...

"HONESTLY, ENOUGH ALREADY!" Leonie chastises me for bumping into her from behind, my mind in my oh so vivid erotic fantasy.

"You're all gaga for that guy," she continues.

We stopped at a greeter station in front of the doors to Peepshow. Taylor is holding bracelets and explaining the differences in the colors: partnered subs wear collars given to them by their Dom; partnered Doms wear gold bracelets; available subs wear red; unattached Doms wear white; voyeurs wear black.

Without looking Leonie in the eye, I select a red

bracelet. If I want to get spanked to ease my nerves for my meeting in the morning, then I have to show my availability, I assure myself.

Leonie, being the best friend that she is to me, doesn't make a comment and selects a black one. I see, The Lion on the hunt.

We remove our Burberry trench coats, hand them to the greeter Jane, and accept the tickets from her.

I had to wear my favorite set from the new collections. The beige, satin-trimmed, embroidered tulle chemise and thong made specifically for me. My size D breasts would never fit the sample. To adjust the piece for my petite frame, I shortened the length to just skim the tops of my thighs. Gold, strappy sandals adorn my feet, adding five inches to my five-foot-five-inch frame. My black hair cascades down my back in soft waves, brushing the curve of my plump bottom. I feel extra sexy and ready to do a scene with a capable caveman—I mean Dom.

Leonie chose the new black lace, strapless jumpsuit that ties above her bosom paired with marabou mules and her hair in a high ponytail.

The statuesque beauty and my curvy, petite self turn heads as Taylor walks us through the room. We pass seating alcoves filled with members in various stages of sex. A main stage and several smaller platforms showcase demonstrations in bondage and edging. We continue through performance rooms with viewing windows where members watch others live their fantasies. A bar that

Taylor points out only serves non-alcoholic mocktails to keep everyone's minds clear.

The atmosphere is all about bacchanalia with the melodic thrum of sensual music and the moans and groans of men and women as the backdrop to intense sexual play. The air is heavy with the scent of perfume, cologne, and sex. I swear that above all, I can detect the caveman's cologne. A faint trail of his scent tickling my nose, adding to my already overstimulated body.

Finished with the tour of this level, we walk down a flight of stairs to a set of heavy wooden double doors with two large, iron circular pulls. A riveting pair oversee the entrance. A man dressed only in a minuscule, black leather jock strap, his enormous bulge slightly covered. A woman in a black latex butt-cheek-baring tube dress, both have black leather collars around their throats.

Taylor explains that this is the Cellar, LEVELS' BDSM dungeon.

I feel a twinge of excitement and my face heats from just thinking about what's behind those imposing doors.

As the couple opens the deceptively light doors, the sights and the sounds that surround us are incredible. The Peepshow is tame compared to the Cellar.

My eyes scan the expansive, grand hall, austere in design. A multi-beamed high ceiling; cobblestone floors; brick walls; lighting that resembles flickering torches in brackets on the walls and in metal stands scattered around the room; an assortment of what looks like Medieval torture devices placed in clusters. My gaze bounces from one area to another. An older man cuffed to one of the several St. Andrew's Crosses, his head thrown back in pure ecstasy. His engorged dick eagerly sucked by a younger man on his knees. A woman in a swing, her thighs glistening with her pussy juices and stretched wide to accommodate the large man standing between them aligning her core to his massive cock. Several men and women attached to hooks hanging from the ceiling in varied positions being whipped by Doms and Dommes with canes, floggers, and paddles extending from their hands. Still others lead naked subs by leashes while they crawl on their hands and knees to one of the partitioned rooms for a bit of privacy. Here and there voyeurs stand watching, mesmerized by the decadent, sexual activities.

The sight has my throbbing pussy so wet that I can feel my juices coating my inner thighs. The aroma of my arousal rising to fill my nose and to join with all the other scents. I shift subconsciously on my feet. Then I look around once more. My gaze reaches the bar on my right where my sight settles on hungry, lust-filled, gray eyes. Once again they magnetize me pulling my soul into the orbit of their black moons.

SEBASTIAN

*F*uck... me.

My rock hard dick weeps pre-cum against the tightened confines of my trousers just at the sight of my Petite Seductress. Standing at the entranced to the Cellar in that see-through getup flaunting her every lush curve, her big, pillowy tits on full display makes me drool. I picture myself suckling her firm nipples as she bounces up and down on my thick, rigid length.

I'm even more riveted by her now than I was when she fell into my arms at the elevator on the private suites' floor upstairs. Her alluring floral scent enveloping me, sharpening my senses. I cannot believe that I couldn't control myself and snarled at Taylor like a possessive jerk. I was already on edge since my mind was on that bad, stupid ass deal that I fucked up and need to fix like yesterday. But as soon as my hands gripped her forearms, even through the barrier of her trench coat, my mind got a jump that reset it.

I felt a jolt shoot down my spine to the tip of my cock, making it stand at full attention to salute the hazel-eyed beauty. My heavy balls demand that I blow my load deep in her pussy, coating her womb with my virile life force.

Damn.

When she and her companion a beautiful supermodel who I easily recognized stepped away, I quickly pulled Taylor aside. I grilled him about my Petite Seductress. Against the privacy rules of LEVELS New York. Yes. But when do I ever let such inconsequential encumbrances impede what I want? Never.

And I want her.

The one piece of information that I could not coerce him into divulging to me was her name. Taylor insisted that detail went too far beyond the privacy boundary, even for me. Since it was the number one rule that members and guests exchange names consensually to keep the integrity of the club intact and everyone secure. Well, that minor detail definitely won't stop me. I determined that she has a week-long All Access trial membership, she's single, and that she's not lovers with the supermodel.

Then, I told him to end their tour in the Cellar instead of at Peepshow, as is his routine. There, I could gauge her reaction to full-on BDSM. If she was hesitant, then I would have to pass no matter how much I'm attracted to her because vanilla lovemaking is not my style. I fuck and dominate, period.

Now, I sit riveted as I watch my Petite Seductress' reaction as she takes in the lascivious sights and sounds of the

Cellar. Her eyes round in awe and not in fear. A heated flush on her face from her excitement. She shifts from foot to foot, discreetly rubbing her thighs together to ease the pressure building from her watching the members play. Her unconscious behavior confirms that she is perfect as my next hookup. Yet I wonder if she's new to the BDSM lifestyle and if she's open to being a sub.

My gaze travels to her slight wrist when she wipes her damp brow. I notice that she wears the red bracelet... Hmmm. So, my Petite Seductress may be virgin to the scene, but she's ready for indoctrination.

I squint and imagine introducing her to the pleasure in the pain, trusting me to take control of her body, to bring her the ultimate sexual satisfaction.

I will make her body my personal playground.

Her feverish gaze once again skips around the room, this time locking with mine as I sit at the bar drinking in the sight of her.

My Petite Seductress' eyes widen even more and she flushes deeper, embarrassed by my witnessing of her sexual arousal by the mere sight of others in promiscuous acts.

A predatory grin slowly spreads across my face. My eyes glint like steel in the torchlight as I rise from my perch on the barstool and stride over to capture my prey.

LOLA

*O*h my God, no.

He's headed towards me. The lusty gleam in his eyes rivets me in place. I'm captured by the raw power that emanates in waves off of this striking man. I can only watch wide-eyed like a rabbit as the wolf approaches me through the crowd. He does not waver for a second. His predatory eyes solely focused on me.

For the second time tonight, my knees wobble and threaten to buckle beneath me.

Where is that strong, independent woman when I need her? I ask my inner *I Am Woman Hear Me Roar*. She's lost out to my body that's inwardly doing a series of jubilant cartwheels, eagerly awaiting his eminent arrival.

"*Le monde est fou!*" Leonie exclaims shaking her head, her swishing ponytail hitting me on the cheek breaking the caveman's magnetic pull on my body.

That's putting it lightly. The Cellar is a crazy world. I peer around once again, a shiver racing down my spine.

And I love it.

"Do you want to remain on this level or return Peepshow? Taylor says they set a demonstration with a popular Domme and her male sub to start in fifteen minutes. I'd love to watch!"

I glance up into Leonie's amber eyes, glowing with ardor. She's just as galvanized by LEVELS as I, its potent draw entices one to step out of their comfort zone and to relish in their sexual fantasies.

I intend to partake.

"Actually—"

"Excuse me."

A quiver instantly shoots through my body, sparked by the deep rumble of my caveman's voice. It ignites my very soul like jet fuel thrown onto a campfire. The slow burn becoming a blazing inferno, scorching everything all around it.

Leonie and I simultaneously pivot on our heels to stare at him, his commanding tone brokering no denial to his call.

"I see that you're wearing the red bracelet."

He gestures to my wrist and I lift it as if he's moving my puppet strings, again. Yes I am, I think dazedly, once more pulled into his spell.

"What do you want?" Leonie demands, hands on her hips.

Our roles have reversed where she's the feisty one who's keeping overly amorous suitors away from me.

With a slow blink, my caveman turns his gaze to Leonie and cocks his eyebrow.

"I appreciate your protectiveness of your friend, but I mean her no harm. I assure you of that fact."

Taylor moves closer to the gray-eyed stranger and smiles reassuringly at Leonie and me.

"*Mademoiselles*, allow me to introduce you to—"

"Baz, and you are?" Interrupts the stranger.

"I'm—"

I quickly cut Leonie off and purposefully glance at her and at Taylor, "It is too soon. So, we'd rather not reveal our names."

"I understand and respect your wishes. Since you chose the red bracelet, I gather that you are interested in being with a Dom?"

I glance away, nervous now that the opportunity for a spanking presents itself. Am I interested? Am I ready? I hesitate. Then, I remember my anonymity and can let go of my inhibitions. I can allow this Dom to dominate me, to release the tension that's inside of me before my meeting tomorrow.

"Yes, I am. I take it you're an experienced Dom?" I question him with a tilt to my head and a raised brow.

"I am a Dom with fifteen years of experience and partnered with many subs. Would you like to see my dossier?"

That's why I sense that LEVELS New York is a safe club. They vet every member and guest and maintain a file on them with periodic background checks and references. The security and privacy measures are unparalleled.

I turn to Taylor who smiles and nods, offering to get my potential paramour's file from the membership office.

I glance at Leonie and she can barely contain her glee. That was a quick change in her stance. I'm not the only one impressed by this Dom.

Finally, I return my gaze to the Dom, scanning his face for veracity. Deep in my soul, I know that he is the one to take me to the next level of my desire to be a sub. If only for this one night.

He holds out his gigantic hand—cocky isn't he—and I place my small one in his. His predatory smile returns and I tremble, my pussy clenches as I expect what the night will bring for me.

We make our way through the members in the Cellar and back through the double doors, two other sentinels comparably attired pull rings from this side. Careful to climb the stairs without stumbling in my sky-high sandals, I tighten my grip on Baz's hand. He looks down at me and smiles reassuringly. This man is beyond gorgeous as his gray eyes sparkle with mischief. I can only imagine what I'm about to experience with him.

We speak no words as we cross the floor at Peepshow and take the elevator upstairs to the private suites. As I stand slightly behind him, I observe him in the elevator doors' reflective surface. He's at least six inches taller than me even in my five-inch heels, so he's well over six feet; his face is a work of art with smoky gray eyes, chiseled jaw, and sexy stubble; his black hair is as thick as his eyelashes and I imagine tugging on it as I climax from him gorging on my pussy juices; his wide powerful shoulders taper to a narrow waist and slim hips, ending in muscular thighs and calves; his enormous feet make me wonder at the size of his cock. The ding of the door opening at our floor brings my eyes back up, only to find that he's smirking at me with a knowing expression in his captivating eyes. Damn, busted.

Baz still holding my hand, leads me down the hallway to the suite on the end. Then he places his hand on the plate to unlock the door before ushering me inside. As I hear the lock engage in acknowledgement of my commitment to this encounter, he breaks the silence.

"Tell me about your experience with BDSM and being a sub."

Baz's questions come as I stand in the middle of what must be his domain alone. I take in the strong, masculine ambience of the decor and the collection of various implements and equipment around the room. My eyes settle on what looks like a pommel horse that's typically used in gymnastics. However, I can sense by the brass rings strategically attached to it that the piece of equipment has a unique use in BDSM. The thought of being cuffed to it, my bare ass exposed to Baz, makes me shift on my feet as my core oozes with need for him.

I turn to Baz. I notice how confident he is standing there in his dress shirt, the top buttons undone and his custom-tailored trousers falling just right on his narrow hips; he laid the jacket and the tie over the wooden valet next to the suite's door.

"I've never been in the lifestyle and I'm not a sub," I pause and gaze directly in his eyes to gauge his reaction. His face remains neutral, not giving away his thoughts.

Not sensing judgement, I continue, "My last lover is a Dom, and he persuaded me to allow him to spank me one night. I… I enjoyed it." I lift my chin defensively and prepare myself for any negative word that he may say in response.

Instead, a low growl emanates from his lips. I blink in surprise at his possessive behavior, but before I can comment, he nods and motions for me to continue, as though he never emitted a sound. Perhaps, I misheard, I think to myself. Then I face the wall lined with whips, canes, and paddles. Slowly, I bring my gaze back to Baz.

"I want to experience that release again. I'm not a sub nor interested in a relationship. I'm a busy woman who doesn't need a Dom nor a man in my life permanently. But, for tonight, I seek the pleasure that I experienced from being spanked."

I stop and ask, "Are you able to give that to me?" There's nothing more for me to say, it's his turn.

He pauses for a moment and runs his thumb over his lower lip, thinking, assessing me and my remarks.

I hold my breath, hoping that he will agree—my body wants him to be the one. Yeah, my roar is definitely on hiatus.

"I can give that to you. However, I want to fuck you,

rough and long. Can you give that to me... along with your trust?"

"Yes."

His gray eyes darken nearly to black, and he licks his full lips.

"You need a safeword that you will use only if you want the play to stop completely."

For a moment, I consider what it should be and decide on the word panther. Baz with his jet black hair, gray eyes, and feline grace reminds me of a sleek and powerful panther. He's definitely one to admire, but not one to cross —my limit ends with him.

"Panther," I say out loud.

Again, a neutral, unreadable face.

"Since you're new to BDSM, we will not jump into the more advanced play. But, I will demand your submission and push your limits, so use your safeword only if you absolutely want all play stop. The point is to explore your sexuality."

I nod my agreement.

"Words, Pet."

He says sharply. His authoritative tone and his use of the word pet makes my pussy juices flow once more and I shift restlessly. I'm ready to get started.

"Yes, Sir," I respond.

His eyes widen and his nostrils flare as if he's turned on by my use of the word sir. Or perhaps, he can smell my arousal because I surely can smell the sweet nectar.

"Crawl to me on your hands and knees, ass high, head low."

I flinch, surprised by his demand.

"If you hesitate, I will punish you. That is your only warning."

As much as it thrills me to imagine him punishing me for my transgressions, I don't know what his form of punishment entails, so I comply.

As I crawl to him, my first response is mortification: who does he think he is to demand that I crawl to him? Then, my feelings shift as my body takes over from my mind: my breathing quickens, my nipples tighten to points, my pussy leaks and contracts. Innately, I hold my position and keep my eyes lowered to the floor when I reach where he stands.

"Such a dutiful girl, Little Pet."

He rubs my head as he praises me and I arch into him, a mewl falling from my lips surprising me.

The tug on my scalp as his fingers twine in my hair pulls my head back, my gaze meeting his as he lifts me to my knees.

"Since the moment you fell into my arms, you have had me hard enough to cut a diamond. Now, you will take every one of my ten inches in your pretty, little mouth. All the way to the back of your throat and suck me off without spilling one single drop."

A gasp escapes from my slacked-jaw mouth. Did he go all the way there with me?

"That is five extra spanks."

I blink and whimper, more in delight at being spanked longer than in trepidation.

As if sensing my desire, Baz chuckles darkly, "You would like that wouldn't you?"

My nod turns into a cry as Baz yanks my hair. "Words, Pet," he admonishes me.

"Yes, Sir, I'd like that very much," I whimper.

"We shall see. Now, take out my hard dick and show me how much you like pleasuring your Dom."

Without the slightest hesitation, I reach up to unbuckle his belt, unzip his pants to lower them past his hips. Directly in my face is the biggest bulge that I have ever seen—grant it, I've only had two lovers, but neither is this huge. His bulging cock tents the black silk of his boxer briefs. I hook my fingers into the waistband and tug them over his dick and down his muscular thighs. It clarifies my wonderment at his shoe size in relation to his cock. Baz is massive.

I swallow and peek up at him through my eyelashes to see an arrogant smirk on his handsome face. The urge to wipe the smugness from him causes me to grasp his cock in one hand and his balls in the other. I heft their weight and stroke them before I lean forward and lick the drop of pre-cum off of the tip with my tongue. I hum around his girth in satisfaction when he groans as I take him to the back of my throat. Sucking dick is my favorite for the power that it gives me over the man. I've made an art out of it.

I glance up again and smile, satisfied that Baz has his

head thrown back and his mouth is hanging open, more groans slipping out.

I turn my attention back to his dick and really go at it. Drawing him in deep with my lips pressed all the way down his shaft to press against his manscaped crotch. I pull back to swirl the tip of my tongue around his bulbous head. Then follow up with a long lick along the vein on the underside of his girth to his heavy balls. To add to the sensation, I suck his full sac into my mouth and stroke it with my tongue. Minutes later, Baz's legs quiver as I hold the backs of his thighs, his six-pack abs tighten, and his cock grows larger, throbbing under my ministrations.

Baz tightens his grip in my hair and locks my head in place as he fucks my throat. His eyes are wild and his lip curls, a guttural snarl ripping from his mouth as an abundant amount of his cum spews down my throat. I remember not to spill a drop, so I seal my lips around his girth and swallow repeatedly.

"Fuck me," Baz groans as his dick—still large even when flaccid—slips from my mouth with a pop and he sinks to his knees staring at me in amazement.

"Damn, where did you learn to suck cock like that? Actually, never mind."

Somewhat piqued, I say defensively, "I've only had two lovers in my entire life, so don't act like I'm some promiscuous tart!"

I stand abruptly, but before I can get to the door, I'm pulled back against his hard chest.

"Please forgive me. I did not mean to offend you."

Baz turns me in his arms, but I keep my eyes on his chest. With the tip of his index finger, he lifts my chin to bring my gaze to his regretful eyes.

"I just don't want to think of you with someone else…"

His words trail off and he looks surprised that he said them as if shocked by the admission. He pulls back and lets go of me, running his hand through his hair.

"Are you using your safeword?"

With his abrupt change in topic, I'm perplexed and pause too long.

"If not, that is ten extra spanks."

With a shiver, I say, "No, Sir, I am not using my safeword."

"Splendid girl, Little Pet. Cum."

I drop to my hands and knees and crawl after him. He stops at the pommel horse and I suck in a breath.

"Stand and undress for me."

I rise with a tremble coursing through me. My fantasy comes to life.

Slowly, I reach under my chemise and shimmy my thong down my legs, kicking it to the side once it reaches the floor. I bring my hands to my neck and trace the edges of the embroidered cups before pinching my nipples through the material with a low moan.

Baz grunts and strokes his hardening cock as he removes the rest of his clothes.

I smile coyly and trail my hands down the sheer panel covering my middle to grasp the hem. Slowly, I lift it up and over my head, my full breasts bounce free. The sudden feel of Baz's hot, wet mouth on my left nipple makes my knees quake and I bite my lower lip to hold back a groan. The powerful pulls as he suckles zing my core. His hands heft the weight of my heavy breasts as he moves from one nipple to the other, lavishing them with equal attention. My head falls back as I cry out in ecstasy—it's been too long since I knew a lover's touch.

I hastily push that thought aside, this isn't about love, it's about release.

His hand skims down my belly and cups my bare mound. His fiery breath tickles my skin as he teases my pussy lips, "All this wetness just for me?"

"Yes, Sir," I moan and grind my mound into his large palm.

"Ow! Oh, ow!"

Five quick spanks to my pussy has me rising onto the balls of my feet and trying to move away from Baz. But his arm tightens around my waist, pinning me in place.

"You did not think I would forget your extra spanks, did you, Little Pet?"

His sneer followed by a pinch to my tender nipple makes me jump—and my pussy contract.

"Lean over the pommel horse. It is time for your spanking," he demands.

My body is ablaze, the inferno is still smoking hot.

I happily drape myself over the horse, my strappy heels lengthening my legs, allowing my toes to skim the floor. My body thrums in anticipation. A slight nag dances at the edges of my mind, questioning my decision to do a scene as a sub with a Dom just to get over my nerves. Is that a plausible excuse? Or do I want to be a sub and not the independent businesswoman? Is it possible to be both?

The sense of Baz's rough hands sliding along the inside of my soft thighs as he lowers himself to the ankle restraints brings me back to the suite. Soft kisses trail after his fingers, lulling me into a stupor. He expertly attaches the cuffs and checks that they're not too tight. A sharp crack of his palm to my left butt cheek dispels the haze and I cry out. Baz glides his hands down my arms and closes the cuffs securely around my wrists, again he checks the fit.

"What is your safeword, Pet?"

"Panther, Sir," I whisper as my muscles tighten to prepare for the blow.

Instead, Baz strokes his palm over my shoulders and down my back.

"Relax, Little Pet. I promise that I will not hurt you more than you can comfortably take. Remember to test your boundaries. The pleasure will follow the pain. Free yourself to receive it," he croons in my ear, his lips brushing the shell.

His palm reaches the curve of my ass and I try to settle, but I'm still tense.

"Thirty plus the five extra. I want you to count them for me."

"Yes, Sir," I whisper.

"Louder, Pet."

I raise my voice and declare, "Yes, Sir!"

The first strike hits my right butt cheek, left, the crease

of my ass and thigh, right, left. I dance on his pommel horse, oddly almost like my fantasy, and count each one out loud.

At fifteen, Baz pauses and slides his thick middle finger along my dripping seam, collecting my juices.

"You want this spanking, Pet. Your little pink pussy swollen and dripping for me."

Another finger joins the first, and he finger fucks me, driving his long fingers into my slippery core. His fingers leave me and I'm bereft. The sound of his groan and tongue licking his fingers clean make me blush.

"So sweet, just as I knew you'd be."

"Oh. Oh. Oh!" I wail as Baz spanks my pussy five times.

The sting morphs into pleasure and I my pussy clenches around his fingers as they slide back into me.

"Fuck!"

I can feel my orgasm rising to the surface and I buck against Baz's hand.

Left, right, left, crease of my ass and thigh, right, left.

"You do not cum until I give you permission. And be still! Control your body."

As the spanking continues, they get harder and the intensity mounts. I can barely concentrate to count and beg Baz to let me cum. Finally, after what seems like a century, I hear those sweet words.

"Cum for me, Little Pet!" Baz commands as he thrusts his engorged cock deep inside of my dripping sheath. I scream as I clench his dick and shudder as I cum.

Baz grips my hips hard enough to leave fingerprints

that will match his palm prints on my ass. He grunts as his hips piston like a jackhammer into my pussy. The sounds of my wetness are loud in his suite.

"Uh. Uh. Uh. Uh," I cry out as Baz increases his pace and pounds into me, pushing me to the brink once more.

"Cum, again!" He shouts.

I babble that I can't take anymore, but Baz is not hearing it. He demands that I cum again as he spanks my stinging butt cheeks.

His dick grows even bigger and throbs as it scours my sheath.

"Cum!"

I grip his dick with all the strength that I have left and scream my release as wave after orgasmic wave hits me. It's so good that I sob and shake my head from side to side, overwhelmed with emotions.

As Baz slams into me one last time and roars his release, at last my mind lets go to float. My mind is free of tension and worry about my meeting in the morning. With a long drawn-out wail from my fifth electrifying orgasm, I give in to the sweet surrender of subspace.

Eventually, I return to myself, aware of my surroundings: Baz is holding me tightly on his lap, sitting against the headboard of the giant bed. My head is against his bare chest and I can hear the beating of his heart.

"How are you?" He asks softly.

The rumble of his voice goes through his chest to my ear.

"Incredible. Sore. Thirsty," I respond with a shy smile, my throat scratchy from my screams.

Baz holds a glass of water to my lips and I gratefully drink all of it.

As the haze lifts more, I realize that we're both still naked. The navy silk sheets caress my bare skin.

"I need to go," I make to get off of his lap, but Baz tightens his grip on my waist.

"That was intense and long. You should stay and get some rest. No one will disturb us. This is my private suite."

The offer is tempting, but I can't allow feelings to develop and I know that I'm vulnerable right now. Plus, it must be late and I need to return to the St. Regis. Breakfast is early and I want a clear head for the meeting.

So, with a heavy heart, I decline Baz's offer and climb off of his lap. The delicious touch of his hands sliding along my flanks, then my hips as I move away tempts me to stay. But, no.

"Would you like to meet tomorrow night?"

I stare at him over my shoulder, surprised that he would ask since we agreed that this would be for only one night, no commitments. I'm further surprised when I answer yes.

* * *

LEONIE DECIDED that she would watch the BDSM demonstration and Taylor offered to keep her company. Not just because he wanted to make sure we enjoyed ourselves, rather *The Lion* completely captivated *him*. She knew my reason for coming to LEVELS. Now that she saw I was in the capable hands of an experienced Dom, Leonie was happy to see me let go.

Stan drove back for me after he took Leonie to the hotel earlier. So, as I ride alone in the Bentayga, I lean my head against the plush headrest. My indescribable scene with my wild, possessive Caveman replays behind my closed eyes.

Tomorrow promises a monumental day and an incredible night.

SEBASTIAN

"Get your head in the game, Steele, and out of your ass!"

The glorious vision of her glistening, pink pussy and tight, puckered hole gets soundly knocked out of my brain. My personal trainer and former MMA champion Borya *The War Defender* Alexeyev delivers a roundhouse kick to my left flank.

Damn... that shit hurts likes a motherfucker.

"First, you're ten minutes late—"

Whack!

"Looking all bleary-eyed—"

Bam Bam!

"Now, I'm beating your weak ass like a *kiska*—"

Before Borya's next series of blows can hit me, I quickly crouch low and use my leg to sweep him off of his feet. The giant Russian lands on his ass with an oomph.

"What were you saying, asshole?" I sneer as I do my best

Mohammad Ali float like a butterfly sting like a bee moves, cracking my neck side to side.

"*Da, mal'chik!*"

Alexeyev punches his fists together as he effortlessly backflips to land on his feet.

"*Da*, that's more like it, Steele. Be here or go jerk off. No room on this mat for *zhopas* with the smell of *kiska* on their breath! Meow. Meow."

Sufficiently chastised and pissed that I'm letting some hookup fuck with my head, I refocus.

I fake a charge at Borya, then at the last second turn and back kick him, the momentum throwing him off balance and causing him to stumble forward. I follow the kick with a few, well-placed punches then taunt him as I float backwards, fists in the air, "I am the greatest!"

It's later than my usual start time of 5:15 a.m. I couldn't sleep after I arrived well past midnight at my duplex penthouse on the fifty-fifth and fifty-fourth floors of The Steele Tower. SI's remarkable gray-tinted glass skyscraper for our headquarters and commercial, retail, and residential properties on Fifth Avenue and Fifty-seventh Street in the heart of Billionaires' Row.

My mind replayed the scene with my Petite Seductress repeatedly, keeping my dick amped up and begging for access deep inside of her tight, wet pussy. From our initial contact with my hands gripping her forearms. To my dick pummeling her pussy, my balls slapping against her clit. To my palms sliding along her small waist and lush thighs as she rose from my bed. I can't shake the need to have her.

It's disturbing since I've never gotten caught up in a tryst before. She's got me all scattered.

Shit, I have to get my mind on straight for my meeting later this morning with a lingerie company based in Paris interested in expanding into the United States. This retail expansion deal must make up for the fiasco. The blight on my record that shall go unnamed and locked away, never seen nor heard from again. No matter what, I can't let that situation or any other disrupt my rise to CEO and Chair next year.

The session with Borya goes on for another hour. The Russian is always ready to hand me my *zhopa*. Workouts with him are brutal and challenge me to bring my A game. I'm forced to focus or get my ass kicked, literally.

"You ended better than you started, Steele. Still weak, but better. Whatever's turning your mind into mush must be worth it. Since you dared to step onto the mat half cocked with me!" Borya says. A deep, rumbling sound that's his version of a laugh. The grimace on his face the closest to a smile that his lips can create.

"Okay, okay, see you tomorrow," I respond and wonder if my Petite Seductress is worth it. Why do I care if she is or if she isn't?

* * *

ASIDE FROM A FULL gym on the first floor of my penthouse duplex, another of the many benefits of living at The STEELE Tower is I can ride the family's private elevator. It links our residences on the fiftieth through fifty-seventh floors to our headquarters on the nineteenth through twenty-ninth floors. The commute to my office is less than five minutes, so despite being late to my workout session, I arrive at my office as usual at seven.

I exit the elevator on the twenty-ninth floor for the executive level where my father, Malcolm, Roger, and I have offices. Our finance and legal departments along with various conference rooms occupy the remaining space. The STEELE divisions have designated floors below along with Harris and Haley's STEELE Technology and Cyber Security.

As always, power surges through me as soon as I enter any of the STEELE global offices. Pride swells in appreciation for my forebears. They laid the groundwork for the following generations to grow SI into a multibillion-dollar, luxury real estate development and management corporation. Each subsequent generation adding to the business' success. As the head of this generation, it is my duty to continue that upward trajectory set by those before me.

Through the gray-tinted, floor-to-ceiling windows, the city stretches out before me with unobstructed views. Central Park to the north, the Hudson River to the west, the East River opposite, and the rest of Manhattan to the south from Midtown to Battery Park. On a beautiful, cloudless day like this morning, the panoramas are riveting.

The decor—as sleek as the exterior—features platinum silk wall treatments, ebony wood floors, dove gray and white leather furniture, crystal light fixtures, Lucite tables, steel accents, and original artwork. The reception area has a spacious desk. Three attractive receptionists with headsets in their ears and custom-tailored light gray dress suits and skin-tone heels that serve as uniforms sit behind it.

The majesty of our power awes all who enter SI's offices.

"Good morning, Mr. Steele!" The trio chorus pleasantly.

"Good morning, Sue, Angela, Katrina," I respond with a nod and a smile.

On my way to my corner suite of offices, I pass Roger's offices and notice that he's in town early. He's based in our Paris branch, but spends about twenty percent of his time here.

"Hey, when did you get in?" I ask him as I stroll up to his desk.

Roger lifts his head and hits me with that intense stare. His gray eyes are just like mine, our family trait.

"Late last night. The investors canceled our meeting because of an ill associate, so I flew out earlier than planned."

He replies as he rises from his chair and comes around the desk to give me a bro hug and slap on the back.

I settle into the chair opposite his desk while he leans against it, crossing his long legs clad in custom-tailored trousers at the ankles, hands resting on the edge.

He catches me up on the happenings with two of the new builds that he's managing in Positano and Monte Carlo. I fill him in on the meeting with Lola's Coterie that

I'm having with my team in a few hours. As the middle child, Roger—*The Responsible* as his childhood nickname implies—seeks to balance everyone and acts as mediator, so I invite him to sit in on the meeting. It's always useful to have his perspective.

My mobile buzzes, interrupting our conversation. I retrieve it from my pants pocket and realize the time is 8:20 already. Tina Nickles, one of my two assistants, texted to ask if I were running late. I type a quick response that I'm in Roger's offices and will be there in ten minutes. Between Tina and Melody Lawson, they keep a tight rein on my schedule because they know how valuable my time is and that I dislike wasting it.

I return to my conversation with Roger for a few more minutes, then head to my offices. The workout session and bonding with my younger brother has me back in the game.

Lola

Oh boy, is my ass sore.

I reposition myself on the seat of Luc's Cullinan, the buttery soft leather not easing the pain from Baz's punishing blows to my bottom. A galvanizing reminder of our incredible play last night.

Even after I soaked in my bathroom's tub at the St. Regis, the blend of essential oils and Epsom salt did not fully ease the tenderness.

Now, I sit here enduring the soreness of my ass. My disappointment at the dull ache in my well-used pussy crying out for Baz's thick, long, tasty dick to fill it. I dreamt of him taking me repeatedly in the Cellar. I awoke this morning at six o'clock not by my alarm. But by a powerful orgasm that ripped through my pussy causing it to clench so tightly that it thrust me upright, crying out at the climax. I shiver just at the memory.

"Is everything all right?" Luc asks me, concern etched on his handsome face.

I feel my cheeks heat of embarrassment as though Luc can read my lewd thoughts.

Out of the corner of my eye, I spot that Leonie grins like the Cheshire Cat and gives me a knowing look with her eyebrow arched.

"I'm fine, just excited to get the meeting started," I respond to Luc, completely ignoring Leonie.

"How are your nerves? Did you satisfy them last night?" Leonie ribs me, suppressing a chuckle.

My face flushes deeper and I reach into my handbag, pretending to retrieve my mobile to avoid looking into Luc's eyes.

"Pretty satisfied, the long soak in the tub did me good," I nod my head in affirmation.

"I'm sure that it was long…" Leonie quips.

Fortunately at that moment, we pull up to The STEELE Tower which is a scant distance from our hotel. Once we're on the sidewalk, I do the decidedly non-New-Yorker move and crane my head back. I look up at the imposing glass building that appears to reach endlessly into the sky—it's magnificent.

We stride into the gray glass and steel lobby that has a three-story atrium with several high-end retail stores. The other stores are just as exclusive and make up the rest of the seven-story, luxury mall, the only one of its kind on New York City's posh Fifth Avenue. I'm determined to make Lola's Coterie New York its newest addition.

Security confirms our appointment with STEELE's president of Retail Properties and escorts us to the elevator for the executive floors on twenty-nine. We're quiet as the elevator speeds nonstop to the floor. The doors open to an opulent reception area with stunning 360-degree views of Manhattan. Once again, I'm suitably impressed by the strength and power that STEELE International exudes.

One of the three receptionists who's not busy on the telephone or speaking with another visitor welcomes us. Then, she informs us that the models are in one of the conference rooms. Our assistants, the glam squad, and the select pieces from the New York and Las Vegas collections are there, too. The receptionist calls for one of the security guards to escort Leonie to the room so she can join the others to prepare for the mini fashion show. Melody, an assistant for Mr. Steele, arrives to take Luc and me to another conference room where the meeting will occur.

"Would you care for some coffee, tea, or bottled water? Pastries and fruit are also available," Melody offers to us.

"Coffee black, *merci*," responds Luc with a charming smile that makes his deep blue eyes glitter like sapphires to which Melody blushes. In an attempt to hide it, she hurries to the breakfront for the beverage.

I head to the sleek, black, wooden table to check the presentations that Blair must have placed at one end. As if on the same wavelength, Blair appears in the doorway and smiles brightly at Luc, then at me.

"Good morning, Monsieur Montaigne!" She chirps.

"Bonjour, Blair."

Not having the patience to deal with Blair flirting with *Le Renard Argenté* before my meeting, I interrupt her before she can say another word.

"Blair, please help me with these," I say pointing at the various remotes that control the conference room's audio-visual system.

Melody assists us and soon we have my laptop connected and working properly. Her mobile chirps and she excuses herself to collect Mr. Steele and his team.

Once the door shuts, I turn to Luc and bite my lower lip as a touch of nerves threatens to rise.

Luc pulls me into his comforting embrace and I wrap my arms around his waist, drawing positive energy from him.

Suddenly, the doors open and we quickly pull apart to face our potential partners.

Sebastian

What the ever-loving fuck is she doing here? Better yet,

who the fuck is that old guy rubbing himself all over my Petite Seductress!

I damn near blow a gasket. The woman who's invaded every fucking cell of my body in less than twenty-four hours has the arms of another man wrapped around her. A man who's abso-fucking-lutely comfortable holding her so damn close. What... The... Fuck.

"—the founder and CEO of Lola's Coterie. Luc Montaigne, CEO of Banque Montaigne and vice chair of Lola's Coterie. Ms. Lewis, Mr. Montaigne, this is Sebastian Steele, the president of Retail Properties."

No one but my traitorous seductress notes that I faltered mid-stride when I entered the room. So Walter Smith, the director of development, continues with the introductions. I missed her first name, but assume it's Lola since the name of the company is the founder's name.

Lola's hazel eyes widen even more than they had last night in the Cellar and she flushes deeply. Obviously, she's as dumbfounded as I. Unconsciously, her hand moves to cover her round ass that I know is still sore and covered in my palm prints.

This is surreal. And fuck me if my dick didn't grow hard.

A lull in the room draws my attention from the little vixen to my team who watch me with curiosity in their eyes. Roger is staring between Lola and me with that damnable intense gaze of his that never misses a thing. He would catch the tension between Lola and me.

I quickly recover and continue to stride over to Lola

and Luc, thankful that my suit jacket prevents anyone from seeing the big bulge in my pants. I give them each a firm handshake—well, I may have squeezed Luc's hand more than necessary. He babbles on about Delcour who made the introduction for this meeting and I let Montaigne know that I'm not impressed by him. The little vixen pipes up about starting the meeting and I check out her luscious hips sway in that tight skirt as she walks to the head of the table. Oh, so the sub wants control.

As I lower myself into the seat opposite Lola, pinning her with a penetrating Dom stare, I remind myself of my earlier pledge. No matter what, I can't let this situation or any other disrupt my rise to CEO and Chair next year. Game on.

LOLA

*H*ow is this even possible? What in the hell did I do to deserve this karma? I ask myself in utter disbelief that Baz is Sebastian Steele, the president of STEELE International, Inc.'s Retail Properties Division. The man who I'm supposed to dazzle with my company's stellar growth and expansion plans. The same man who spanked my ass, saw my pussy, and fucked me raw.

Holy shit...

His expression and the falter in his stride, show that he can't believe this either. What are the chances that we would encounter one another at a BDSM club; share an intense scene and have crazy sex; later come face-to-face at a business meeting the next morning? Incredible.

The thought reminds me of my sore butt. I didn't even realize that I touched my ass until the arrogant smirk on his face appeared. Baz, I mean Sebastian... didn't miss the subtle movement.

I bite my lower lip in consternation as I wearily eye him strutting towards me.

The feel of his palm touching mine in a firm handshake causes a zing of electricity to shoot up my arm straight to my core. Against my will, my pussy obediently clenches for its Dom. The expression in his eyes turns feral at the contact before returning to neutral. Once again, like a puppet on a string, I shake his hand.

As if sensing my discomfort, Luc steps forward and holds his hand out to Sebastian.

"Good morning, Monsieur Steele, it's a pleasure to meet you. Pierre Delcour speaks highly of you and STEELE International."

"Yes, Monsieur Delcour is an honorable man, Monsieur Montaigne," Sebastian responds with a hint of a growl in his tone. "Let's determine if you are, too."

I glance to Luc as his face slightly grimaces, then I notice how tightly Sebastian is gripping Luc's hand. Sebastian's unprovoked aggression snaps me out of my stupor—this isn't the Cellar and I'm not a sub. Who the hell does he think he is behaving this way? I didn't come this far to let some caveman frazzle me.

"Mr. Steele, Luc and I appreciate you and your team meeting with us on such brief notice. Shall we get started?"

Without waiting for Sebastian's response, I strut to the head of the table and signal to Blair to close the doors. I begin the presentation once everyone settles in their seats. Sebastian sits opposite me, his gray eyes unreadable, his face set in a neutral expression. No sign of what happened last night impacting him today, hmmm. Unlike me so, I take a deep breath to re-center my thoughts and proceed as Luc and I practiced. My gaze travels to each person seated around the table to encourage their engagement during my thirty-minute pitch. After I finish, Luc's assistant opens the door to start the mini fashion show. As each model enters, I explain the relevancy of the piece for the specific boutique location and the craftsmanship that is the hallmark of my designs. Leonie, as my muse, begins and ends the show with her trademark predatory gait and mesmerizing aura.

At that point, Luc takes over for the financial portion of the presentation. I sit in awe of him and his innate ability to charm and to win over people so easily. The confidence that Luc exudes makes everyone around the table sit up straighter after being wowed by my story and by the models. After he's completed the details on the growth rate and expansion numbers, we answer the team's questions without a hitch.

Two hours later, the meeting ends with Sebastian rising from the table and announcing they will get back to us in a few days, before he abruptly leaves the room. Throughout the entire presentation, he sat there stoically and mum. I couldn't gauge his reaction, even when the scantily clad models with Leonie in the lead pranced around the conference room. That man confounds me!

Luc waits until Sebastian's team and his brother Roger exit the room before turning to me with a raised eyebrow.

"Je ne tolère pas l'impolitesse," he scoffs, the corner of his upper lip curled in disgust.

I can't stand rudeness either I nod my head in agreement with him and gather my laptop and portfolio. Blair and Luc's assistant handle the rest of the items in silence.

"Well, Mr. Steele may have been a cold fish, but we impressed his team and engaged them. I'm pleased with the presentation and I know that we did our best. Like my father used to say, 'Nothing beats a failure, but a try.' Thank you everyone," I smile.

Despite my mind racing, trying to figure out my next move and holding back my disappointment. I expected more than a cold brush-off.

Does he think less of me since I played a sub for him last night and now he can't perceive me as a serious businesswoman? Would he have had more respect for me if I hadn't given him head like a professional? Should I have pulled him aside and cleared things up? Why the fuck did I go to that damn sex club?

"Did you notice his brother Roger's face when Leonie entered the room?" Luc asks.

I shake my head no. My focus was on the meeting and trying to get a read on Sebastian to notice his brother—the president of Residential or something—and Leonie. Besides, it's unusual if a man doesn't drool when he sees her.

Melody reappears as we finish gathering our belongings and walks us towards the elevator. As we pass a set of offices, Sebastian is leaning against his desk laughing with some red head standing in front of him. His gaze briefly meets mine without acknowledgment of me before he looks back at her when she places her hand on his chest. He laughs even more at something she says in his ear.

My vision goes red, and my brain explodes.

SEBASTIAN

*L*ook at the vixen teetering over here in those fuck-me shoes, her hazel eyes trained on me, her heart-shaped face red in anger. I want to bite those tightly pressed lips. The spitfire has my eager dick expanding.

Poor Tina didn't stand a chance as Lola sidestepped her way around my assistant as she fruitlessly attempted to block Lola from barging into my office.

"Who the hell do you think you are, asshole?" Lola demands, hands on hips and feet planted wide on the floor. Her fight stance beats Borya's by aces.

"Please excuse the interruption, Chloe. We'll continue our meeting momentarily," I tell her. I never take my eyes from Lola. Who looks as though she's about to throw Chloe out of my office by her long, red hair if she doesn't leave fast enough.

"I'm so sorry, Mr. Steele!" a flustered Tina starts, "Ms. Lewis, please come with me."

The scathing look that Lola gives Tina makes me shudder just as much as Tina trembles in fear.

"It's all right, Tina," I assure her. "I'll handle Ms. Lewis."

"Handle... Handle? I'll give you something to handle, you jerk!" Lola screeches as Chloe and Tina scurry out of the office giving Lola a wide berth. They're followed by Melody, who had appeared at the door openmouthed and wide-eyed. As she leaves, she slowly shuts the door watching me for a sign to call security. I shake my head and gesture for her to go.

I peer beyond Lola to see more shocked expressions on the faces of Luc, Leonie, Roger, and the team from the meeting. Still others stare from their spaces. The situation prompts me to walk around my desk. Where I press the buttons to darken the glass walls of my office and remotely lock the door. This provides much-needed privacy for our unexpected encounter. As loudly as Lola is speaking, I'm glad that my office is soundproof, too. As she continues her rant, she stands in front of me poking my chest with her long, red fingernail in emphasis.

"Don't you dare think less of me because of what happened last night! I'm a successful businesswoman who deserves respect! I will not allow you to discount my achievements and blow off my expansion plans! Sitting in that room all high and mighty, as though you had more important things—"

I swipe the surface of my desk clean. The items hit the

floor with a crash. I deftly grab the wrist of her jabbing hand, spin her around, and put her hands on her lower back. I press her against the top of my desk with my torso.

"Are you forgetting who's the Dom and who's the sub here?" I growl into her ear, satisfied when she trembles beneath me and expels a heavy breath. I push my hips into her plump ass, my thick cock wedged against her crack.

"Well, let me remind you, Ms. Lewis," I tell her gruffly and stand.

The snap of my large palm spanking both cheeks of her ass slides Lola across the surface. I remove my tie and secure both of her wrists against her lower back. I wrap the fingers of my left hand around the back of her neck to hold her in place. My right hand delivers a quick succession of smacks that have Lola dancing up on her toes. She squirms to dodge the startling blows.

"Don't you dare!" She splutters attempting to rise from the position. "I did not give you permission to spank me and you are not my Dom and I am not your sub!"

My hand stops midair as I realize with a start that I want to be her Dom and I want her to be my sub. I want my Petite Seductress for more than one night. My body craves her, I need to have more of her. I conclude that I have two choices. Ignore my inner caveman who wants to claim her and walk away with just that one glorious night. Or give in to the feral beast and fuck her out of my head while she's here this week.

In the brief span of time for my thoughts to form, she takes advantage of the break in the spanking to rise and face me. The breathtaking blow from her head butting my chest brings my focus back to Lola. She's stunning with her eyes bright and her cheeks flushed in anger and thinly veiled passion.

She's wrong in her conclusion that I think less of her because we had a Dom/sub scene and intense sex. No. Lola is a brilliant, determined woman who accomplished a huge and rapid success despite the tragic loss of her parents. I learned those details from the synopsis that my development team assembled on her company and on her personal life. The expansion plan is spot-on and would be a positive addition to the profitable roster of STEELE retail partners. It wasn't a delay tactic nor a dismissal when I told them that my team would be in touch. The details that Lola presented today need an in-depth review by my team, finance, and legal. More than likely, they will have revisions and recommendations that will require a follow-up meeting. That's all a part of the negotiations, but there's no doubt that we'll move forward with the deal. It promises to make up for my recent mishap. Especially if we expand into Los Angeles and Miami in the United States and Abu Dhabi and Dubai in the United Arab Emirates. Those epicenters for the wealthy who appreciate fine craftsmanship and sexy lingerie. I shake my head and snort at her false assumption.

"Oh, so now you're laughing at me? It's not enough to make a fool out of me, but to add insult to—"

I silence her newest tirade with a knee-jellifying, ground-shaking kiss that renders her speechless. Lola's taste is addictive and I seal my decision with our lips crushed together—I haven't had enough of her and I damn sure need more than one night.

Gently, I pull back and watch Lola's beautiful, hazel eyes flutter open to gaze into mine. In that moment, I see and sense her need to have love and to give into someone whom she can trust. It may have to do with the loss of her parents at such a young age and not having any siblings or other relatives to comfort her. Or the loneliness of chasing her business success. I can relate with the loneliness, but ignore it. No wonder Montaigne latched onto her—old, scheming bastard. An overwhelming instinct of protectiveness for Lola takes over me. I brush her soft cheek with the pad of my thumb and cup her face, holding our stare.

"Lola, you are mistaken. What you shared with me last night was a gift that I cherish. You put your trust in me and I value and respect you for it."

As she attempts to interrupt me, I put my thumb to her kiss-swollen lips and continue.

"You decided that you wanted to do a scene with me during which you wanted a spanking. The sex was as much for your satisfaction as it was for mine—I pushed you to your limit for orgasms before I allowed myself release. You learn that a sub holds all the power, not the Dom."

I remove my thumb from her lips to allow her to speak.

"Then, why were you so aggressive when you saw me and closed off during the meeting? You walked out without even a glance my way," Lola laments, her beautiful face set in a scowl of frustration.

I pause and reflect on my behavior and the reasons for it. The realization that I'm jealous of her relationship with Montaigne and that jealousy being the impetus for my actions makes me uneasy. I don't want to develop feelings for Lola for many reasons: I don't mix business with pleasure; I'm not interested in a relationship; I have a business to grow. The one exception is to fuck her despite our pending business deal. That she isn't interested in a relationship either, as she stated last night. Then proved when she left even though I offered for her to stay validates the exception for my next offer.

"As per the norm, my team vetted your company prior to our meeting, so we knew what to expect. The specifics you presented today require an in-depth review. More than likely, a follow-up meeting will be necessary to discuss revisions and recommendations. All necessary before we move forward with the deal."

I allow her time to cogitate.

With a nod of acceptance, she tries to slip out of my embrace. But I hold her tighter and she looks up at me questioningly.

"I have an offer for you," I start and my Petite Seductress lifts her elegant brow further.

"Really... do tell," she smirks.

"Let's set the deal aside and leave it to our teams to hash things out until we need to make the ultimate decision. I propose that you and I spend our time more pleasantly," I respond, then pause again to judge her reaction.

"What do you have in mind?" She purrs with a tilt to her head, eyeing me through her long, dark lashes.

"That for the week you're here, I teach you the beauty of a Dom/sub relationship and you get thorough use of your LEVELS New York guest membership."

Her hazel eyes darken to black as desire runs through her body. The telltale scent of her arousal from the spanking a moment ago grows stronger when she shifts from foot to foot. She rubs her thighs together to soothe the ache that's built in her core.

It intrigues my Pet.

* * *

I CAN'T BELIEVE I'm anxiously sitting at the Cellar's bar hoping that Lola will meet me here. I'll think about it, she told me. Really... Even while her nipples peaked against the silk of her blouse and her body quivered at the thought. What the fuck?

Now, who's playing hard to get. Except I'm the one who's hard. So hard that my pent-up dick is about to punch a sizable hole in my trousers and blind me with the force of my balls unleashing. I've been on edge since ten o'clock this morning, eleven hours now—not to mention since she left me in bed last night. Shit, Lola even refused to let me walk her to her car, not wanting anyone to see us together as I recall. Annoyed that she didn't want people to know that we spent time together. Further annoyed that I'm annoyed.

Lola is fifteen minutes late. If she doesn't show up in

three minutes, I will split in two the sexy Milk Chocolate Bunny. She's been eye fucking me this whole time. Even after I showed her the gold bracelet and reminded her it matches me with a sub for the night.

My mind is on a nonstop Lola Loop: thinking of her soft coos as I finger fucked her; remembering how good her tight cunt seemed wrapped around my swollen dick; and most of all, the sweet taste of her juices. Tonight I have to feast on her honeypot.

The sweet thing walks towards me and I give her an encouraging look since at this point Lola's missed the deadline. Moments before the tasty delight reaches me, Lola saunters into the Cellar. She looks beyond fuckable in a chestnut brown colored, leather bustier that pushes her succulent tits to her throat, a skimpy silk thong, and a pair of thigh-high leather boots.

Damn, my dick jumps and weeps as I groan out loud.

Just as we make eye contact, Lola gets stopped by that bastard Patrick Rockett, another Dom and the CEO of STEELE's biggest competitor Rockett Construction before she reaches me. That motherfucker is a pain in my ass. He's already fucked me over with that poor ass deal, sliding in and lowballing the contract. Now, he's after my Petite Seductress. I don't think so, asshole.

"Hi, looks like your sub didn't show up. Her loss is my gain—" starts the Milk Chocolate Bunny.

"Excuse me, she's here," I respond, rising from the barstool without taking my eyes off of Rockett. He's damn near drooling on Lola when she laughs at some inane thing he's said in her ear.

As the bunny follows my trail of sight, she adds, "Well, she's hooked up with Pat—"

"No," I bark at her, my blood boiling at the thought of Rockett taking what's mine, again. Then, a sense of contrition hits me when she steps back in surprise at my sharp tone. "I apologize. Excuse me," I quickly add, then stalk over to Lola and Rockett.

"—I already told you I'm meeting someone—" Lola is telling him.

"Rockett, the lady is with me," I cut in and position myself between him and Lola, forcing Rockett to back up. I've got an inch on him even if he outweighs me by about 20 pounds of muscle still fit from his rugby days. I'm swifter and a trained fighter.

"Damn, mate, no need to get in my face," he responds with a sneer.

"Wanna be sure you're clear," I retort and glare at him until he backs down mumbling about me being a sore ass over the deal. I ignore him. My Pet is here now, even though in the back of my mind a niggle reminds me I'm a wimp for allowing more feelings where there should be none.

I shake it off and face my Petite Seductress, who's even more bewitching up close. She's added some eye makeup that enhances the flecks of gold in her hazel orbs. If I'm not careful, I could get lost in their depths especially as Lola stares at me like I'm her protector.

"Are you all right?" I ask, noticing a bit of unexpected, but pleasant warmth at the thought.

"Yes, he just wouldn't take no for an answer," She sighs in frustration. "Colossal jerk."

"Yeah, he is a colossal jerk. Come, we'll use one of the private areas... No need for an audience," I tell Lola. I make a mental note to tell Taylor to remind Rockett of LEVELS' rules of engagement.

I put my hand on Lola's waist, my fingers brushing against her soft skin exposed between the bustier and the thong. I guide her to one of the Cellar's alcoves separated from the main hall by heavy blood-red velvet curtains held by metal links suspended from the ceiling. Within each alcove a multitude of BDSM toys and equipment offer various levels of pleasure and pain. I choose an alcove with my favorite piece—the St. Andrew's Cross.

"Oh, of course, we don't want that woman to have more of a reason to eye fuck you," Lola mocks with a tilt to her head and her lips pursed.

I smack her bottom twice and nearly cum as it jiggles and my palm print blooms red on her still sensitive skin. As I pull her back to my front, I growl in her ear, "Are you sassing me, Pet?"

"Well, Sir"—she emphasizes the sir cheekily—"I'm merely pointing out the obvious."

I bend my knees and grind my hard cock into her ass while I press the flat of my hand against her mound, locking her ass to my pelvis.

"I'll tell you what is obvious. I will show you another

use for your cocky mouth. Then you are getting this plump ass paddled. After which I will keep you on the edge until you beg me to cum on my dick."

I warn the vixen, the sound of her soft mewls zinging my balls.

Enough time wasted. I stand to my full height—Lola teeters on those sky-high boots—return my hand to her waist and walk us to the alcove. Time to start our evening.

LOLA

*H*oly shit! My pussy creams not only from the wild vision that Baz depicts. But from his massive cock grinding into my ass and his gigantic hand cupping my mound. His long fingers stroking my engorged clit through my thin, silk thong. I tremble and a mewl escapes my parted lips on a lengthy sigh. Damn, I can't wait to have Baz fill me and take me roughly.

I agreed to his offer to introduce me to the Dom/sub world so I can get my fill of him in more ways than one and to satisfy my curiosity. The spanking Simon gave me opened my body to pleasure and release that I never knew existed. The key with Baz is to remember that this is only for the week and that I don't have the time for a relationship—my relationship status is Lola's Coterie. I can't allow Baz's training to impact our business deal negatively. Fortunately, he seems just as keen as I am to keep things purely sexual. I must stay focused and not develop any feelings for him. Easier said than done, especially when Baz has my body buzzing just from his words and from his touch. My inner cheerleader urges me to stay in the moment and to have fun, business completed for the day.

"So, what do you have in mind, Sir?" I ask. He guides me to a secluded corner of the Cellar where an alcove with ominous red velvet curtains held open by gold cords beckon us to enter.

"I told you, your mouth needs filling and your ass needs punishment," he retorts looking down at me with a smirk. His gray eyes filled with lust, shining like liquid platinum. Damn, is he the most vampish man I've ever met?

Without further interruptions, we reach the private alcove and Baz loosens the curtains from their cords. As they flow closed, he turns and his eyes gleam at me in the dim space lit by a pair of torches in metal stands. I peel my eyes from his lust-filled gaze and take in my surroundings.

A standing wooden cross that has cuffs on the four corners—similar to the one Baz has in his corner suite upstairs—dominates the area; a leather bench is along the stone wall; an antique wooden chest sits beside the bench; my eyes widen and I gasp when I recognize different whips, crops, and... a few paddles. Some paddles are smooth wood, while others have holes or studs on their surfaces. The sizes vary from as large as a cricket bat to as small as an oven mitt. Instinctively, I cover my bottom with my hands and glance at Baz who's studying me with an intense stare. Oh dear, why did I mouth off.

"Come here, Pet," Baz chides.

I gulp and keep eye contact with him as I walk in his direction. I pray that my shaky knees won't give out and I collapse into an undignified heap at his feet.

"Ah… Ah… Ah," Baz intones with a wag of his long finger and a shake of his gorgeous head.

With a tilt to my head, I pause in the middle of my stride and ponder what I'm doing wrong. Then, it hits me… I'm a sub for all intents and purposes now, and subs don't walk and keep their eyes level with their Dom. As gracefully as possible in my tall boots, I drop to my hands and knees. I attempt to recapture the moment from last night when I crawled to Baz. I keep my ass high and my head low. Once I reach him, I sit back on my haunches and await his next command. Am I a bitch in heat or a successful businesswoman, I question myself. Again, my inner cheerleader tells me to leave it at the door and to fulfill my desires.

"Good, girl, Little Pet," Baz croons with a smile on his handsome face. I notice that he's shaved the five o'clock shadow that he had earlier today and last night. This guy's face is a work of art. His sculpted cheekbones, strong jawline, and nose that he must have broken at some point and it healed slightly crooked gives him a more edgy and less pretty boy appearance. His full lips are so kissable that I lick my own and bite my lower one to hold back the moan that's threatening to burst forth. I quiver in anticipation.

"You were so sassy a minute ago and I warned you what

was in store for your flippant mouth," Baz reminds me with a smirk. "Time for your first lesson, a sub does not talk back to their Dom nor do they flirt with other Doms—"

"I wasn't flirting with that guy!" I protest. "He was—"

"Lesson number two, a sub does not interrupt their Dom and never yells at them," Baz chastises me. "For those grievances, you will receive five extra strikes of my paddle. But first, it's time for you to fill this hole with every inch of my length."

As Baz traces my lips with his fingertip, my mouth waters from the memory of how good he tasted, like saltwater taffy from the Jersey Shore, sweet and salty. I lick my lips in anticipation and reach up to open his fly.

"I apologize, Sir, please allow me to make up for my naughty behavior," I purr with a voice so thick with lust that I barely recognize it as my own.

Baz grunts his approval. I slowly unzip his trousers exposing his black silk boxer briefs stretched to capacity by his dick so hard and ready to be free it's pulsating behind the material. I happily uncage the Beast and push Baz's pants and briefs down his muscular thighs. A drop of precum greets me once his massive cock springs free, nearly taking my eye out. Mmm mmm.

Without hesitation, I set to work, cupping his heavy sac as I flick the droplet onto my tongue, savoring his salty-sweet taste and musky scent with a groan. I swirl my tongue around his swollen tip and massage his balls before I wrap my other hand around the base of his girth. In tandem, humming, I move my mouth lower on his head as one hand strokes his dick and the other squeezes his balls. Baz grunts in appreciation. A quick upward glance and I see he's watching me with heavy-lidded eyes black with lust, mouth parted in absolute bliss. His look encourages me to take him deeper into my mouth until his bulbous tip hits the back of my throat. He groans in response, his fingers fisting my hair holding my head at the perfect angle for him to fuck my face.

"Damn, Pet, your mouth feels so good. I've been hard all day for you. Fuck!"

His hips jerking forward, fucking my mouth in earnest follows Baz's exclamation. I meet his cries with my moans reverberating around his cock, driving him further into oblivion before he cries out.

"Fuck, Pet, I'm going to cum so hard. Fuck! This is how you use your mouth with a Dom. No… more… sassing… me!" He punctuates each word with a forceful thrust.

Tears form in my eyes. I have to concentrate to keep my breathing at pace with his thrusts since Baz is holding my head so tightly that my scalp stings and I groan in pain.

"Yes, Pet! That's it! Take it… Take every fucking one of my ten inches. Fuuuuuuuck!"

With that, Baz's dick expands in size and pulsates with rope after rope of his cum shooting down my throat. He locks my lips to his crotch and jerks his hips to get every drop out and into my mouth. I swallow profuse amounts of his seed—delicious…

As Baz's length lessens, he pulls his dick from my

mouth. I suck on it until it comes away with a pop, a trail of my spit connecting my lips to his tip. I smirk and lick my lips, satisfied that I had a powerful hold over such an Alpha male that his knees shook and he threw his head back completely undone. Now, I understand what Baz means by the sub has all the power. My inner cheerleader does a series of cartwheels in jubilation.

As Baz tucks himself back into his pants, he stares at me with a dazed look. Then shakes his head as if trying to rid his mind of some unwanted thought. I sit back on my haunches and daintily wipe my mouth with my fingers. Then wantonly lick the cum that's there into my mouth. His eyes darken further.

"Now that I used your mouth suitably, it is time for your spanking."

Baz holds his hand out to help me from the floor—used, ha, I love sucking his dick—and leads me to the cross.

"This is the St. Andrew's Cross," Baz starts as he positions me with my front to the cross and my back to him.

"We place subs on the cross for various reasons. Tonight, it's holding you in place while I administer your punishment, naughty, little girl," he continues as he buckles red, suede-lined leather cuffs to my wrists and ankles.

"Tell me why you're being punished, Pet," Baz quizzes me.

"You're punishing me because I was sassy when I commented that other woman would have another reason to eye fuck you if we stayed in the main hall for our training session," I answer snarkily.

"Ow," I yelp when Baz smacks my bottom unexpectedly.

"Another lesson. How do you address me and in what type of tone?" He barks.

I know right away that my tone wasn't submissive. But I take a moment to realize that I didn't end my response with Sir, so I add it to the sentence and answer contritely. After a placated grunt, I hear Baz walk away from me. My mind runs wild as I think of which paddle he'll choose for my punishment. Will it be the small one that has holes in it, the large one with indentations, or the medium one that's plain? All too soon, Baz is back and the hardness of one paddle against my skin makes me explode with desire as he rubs it along my thighs and buttocks.

"You are new to BDSM, Little Pet. So I will not take you to the extremes with one of the more advanced paddles. Tonight, I will use a classic one made of wood and only six inches in length and 5 inches wide. I will administer ten strikes for the punishment and five more for your insolence. I want you to stay still and count for me. Absorb the pain and take your mind off of it by focusing on the numbers. Do you understand?"

Baz asks as if I have a choice. Actually I do as he reminded me this afternoon, that the whole situation is my decision and he will respect my desires.

"Yes, Sir, I understand," I respond, anxious about the pain level. Yet giddy to reach subspace knowing that I can trust Baz.

"What is your safeword, Little Pet?" Baz asks me, while

ripping the silk thong off and rubbing the paddle against my bare skin.

"Panther, Sir," I moan as my juices flow down my legs.

"Good, girl."

Whack. Whack. Whack. Whack. Whack. Whack. Whack.

I try my best to stay still and to count as Baz unleashes blow after blow on my bottom. The impact of them sending shock waves through my body, radiating from my ass to my hands and feet. I lean into the St. Andrew's Cross, thankful that it is sturdy and won't let me crumble to the floor. Once we reach the seventh blow, I'm not sure how much more I can take. As if sensing my distress, Baz pauses.

"You are doing well. Are you still with me, Little Pet? Or do you want to safeword? Then we stop right now."

The pause gives me time to re-collect myself and I shake my head no.

"Words, Pet," Baz admonishes my non-verbal response.

"No, Sir, I don't want to stop," I vocally answer, my juices slipping to a puddle below the cross. It hurts, but the pain is morphing into pleasure, the release that I crave. "Please don't stop, Sir!"

The last few hits send me into a place where I can just let go and not worry about business, being lonely, my parents, fighting my desires—I'm free.

I WAKE to strong fingers smoothing a cool gel onto my heated buttocks and thighs. I lie face down with my head resting on my hands on the leather bench. A low hiss issues from my parted lips when Baz's fingers touch a sore spot on my left cheek. I open my eyes and push against the bench to sit up, but a firm press between my shoulder blades prevents me from rising far from the soft leather.

"Lie down. I am almost done massaging the salve into your skin. It will not hurt much longer," Baz commands and assures me at the same time. "This is aftercare when a Dom tends to their sub once the scene is over. How do you feel otherwise?"

I don't want to keep my Dom waiting too long for my answer. So, a quick head-to-toe scan of my body reveals that other than my bruised rear, I'm pretty relaxed. Albeit fuzzy in the brain.

"Good—" I wince when Baz touches the crease where my thigh meets my ass. "Except for a few painful areas on my rear, Sir."

"Mmm mmm," Baz responds in a low rumble that makes my pussy clench and weep all over again. "Enjoy this moment of relaxation now because your punishment continues shortly."

I whimper and adjust my position on the bench. Three rapid smacks to my pussy makes me yowl and squirm.

"Enough!" Baz demands. "Time is up. Follow me."

Gingerly, I sit up on the bench, certain not to put too much pressure on my punished rear. As I drop to my knees, I realize that the salve has lessened the sting from the paddle. With an appreciative sigh, I crawl behind Baz until he stops at the St. Andrew's Cross.

"Not again!" I wail, kneeling up to stand. "It's too soon and my—"

Baz cuts my words off when he wraps his fingers around my throat and leans in so close that our noses touch.

"You will not tell your Dom what is best for your punishment, nor will you raise your voice to me!"

As he keeps his grip firm on my neck, Baz continues in a dangerous whisper, "Understood, Pet?"

At the sensation of his fingers applying pressure to impede my breath and the fury glowing in his gray eyes, my traitorous body quivers with pleasure. Despite my brain, yelling at me to tell Baz to fuck the hell off.

I nod.

"I will have your words, Pet!" Baz thunders at me.

"Ye... Yesss, Sir," I stutter.

Still holding my throat, Baz stands. I clumsily rise to my feet. A sense of shame at disappointing my Dom washes over me. The burn of tears behind my eyes.

"You will learn, and quickly, what is correct and what is wrong. Or, you will not sit on your plump bottom for the rest of this week."

Both of us suck in a breath—me at the thought of the pain and the pleasure of his promise. While Baz looks taken aback by the reminder of this being for a week—at least my inner cheerleader hopes that's the reason.

As he regains his composure, Baz continues, "Stand with your back to the cross, Pet."

Immediately, I obey his command and get into position, careful not to let my butt cheeks come into contact with the hard wood. I keep my gaze at his chest while I await Baz's next form of punishment. Without delay, he cuffs my wrists and as he lowers himself to a squat; he trails the tips of his fingers along my inner thighs and calves. Once my ankles are secure, Baz buries his nose in my folds and inhales deeply.

"Oh, Pet, your arousal smells divine," he croons, then with a lick to my pussy lips, he groans. "So sweet, just like honey. Tell me your pussy is my personal honeypot, Pet. All mine!"

Baz's deep, passionate growl sends shivers up and down my spine, a gasp falling from my lips when his tongue flicks my swollen clit. A not so gentle nip to it makes me jump and bump my butt against the cross.

"Nooo," I wail as the pain radiates through me.

I open my eyes when Baz suddenly stops his ministrations to my core and stands before me, a frown on his face.

"No? No, your pussy is not mine? Then, who does it belong to?" He snarls, eyes blazing.

I gasp and quickly respond, "To you, Sir. To you! I hit my butt on the wood and it hurt. That's why I cried out no!" I insist to compel him to return to devouring my pussy.

With a nod, Baz turns and walks to the wooden chest. I crane my neck to see what he's removing from it, but can't get an unimpeded view from this angle. When he returns, he's holding a red silk scarf and his trouser pockets are full.

"Edging is orgasm control where at the peak of arousal the Dom refuses to grant the sub release, preventing one from going over the edge to climax. I will keep you at a top level of arousal for an extended period. If you cum without my permission, I will punish you. Do you understand?" Baz gazes intently at me.

The thought of not being able to cum coupled with knowing that Baz is so good, that I'm scared I won't be able to hold on to my orgasm. I look away from his captivating gray eyes to think without his influence. The sounds of others in throes of passion fill my ears and makes me want more. Decision made, I look back at him.

"Yes, Sir," I respond, my curiosity overtaking my nerves.

"I will deprive you of three of your senses."

He holds up the blindfold and presents ear plugs from one of his pockets.

"I bound your hands so you cannot touch. Your sight and sound are next. I want you to only feel what I am doing to you with no distractions. It will be intense, so use your safeword if you want me to stop completely. Remember to push beyond your limits as much as you are comfortable."

"Yes, Sir," I reply with an affirmative nod for double surety.

With my confirmation, Baz places the earplugs in and pauses with the scarf in front of my eyes. I smile shyly at him and he places the soft material around my head and ties it securely.

His lips crush mine. I gasp at the sudden kiss and he pushes his tongue past my open lips. Our tongues duel and mate as he dominates my mouth. The sensation of his thick fingers sliding along my pussy lips as he nips the lips on my face draws a moan from me. His tongue and two of his fingers act in tandem as he repeatedly plunders my mouth and my pussy. When he adds a third thick finger, I'm amazed that my juices gush in a torrent and the stirrings of an orgasm surface. I bite back a scream as I attempt to rein in my climax. My pussy walls clench around Baz's fingers and I pant into his open mouth. Suddenly, three smacks hit my pussy and my orgasm retreats from the shocking pain. I whimper and toss my head from side to side in irritation.

Warm wetness engulfs my left nipple. I arch my back into the ecstasy of Baz's mouth suckling my breast, the suction intense, bordering on painful.

"Aaahhh," I moan when he fondles my right breast, testing its weight in his palm before pinching my nipple between his fingers. A sharp bite to my left nipple makes me shudder and cry out. Baz's mouth immediately moves to my right nipple and suckles relentlessly until another sharp bite on that nipple makes me squeal. Kisses to each nipple followed by kisses and nips trailing down my belly to my mound dulls the pain in my nipples.

Baz's tantalizing tongue plays my pussy like a fine instrument and makes me sing mezzo-soprano in absolute pleasure. He pulls my engorged clit into his mouth and nips it before a sharp bite closes around it and I wail in agony that morphs into pleasure. Baz returns to his concerto and I return to the brink, yet again. This time, I hold on longer than before. Deep breaths help me maintain a bit of control over my orgasm. Baz adds his fingers to my pussy, stroking them in and out. My juices coat them more with each thrust and my orgasm builds with their plundering.

Suddenly, he slides his hands above my core into virgin territory—my asshole. I jerk and attempt to lift off of the cross once again inflaming my butt when it strikes the wood. I'm pinned into place against the cross by Baz's other hand on my hip. All the while, he continues his path to my forbidden hole and his tongue laves my clit, scooping out my honey. I clench my fists and my pussy walls with a shout when he slides one finger to the knuckle inside of my ass. I pull against the cuffs and jerk from his hand on my hip as his finger goes deeper, and the pain increases. The muscles of my hole resist Baz's dark trespass. Once he fully seats his finger deep within me, I pant and try to breathe deeply—until he thrusts his finger and add the second one, stretching my puckered hole. As quickly as the pain hit, it changes into pleasure and I moan and beg.

"Baz, ppp... please let me cum," I wail. "I can't hold on anymore!" I cry as he speeds up his finger and his tongue. It's pleasurable torture and I can't hold it anymore.

Just as the orgasm under the surface rises, Baz stands, removes his finger from my ass, and tugs on my nipples and clit. The pain is excruciating and I scream as blood rushes back to the sensitive areas. What. The. Fuck. Was. That.

Before I can even speculate on the possible causes, Baz's mouth surrounds one of my tender nipples. Then the bulbous head of his hard cock at my pussy entrance pressing between my folds with a demanding urgency. I wail and try to match his pistoning strokes, thankful that I'm so wet that his massive dick glides unimpeded through my core.

"Uh. Uh. Uh. Uh."

Faced with Baz's unrelenting onslaught, I can only give into my orgasm as it breaks the surface and crashes through me. My body convulses and I scream through wave after wave of my unbound release. I've never cum so hard in my life and revel in the unending pleasure until it becomes too much and I beg Baz to stop.

"Please, Baz, no more... I can't take another orgasm," I wail as tears fall from my eyes.

Baz ignores my pleas as he continues to pump into me like a machine, still hard, his pelvis crushing mine, his heavy balls slapping my pussy lips. I tighten up again as another set of orgasms rips through me and I cry out.

"Oh! Oh! Oh! Oh!"

Just before my last orgasm crests, I clench as tight as my ravished pussy can on Baz's cock. I'm rewarded with his dick expanding and jetting his seed into the condom. Another round of orgasms triggered as my pussy milks his cock for every drop.

Breathless and spent, my head hangs and I pass out.

SEBASTIAN

his stunning beauty in my arms is really getting under my skin. It's not just the earth-shattering sex. But the combination of how Lola's body responds to me as a sub and how she still fights me with the spunk of her independent-woman mind. I've never experienced a woman who challenges me and I want to stay buried deep inside of her. Hell, if I'm perfectly honest with myself, Lola is the first woman I want to go bare with. I have the urge to mark her with my scent and to coat her womb repeatedly with copious amounts of my seed. I won't stop until her womb grows my baby. Lola is the one who could bear my heir as the leader of the next generation of the STEELE Dynasty. I know this is a dangerous territory that I'm diving into, but I can't ignore these sensations. Screw that, fucking her this week will push these crazy thoughts out of my head—I'm just caught up in this climatic moment.

A small sigh draws my attention to my Petite Seductress who's now staring at me with eyes full of ardor as she savors the afterglow of subspace. I stroke her cheek with my thumb and smile when she stretches like a cat, her luscious tits lifting to my face. I can't resist drawing one of her succulent nipples into my mouth and she mews, tangling her fingers in my hair to hold me close to her bosom. Damn, my dick jumps and I want to take her again and again. I shake off the thought since she's had two rough nights and hasn't been sexually active in a while. Instead, I satisfy my craving by toying with her breasts. Neither of us is ready to stop.

"Oh, Baz," she purrs. "You feel so good, baby… Please don't stop… Fuck!"

In the back of my mind, I know that I should correct her for calling me by my nickname instead of by sir. But I don't want to—it sounds right, just as right as her calling me baby.

Nope—I'm screwed big time.

My fingers slowly ghost over her belly and cup her mons—Mine! Before I slide them along her puffy pussy lips swollen from the pounding that I gave her. Yet they're still wet and getting more moist as her arousal increases. Tenderly, I slide one of my fingers into her core, slowly rubbing her G-spot. I increase the rhythm and use my thumb to stroke her distended clit until Lola breaks beautifully for me.

"Mmmmmm… Ooo… Baz… Right there… Oo… Oo… Oo… Aaaaaahhhh… Yes!"

Lola's writhing and her wanton wail force cum to ooze down my turgid shaft and coat my balls that ache to fill her with my displaced seed. I lift her languid form. Then crush her to my chest burying my face in her soft hair inhaling the aroma of her floral perfume mixed with our scent of carnal sex. Our synchronized heartbeats pulse rapidly from our desire and reverberate through my mind, body, and soul leaving an indelible mark. I'm silenced while I process our connection.

After a few minutes, Lola wraps her slim arms around my neck and cuddles into my chest. Sweet sounds of her contentment slip past her lips as she adjusts her position.

"That was amazing, Sir," she coos. "Thank you so much."

With a kiss to my neck, Lola rises, but I hold her firmly in place on my lap—no repeat of last night with her skipping out so quickly. It hits me she's returned to the more formal sir, than Baz or baby of moments ago. Before I can question whether or not I'm disappointed in the change, I issue a command.

"Be still, Little Pet," I tell Lola. "Your aftercare is not over. Your body needs to reacclimate from our play. How do you feel?"

With an audible sigh—there's her independent woman breaking past my sub—Lola lifts her head to look me in the eyes. Gone is the ardor of subspace.

"Very good, Sir. Relaxed and clearheaded," she responds, then looks over her shoulder towards the drawn curtains, her wish to leave obvious in her agita.

Just as well since I need to stay in control and not allow impulsive behavior to lead me astray.

"Excellent, Pet," I tell Lola. "However, I sense that you are impatient to leave. Did I not treat you well…"

A flush of embarrassment colors Lola's face and she stammers a quick response.

"Oh, you treated me very well, Sir! I didn't mean to imply otherwise. It's just that…"

Lola's blush darkens and spreads to her chest, her hands twisting in her lap.

"What is it, Little Pet?" I ask her. "Subs should always be truthful. They hide nothing from their Doms."

As she peers up at me from beneath her lashes, Lola murmurs that she's embarrassed that others in the Cellar heard her passionate cries and will think she's a loose woman. I stroke her hair to gentle her and smile when she fully lifts her gaze to mine. The worry that's in the depths of Lola's eyes is real—she's truly concerned that others will think less of her. When in reality, everyone at LEVELS is here for the hedonistic atmosphere where they are free to explore their desires safely.

"No need to worry, Little Pet," I say as I continue stroking her long, wavy raven-colored hair. "Members and guests are in the same position as you—no pun intended— so we do not judge one another. LEVELS is a welcoming environment. Does that make you feel more comfortable?"

With a nod and a coy smile, Lola responds with an affirmative hum, slipping her arms around my waist and nuzzling her lips against my hard pecs.

We continue to sit quietly, absorbed in our separate thoughts. The sounds of the Cellar activities no longer white noise in the background: a woman's piercing scream followed by her plaintive moans; a man's guttural shouts of release; the slap of leather meeting skin; the soft sobs of desperation floating to us just beyond the curtains. No, Lola need not concern herself with shocked faces upon our departure from this private alcove when we leave our little bubble.

My mind drifts to my calendar to decide what time is best to meet Lola tomorrow night. She has so much more to learn and I'm eager to test her pain levels since she responded so nicely to the nipple and clit clamps. The set that I used tonight were entry level. The weighted clamps will bring Lola closer to her limits. Just as I'm envisioning how lovely Lola will look tied to my bed upstairs spread-eagle with her juices glistening on her pink pussy and her tight puckered hole on display before me, it shatters when I remember that I have a charity gala to attend. STEELE International is the patron sponsor, so I can't decline the invitation. I sigh in annoyance.

"Are you all right, Sir?" Lola asks as she pulls her torso away from my chest—I miss the warmth of her embrace.

"I have a charity gala tomorrow night that I must attend since STEELE is the patron, so we cannot play tomorrow. Unfortunately, your lessons will have to skip a day, Little Pet," I respond, stroking her back to get some skin-to-skin contact with her.

"Oh," Lola pouts, her full bottom lip poking out. I can't

resist the temptation to bite it before I soothe the sting with a deep kiss that has Lola going from a squeal to a sigh of bliss.

An interesting idea pops into my head as I kiss her sweet lips. I can invite Lola as my guest, an opportunity for her to engage with New York's elite before her boutique opens. Yeah, I'll just keep telling myself it's for business and not because I can't go a day without seeing her curvy ass.

"You should come with me as my guest so you can mingle with the attendees influential in the city and beyond," I start, gaining belief that it's only for business. "They will be good to know since you're opening Lola's Coterie here." I add as further encouragement.

Lola looks hesitant and studies my face for a moment, trying to decide whether I'm asking as a date or truly as business. I struggle to maintain a neutral expression—I want her to say yes. Decision made, Lola nods and with an equally neutral face responds that it's a smart business move. We discuss details. I offer to buy her a dress and accessories since it's a formal event, and she didn't travel with a gown. To which, Lola bristles and frowns before telling me she can take care of her clothes. I refrain from spanking her for her attitude because again she intrigues me, switching from sub to sass like a pendulum. We discuss the logistics and put on our clothes to leave the club.

As we walk through the Cellar and out to our awaiting cars, I possessively keep my hand on Lola's lower back. I guide her past members, some of whom follow us with their gazes. My eyes land on Rockett who's also eyeing us. I smirk at him—there's no denying that it was me making Lola scream in pleasure.

LOLA

*A*nother day my ass and pussy are sore—that damn Sebastian Steele whose hand and cock are like steel.

I attempt to sit comfortably on the buttery soft desk chair. My temporary workplace is in one of the guest offices at Luc's Banque Montaigne United States headquarters in Midtown on Park Avenue. The navy blue, ribbed-knit, midi dress I chose has enough stretch in the material to prevent any chafing and hugs my curves for a little vavavavoom action. Paired with stilettos and my hair in a high ponytail add height to my petite figure. From the appreciative looks that I garnered as I left the St. Regis, followed Luc through his building, and to the office, confirm that men approve my outfit of choice. I feel good, even if achy.

"—halt production and set the date back or use the lace from the last collection?"

My body is in the office. But my mind is back in the Cellar, reliving the nirvana that I found twice upon waking in Baz's arms after he forced multiple orgasms from my quivering pussy. Pure rapture. The elated smile playing on my lips dips when I notice Blair staring questioningly at me.

"Excuse me a moment," I tell her as I gingerly rise from the chair and walk to the en suite bathroom. First, I have to clear my head. Then get back to work. I dab my eyes with a damp washcloth—thank goodness for waterproof makeup —and the back of my neck, hot from the lustful thoughts. I gently massage my ass to ease some dull pain before I return to the chair.

"What were you telling me, Blair?" I ask once I'm perched on the seat.

Blair smiles and repeats the situation to me. The artisan being upset with the quality of the lace. How Blair tried calling the atelier, but Pierre—Monsieur Thibault's son who runs the business side for him—was not available. Lola's Coterie is my top priority, not reminiscing about earth-shattering sex. So, I roll my shoulders back and forth a few times to ease the tension, then get to work.

* * *

JUST BEFORE NOON, I hear the sexy baritone of Luc's voice as he speaks to Blair in his native French. If he were anyone but my mentor, I would swoon as often as Blair does whenever he's near. *Le Renard Argenté*. I laugh to myself, then glance up when Luc saunters into the office and lowers his tall frame into a chair opposite my desk.

"And how are you, *petite chérie?*" Luc asks me, his dark blue eyes twinkling with mirth from his conversation with Blair.

"Well, I'm fine, *Renard Argenté,*" I tease him with a smirk. "How are you is the better question?" I continue, raising my eyebrow and glancing towards the office door at Blair's desk for emphasis before returning my gaze to him.

Luc clears his throat, tugging at the Full Windsor Knot of his tie as he shifts in the seat.

"Comfortable?" I ask sweetly, bringing my hands up to rest my chin on top of them, awaiting his response.

"Indeed, I am."

Ever the aristocratic gentleman to not discuss another's private life, Luc parries my question with one of his own.

"Leonie tells me you've been attending lessons these past two nights. Something about improving your learning curve?"

Now, it's my turn to squirm and I bump my rear against the base of the armrest and yelp.

"Are you truly all right, *petite—*" Luc starts.

But thankfully, my mobile buzzes with a text from Leonie informing me she's in the Bentayga outside of Luc's building.

"Oh, that's Leonie. I have to meet her to pick out an outfit for tonight's gala. The one I told you Sebastian invited me to mingle with influential people," I hurriedly tell Luc as I grab my handbag and practically run out of the office. I don't wait for his response—I feel like a naughty teenager about to get reprimanded by her father—and rush past Blair to head to the elevators.

* * *

"*Oui, fermez la bouche, Leonie!*" I exclaim when I slide into the back of the Bentley SUV without so much as a bonjour to my big mouth best friend. "Why did you insinuate anything to Luc about my lessons?" I stress the word lessons with air quotes and an exaggerated eye roll.

Leonie's melodic laughter rings out in the luxury SUV while Stan attempts to maintain a professionally neutral expression. My accomplice who drives me to LEVELS New York for my trysts with Sebastian is a two-faced Janus. I glare at Stan through the rearview mirror and watch as his neck reddens at the collar of his suit jacket, his eyes refusing to meet mine in the mirror. I slam my back against the seat and fold my arms under my breasts with a huff. Then suck in a sharp breath when I hit my bum on the seatbelt buckle. Leonie doubles over, laughing even harder than before. As she wipes tears from her eyes, she turns to me and giggles.

"*Je suis désolé, Chérie!*" Leonie swears with her hand over her heart.

"Yeah, well, you are sorry and you better keep your mouth shut," I grumble as I rub my rear.

Since we have had little time to talk, Leonie fills me in on her activities over the past two days: her rounds at New York's most prestigious design houses; a visit to the New York office of her modeling agency; an interview at *Vogue*; prep work for the PSA commercial she's shooting tomorrow that encourages adolescent girls to follow their dreams.

Just as the SUV stops on Fifth Avenue and Fifty-seventh Street, Leonie briefly mentions Roger Steele. She became unsettled when he stared at her so intensely during the fashion show at our meeting. With no time to delve deeper, we lose the comment as we slide out of the Bentley.

It's good to catch up with Leonie. But my spirits really lift when we step onto the hallowed ground of Bergdorf Goodman—the venerated retail mecca of class, elegance, and sophistication for women, men, children, and home. It's situated directly across from The STEELE Tower. The thought of Baz adds to my upliftment. I'm surprised, but I can admit that Baz makes me happy. With a smile playing on my lips, Leonie and I begin the hunt for a showstopper gown that will turn heads and make my re-entry into Manhattan's elite spectacular.

"Oh, *Chérie*," Leonie coos as we eat a late lunch at BG Restaurant on the seventh floor of Bergdorf's overlooking Central Park. "You will make Sebastian turn back into that crazy, possessive caveman when he sees you in your dress!"

I bite my lower lip to hold back a moan as I think of Sir spanking me for wearing the hourglass-enhancing, irides-cent orange and gold sequin gown. It definitely checks off my boxes for an ultra glamorous scene-stealer with its long sleeves, dramatic padded shoulders, and pooling train. The exquisite gown will definitely make me stand out on the red carpet.

"I know," I cry gleefully as I clap my hands together and dance in my chair, unable to contain my excitement—damn my sore ass.

* * *

It's just 6:30 p.m. So Baz isn't late, but still I wait anxiously for him to arrive at the Presidential Suite that Leonie and I share at the St. Regis New York. An hour ago, the glam squad completed my styling, stressing the gold flecks in my hazel eyes to complement the tonal colors of my gown; my hair blown stick straight floats down my back to the curve of my ass like an arrow for Sir's strong palm. I recheck the contents of my new sleek-shaped and innovative-designed evening clutch made from gold satin and 18-karat gold-plated aluminum. When at last the butler announces Baz's arrival, I pivot in my Aquazurra gold, mirrored-leather sandals with slender, foot-framing straps to face him.

Baz's wolfish gray eyes lift from staring at my round ass before I turned around to slide seductively over my body. His gaze travels from the top of my head to the hem of my gown. His eyes brighten with unmistakable lust when his gaze slows at my hips. Baz's nostrils flare as though he's inhaling my essence. Then licks his full lips as though he tastes my unencumbered arousal on his tongue. Scandalously, I went sans lingerie. Baz slides his palm over the front of his bespoke tuxedo jacket, smoothing his hand against the noticeable bulge forming in his perfectly tailored trousers.

I've definitely brought out Captain Caveman—again.

SEBASTIAN

*D*amn, my Petite Seductress went all out tonight. That dress makes her look like a golden, shimmering mermaid basking in the setting sun. Like a siren, she calls me to my death—the end of my playboy days is neigh if my dick has any say in the matter. Absentmindedly, I rub my growing cock that, with a mind of its own, lengthened when my eyes took in the glorious sight of Lola's ass encased in her hip-hugging dress. When she turned, I almost let loose with a wolf whistle and growled my approval—my dick stood up at attention, silently weeping a salute to my bewitching goddess.

"Good evening, Mr. Steele," she purrs with sinful lips curled up in a smirk, fully aware of my body's response to her exquisite beauty. "You look delicious in your tuxedo."

"Tha—" I begin, but have to clear my throat since my voice was too thick to be coherent with my cock remembering those lips wrapped snuggly around its girth.

I try again, "Thank you, Ms. Lewis. You are a divine sight. Shall we?"

I walk towards her with my elbow bent in suggestion that we depart. My Petite Seductress smiles at me from under her eyelashes—her hazel eyes dazzle me—and hooks her arm through mine. With a nod, I return her smile and we exit the suite.

As we sit in the back of my chauffeured Mercedes-Maybach S 650 Sedan the proximity to Lola drives me mad. Her perfume teases my nose. Her thigh brushes against mine as she re-crosses her legs. If I'm not mistaken, I swear that I can detect a hint of her arousal as she sits beside me. I want to pull her across my lap and spank her for wearing such an alluring dress. It hugs her ample curves than trails behind her, guiding my eyes up to her ass. She captivates me.

Unfortunately, I extended this invitation as a business opportunity, not as a date. Even more annoying, I'm sure the same people, the men specifically, that I wanted Lola to mingle with will ogle her. Their fantasies about gripping her hips as they pound into her tantalizing pussy makes my head explode.

"Fuck!" I growl.

"What's the matter?" A bewildered Lola asks me.

It's only then that I realize I spoke aloud. Damn, I'm definitely losing it.

"Nothing, babe," I respond, shaking my head and caressing her cheek with my thumb to soothe her.

Lola stares at me wide-eyed and again I realize that I

spoke out loud what should have remained in my head or not even in my head. I called Lola babe. I quickly shift in my seat and press the intercom to ask my driver Michael how far we are from the venue. I refuse to make eye contact with Lola even though I feel her staring at me, waiting for me to address the term of endearment. Not happening.

"We're behind a queue of cars waiting for the valets, Mr. Steele. It should only be a few minutes," Michael informs me.

The annual gala raises funds for the nonprofit children's hospital that's one of the few organizations outside of STEELE Foundation's roster that I support. My mother Shelley runs our family's foundation that builds and manages attractive, affordable housing for urban, lower-income families. The name is a play on the house foundation, being strong and supportive like steel.

The children's hospital is a favorite of mine since I volunteered there as a teenager and witnessed firsthand the importance of quality healthcare for all children. Our mother insisted that we did more than as she called it "lounge around the pool working on our tans" during the summer. I'm thankful that she was so determined to have us experience life beyond that of typical offspring of the über-wealthy.

The Maybach pulls up to the front of STEELE42, one of our award-winning entertainment venues. It specializes in weddings, parties, and galas for society's best both in the United States and abroad. A buzz surrounds the area with paparazzi and news crews angling for the best shots and interviews on the red carpet. The energy is high and reaches into the sedan, drawing us out as a valet opens Lola's door and Michael opens mine.

Lights flash and the photographers yell my name to turn my head in their direction. As I reach Lola, I can't help but smile at her radiance—she looks spectacular with the lightbulbs flashing off of her iridescent gown. I will have the best-dressed woman on my arm tonight. Lola smiles as her hand wraps around my forearm and like a pro saunters along the red carpet. When the paps call for her to pose, as a good sub should, she looks to me for approval, then poses like the best supermodel. My dick aches for her.

Once we arrive inside, we stop and chat with other attendees. I introduce Lola to key guests and mention her lingerie boutique. The women love it. Some of whom are already familiar with it and have pieces from Lola's Coterie. Their excitement to meet the creator palpable. The men as expected nonchalantly check Lola out and I struggle not to deck someone.

"Oh, Sebastian, this is a beautiful venue. Are all the STEELE properties as refined?" Lola asks, looking up at the vaulted ceiling where the constellations twinkle in the dim lighting. I want to lave her throat and suck on it until I leave my bright red mark as a warning to others to back the fuck off.

"Yes, they are," I reply instead. "This is one of my favorites. It was a bank and when we refurbished it, we strove to keep the integrity of the space. We kept the original ceiling, columns, teller windows on the sides, the vault, and more original details."

"It's impressive," she murmurs.

We spend the evening mingling during the cocktail hour, chatting with potential shoppers. We place bids on a few interesting items from the silent auction. Then, eating a fantastic dinner—Lucien's catering division handles the food and drink.

"Excuse me," Lola says to me and the other guests at our table.

"Where are you going?" I have to pause as I realize how needy I sound.

"I just need to freshen up. Don't worry, I'll be right back," Lola says as she rises and I follow suit to pull out her chair.

I watch my Petite Seductress glide past tables with eyes that follow her movements and growl. Suddenly, a red satin gown blocks my view. I glance up for the source, I see Kimberly, the LEVELS New York member that I fucked a few weeks ago.

"Baz, it is you," Kimberly purrs as she sits in the still warm seat that Lola just vacated. "What a lovely surprise!"

"Hello, Kimberly, how are you?" I try for polite since I don't want to upset her again.

"Better now that I'm with you," she responds rubbing my thigh way too close to my crotch. As she inches her fingertips higher, Kimberly leans towards me to whisper in my ear.

"How about we skip this stuffy gathering and head to

Peepshow for better entertainment?" She says before licking the shell of my ear with the tip of her tongue.

Kimberly mistakes the shudder of revulsion that runs through me at the thought of being intimate with her or anyone besides Lola and places her palm on my crotch. Just as my hand grabs her wrist I hear a cry of pain from Kimberly.

"Pardon me, I forgot my clutch."

Unbeknownst to Kimberly and me, Lola returned to the table. Judging by how Kimberly cradles her foot, Lola must have stepped on it with her pointy heel when she took her bag off of the table. With a balls-shrinking stare directed at me, Lola storms away and straight into Rockett. Fuck me.

"Whoa, there, lass," Rockett tells Lola as he grips her forearms to keep her from tumbling backwards from bumping into his hard body.

"Oh, excuse me," Lola responds as she presses her palms against his chest.

"Well, let's take this tango to the dance floor!" Rockett laughs and throwing a glare at me over her shoulder, Lola lets him lead her away.

Lola

I cannot believe that Sebastian would flirt with that woman and let her grope his junk as soon as I left the table. I saw her eye fucking him from across the room. He's like a fucking magnet for women. Well, two can play that game, I grouse to myself as Patrick expertly spins me on the dance floor. He's actually handsome in his tuxedo and his big, muscular body is impressive. Not to mention his sexy Scottish accent. How Jamie Fraser!

As I chance a peek in the table's direction where Sebastian and I are sitting, I see him scowling, his gray eyes black with anger as his eyes lock with mine. With a smile, I return my attention to Patrick and try to ignore the pang in my chest.

Sebastian

That... fucking... Rockett.

He always shows up at the worse fucking times. He thinks he's hot shit, twirling my girl around and holding her close under the pretense of dancing. If he grinds his dick in her, I'll kick his ass right here, right now.

Not to mention Kimberly—cockblocker once again. Her babble continues on some mundane topic. Who the fuck knows or cares? When all I can see is red as I watch Lola in the arms of another man, my enemy to boot. Without even acknowledging Kimberly, I stalk over to the laughing pair.

"Lola, a word," I tell her as I clasp her elbow and pivot to walk off of the dance floor. A tug back makes me turn around to see Lola's hazel eyes blazing and her face contorted in rage. With a snarl, she yanks her elbow free.

"Take your hand off of me—" Lola starts, and I flash back to my office, the scene of her previous tirade.

Quick to defuse the situation, I grab her by the waist and crush my lips to hers, not giving a damn who sees, or that this is a business engagement.

I feel Lola melt into me and with a sigh open her mouth to give my probing tongue entry. As we continue our unplanned, passionate kiss, Rockett, Kimberly, the gala, and the world fade to nothing—all we know is the other. At that moment, I decide I'm all in with Lola, my Petite Seductress.

LOLA

he week ends where we started—in the conference room at The STEELE Tower with the same cast of characters as our first meeting. This time, Dom Pérignon Rosé Vintage 2005—somehow Baz knows my favorite champagne—flows as we sign the contracts for Lola's Coterie and STEELE International, Inc.'s multiyear, multimillion-dollar partnership. My expansion into the United States is in place with New York City and Las Vegas in four months. Amazingly Los Angeles, Miami, Abu Dhabi, and Dubai within the year, too. I'm so thrilled that I dance around the table with Leonie while Luc and Sebastian laugh and Roger stares—Leonie is right, he's intense.

Not only is my company on track, but I've had an unbelievable time with Baz. We spend every night at LEVELS New York furthering my Dom/sub lessons and pushing past my limits—who knew I was such a hedonist. Sometimes, I still hesitate when Baz commands me since my mind wants to have a say in the matter. Or I'll flat-out refuse, mainly because I'm yearning for the pleasure of his punishment. But, I'm learning to let go and just feel as Baz demands.

I glance across the room at him and shiver when his pupils dilate and his gray eyes turn black with desire for me. I'm wearing a pink sapphire suit with a pencil skirt and a waist-length jacket, a matching lace bralette, nude high heels, and flesh-tone silk stockings. I purposefully wore the fitted outfit to tease him right within the walls of his empire. I'm the sub and I hold all the power, that lesson I've definitely mastered.

"I'm so excited for you, *Chérie*," Leonie squeals and hugs me close. "Your dreams are coming true!"

"I know!" I exclaim. "It's so awesome! We have so much to do! I can't wait to get started." I continue and hug her back.

"*Oui, petite chérie*, but no need to think of it all at this very moment," Luc interrupts as he joins us and pulls me in for a warm embrace. "*Jouissance du présent!* Let's have dinner tonight at Per Se, your favorite New York restaurant, to celebrate."

My heart drops when I realize that I have to decline since I already have plans with Baz. I feel even worse since I have spent no time with Leonie and Luc the entire week. I only see Leonie in the suite and Luc at the office in passing. Only brief pleasantries—every non-work moment is with Baz.

"Lola and I already have plans for this evening," Sebastian cuts into the conversation, staring challengingly at Luc while placing a possessive hand on my lower back.

They contentiously eye each other like two Alpha lions fighting to claim the last lioness in the Serengeti. My insides tingle knowing that Baz wants me so much that he'll square off with my beloved Luc. My instinct tells me that Luc is only tolerating Sebastian for my sake. Their initial introduction did not sit well with Luc at all. He may be a tad jealous of the personal time that I'm spending with Sebastian.

"*WHAT ARE you doing that you can't have dinner with me, again?" Luc asks after I tell him I have plans for the evening.*

"I'm meeting with Sebastian. You know that I told you he's introducing me to people who are worth connecting with—"

Luc cuts off my response.

"Bof! He isn't the only one who knows people to introduce you to, you know that, Lola. I think you're getting too involved with him, especially since we haven't completed the deal yet. Do you think that's a wise decision?"

Somehow, Luc twists it around and makes me guilty for not putting Lola's Coterie ahead of my personal life. I'm sure that he knows I'm not spending time with Sebastian for business. But Luc is too much of a gentleman to call me out on my half-truths.

"Okay, let's have dinner tonight. Just give me a moment to tell Sebastian that I can't make it," I give in to Luc. I owe him so much and I wouldn't be here pitching a deal if not for his contact.

It pissed off Sebastian rightfully so that as he said I chose Luc over him. Damn these men in my life...

AS I WATCH the two of them puff up, I wonder if Sebastian is in my life. Or am I just a conquest for him—the playboy as my obsessive Google searches revealed. What I know for sure is over this week, he's made me admit to myself I am lonely and I want a good, strong man in my life. If it's Sebastian I can't say for sure, but my inner cheerleader is gleefully doing jumping splits and waving her pompoms in the air.

"How about you, Luc, Leonie, Roger, Blair, and I celebrate the deal over dinner and afterwards the two of us can continue with our plans?" I hopefully suggest to Sebastian as a compromise.

Sebastian rolls his eyes and Luc grunts. I take the reactions as their agreement since they didn't say no nor did they duke it out. So, I grab two fresh glasses of Dom from the sideboard and continue my merry dance around the conference room with Leonie. I will not let their overabundant testosterone ruin my joy.

AGAIN, hoping to keep the men in my life appeased and not ripping each other's throats out, I organize the rides to Per Se. Sebastian and Roger riding in Baz's S 650. Luc and Blair in his Cullinan. Leonie and me in my Bentayga. We plan to meet at the restaurant at eight o'clock. Leonie and I arrive last—both of us took extra care with our looks and attire. I wonder at the reason for Leonie's primping, but then notice the appreciative eye that Roger gives to her as we walk towards the bar where the others gathered. My eyes scan the group for Baz, but don't see him.

"Where's Sebastian?" I ask, hating that I sound whiny.

Roger shifts uncomfortably as he stands next to the barstool he vacated for Leonie to sit and looks over my shoulder. I follow his gaze and see Sebastian off to the side in an animated conversation with a gorgeous blonde woman who has her hand on his chest. A slight cough from Roger draws my attention away from the good-looking couple. Luc just raises his eyebrow and folds his arms across his chest. Blair standing next to him looks at me worriedly.

"*Le playboy occupé à une autre tâche à ce moment,*" Leonie spits out while she glares at Sebastian.

"Come, we will sit. I reserved the private East Room for our *fête*. Tonight, we celebrate your success, *petite chérie*. Nothing else matters, *non?*" Luc says and places his hand on my lower back to guide me to the maître d'.

I allow Luc to take control of the embarrassing situation while I attempt to restrain the tears that burn behind my eyes. I refuse to let them fall. Fuck Sebastian.

I sit between Luc and Leonie—my support for so long. Then peruse the menu to occupy my hands and to take my mind off of the pang in my chest. It doesn't matter anyway since this is the last night of our agreed upon D/s lessons; I remind myself. I just hate that I've allowed Sebastian past the wall I built to keep my heart safe from pain the night of my parents' death.

"Oh, the oysters and pearls are on the tasting menu tonight. Your favorite!" Leonie says, nudging me and smiling. "I can't wait to savor the flavors of the hand-cut tagliatelle. *C'est magnifique*!!" She closes her amber eyes and kisses her fingertips for emphasis.

The server is collecting our drink orders when Sebastian finally enters the room, his eyes search the table until his gaze lands on mine. I glance away, still hurt that he would so blatantly flirt with another woman in front of everyone and knowing that I was arriving soon. This answers my questions. I was just a conquest for the Dom playboy.

Sebastian sits in the chair opposite mine at the circular table and continues to stare at me, trying to get my attention. I dutifully ignore him and turn to stare out of the window at the stunning views of the Manhattan skyline and Central Park clear across Columbus Circle to Fifth Avenue. The other side of the East Room is a glass panel that overlooks the restaurant's main dining room. But prior to our arrival, Luc had the staff close the silk drapes for privacy.

The festivities proceed first, with Leonie and Luc offering toasts—Sebastian's toast is irrelevant and I choose not to listen. Then they present the savory dishes for the nine-course meal. Just before they serve the cheese dish, I excuse myself to go to the ladies' room and whisper to Leonie that I'm fine to go alone.

As I'm reapplying my lipstick, the door to the bathroom's antechamber opens and Sebastian walks in, locking it behind him. With a determined expression on his handsome face, he strides over to me. I attempt to duck around him, but he cages me in between his arms with my butt against the counter below the mirror.

"Get out of my way!" I seethe through my clenched teeth as I push into his hard chest. A futile effort to move his solid body that towers over me.

"No! You've ignored me all night—" Sebastian starts.

"Well, that's just rich, isn't it... I ignored you all night?" I snarl and try to knee him in his philandering balls. Unfortunately, he deftly blocks my blow and smashes his pelvis into mine. His thick shaft presses up and against my mons, eliciting a strangled moan from my pursed lips as his tip hits my clit.

"Fuck you, Sebastian!"

"Yeah, Pet, that is exactly what you will do... fuck... me."

He thrusts his hard cock against my mound with each word. Then flips me to face the opposite direction. Sebastian yanks the bottom of my dress over my head, bends me across the counter, rips off my thong, and kicks my legs apart.

"You... ignore... me... all... night... because... you... are... pissed... that... I... am... speaking... to... another... woman..."

Sebastian lands hard smacks to my ass between each word that he utters out of his mouth. He continues to berate me for not giving him a chance to explain. I dance on my toes and squirm to avoid the punishing slaps to no avail. My ass is on fire and I can't hold back a wail when his fingers spank my dripping pussy.

"Enough, Sebastian," I cry.

"No, it is not enough!" He growls in my ear as I hear him unzip his trousers before he slams his gigantic cock past my wet, swollen folds to enter my core.

He's so deep that his bulbous tip hits my cervix. Like a madman, Sebastian pistons his hips, jamming my pelvis into the counter until I grasp the edge as a counterbalance. The sounds of our grunts and my juices sluicing fill the air along with the scent of our feral sex.

I can't help my body's response to Baz's brutal assault: a sheen of sweat and goosebumps break out across my skin; my heart races; my pussy walls suck him in to take every inch deeper with each thrust. I mewl when his long, middle finger swipes my seam collecting the dew dripping down my spread thighs. I moan in pleasure until I yelp when Baz presses that same finger against my puckered hole. Ignoring my pleas, he pushes past the rings of muscle until he encases his finger completely in my ass. His colossal cock in my pussy and his thick finger in my bottom hole leaves little room in my core.

"So tight, Pet," Sebastian hisses in my ear as he flattens my body to the counter with his heavy torso. "Tonight, I will take your last hole."

The words rumble through me as his dick swells and pulses before one last deep thrust that lifts me clear off the ground. His roar of release sends a zing to my core, stimulating my walls to milk every drop of his seed. For a moment, we collapse onto the counter and pant.

Sebastian slowly stands and as he withdraws from my sheath, his cum oozes out and drips to the floor—my pussy clenches to re-collect the spillage.

"Shit!" Sebastian exclaims.

I hastily rise and adjust my rumpled dress.

"What? You suffer remorse for forcing yourself on me, asshole?" I retort, still pugnacious despite my body thrumming with delight.

"I didn't wear a condom, and I came bare inside of you." Sebastian responds sheepishly, looking at me with wide eyes. "I've always worn a condom... I don't know what came over me... I—" He mumbles more to himself than to me.

He walks into the bathroom and returns with a damp linen cloth that he hands to me. I stare at it, then at him before snatching the cloth to clean myself.

"I'm on birth control. No need to get your panties in a bunch. I'm the one that should worry since you're a man-whore who can't keep it in his pants!" I chastise him with a glare, wiping our combined juices leaking from my pussy and from between my thighs. "I've only had two lovers and can guarantee that I don't have any sexually transmitted anything. Who knows about you," I add pointedly.

When Sebastian doesn't respond, I glance up to see him gazing at me with an unreadable expression on his face. He's so damn sexy, hair mussed, flushed skin, darkened gray eyes. I shake my head and sigh—if only.

"Whatever," I say as I toss the soiled cloth in the bin and limp towards the door—damn, did he ravage me. Sebastian's hand whips out and he stops me mid-step.

"I'm clean... I get tested regularly. It's just that I've never been bare in my life and my behavior shocked me. I apologize, Lola. Do you forgive me?"

The sorrowful expression on Baz's face takes me aback and I can't stop my hand from cradling his face. He closes his eyes, takes a deep breath, and nuzzles his cheek into my palm. I study his face and can sense that he's truly unsettled. If my instinct is correct, it's because he's falling for me and it shocks him. We stay that way until Baz opens his eyes and gazes down at me.

"I know it's your celebration party, but can we go now? I want to be alone with you."

His gray eyes nervously slide across my face, trying to judge my reaction.

I could let him hang out there, but I have the urge to be alone with him, too. Is it too fast? Am I getting too involved with Sebastian? Will he hurt me? If I were a fortuneteller, maybe I could answer my questions, but I'm not. So, I won't repair the crack in the wall around my heart just yet. I want to see where this—whatever this is—takes us.

"Yes, Baz," I give in.

SEBASTIAN

I've seriously lost my shit, but I don't mind. It felt damn good to fill Lola's womb with my seed. Perhaps it was my subconscious that made me follow her to the bathroom and take her so thoroughly and bareback. Because that's what I really want—Lola's belly big with my baby. Lola as the mother of my child would lock her to me forever. No, that's not so bad, I muse—the caveman in me beats on his chest in triumph at the conquest of his mate. I'm glad that I didn't let that jerk Luc stop me from following Lola.

However, I regret hurting her feelings by getting caught up with Bridget Heimonen, the Finnish model that I played with at Peepshow last week. I didn't fuck her, just toyed with her a bit and that's why she accosted me demanding more as soon as I walked into the restaurant—what luck. Definitely a stunner, but not my type. Hell, no one's my type anymore.

Only Lola has got to me, the real me inside, beyond my playboy exterior. I thought in a week I could fight the instant, soul-stirring attraction. Just fuck her out of my system under the guise of training her to be a sub and to enjoy the pleasures of a Dom/sub relationship. Never have I desired a woman more. She challenges me at every turn. Her body makes her an adept pupil—despite her protests—easily responding to stimuli of all kinds. But her intellect and emotional fortitude combined with her innate submissiveness make Lola superior to all those who came before her, including Bridget. Not a day goes by that I don't think about Lola and want more from her.

"Why are we stopping here?" My Petite Seductress asks as she peeks out of the sedan's window, tilting her head back to get a glimpse of The STEELE Tower's upper floors.

I didn't tell her we were going to my penthouse and not to LEVELS New York. I wanted to get her out of Per Se without a scene or any delay. So I just let her assume that we were going to the club. My intentions for bringing Lola to my home is to see how we interact in my personal space. We need time together beyond public places like the office, the club, social gatherings, or restaurants. If this can be more, then I have to be sure that we can be together intimately. Not only sexually.

It's also a place no woman besides my female family members have been. I only have sex at LEVELS or a hotel. This is special.

* * *

THE DOORMAN OPENS Lola's door before I'm forced to admit the truth. I hop out and take her hand as she stands in bewilderment. Swiftly walking through the grand doors for the residence side of the Tower, I nod as the concierges greet me. Distracted by the opulence of the lobby, Lola scurries along beside me, turning her head in every direction. I don't slow my pace until we reach my family's private elevator and gently tug her through the open doors. As they close, I place my hand on the plate to select the main level of my duplex on the fifty-fifth floor.

"Sebastian, where are we going? This looks like residences and not your headquarters," Lola demands, trying to pull her hand loose from my firm clasp, garnering my immediate attention. I refuse to let her hand go.

"I said that I want to be alone with you, Lola."

I respond not answering her question instead mentally urging the high-speed elevator to hurry before Lola's quarrelsome nature breaks through disrupting my plan.

"Thanks for the non-answer," she retorts with a raised eyebrow and pursed lips.

In response, I grab her wrists to pull her arms over her head and push her into the corner of the elevator with my much larger body. A small oomph pops out of Lola and I bend down to bite her luscious lip into my mouth. I groan at the contact and rock my hips rhythmically into her pelvis. The all-encompassing kiss leaves her breathless and pliable in my arms. I need Lola in a blissful state to prepare her for my next offer.

We kiss—her flavorful taste a mixture of the rich foods

and fruity wine that she had at dinner tantalizing me. The doors ping open to the foyer at the entrance of my penthouse duplex high above the rooftops of Manhattan. I bite Lola's lip as I slowly pull away from her delectable, curvy body and pin her with my lust-filled gaze once her eyes open—she's soft and loose, perfect. I grasp her hand in mine again and place my palm on the plate next to the door to trigger the lock. Then gesture for Lola to enter ahead of me knowing that the 360-degree, unencumbered view from the expanse of wall-to-wall, floor-to-ceiling windows will astonish her. She won't have time to question me further.

As if on cue, Lola sucks in her breath at the sight and teeters over in her fuck-me heels to the wall of windows that faces south. The famous skyline is breathtaking in its magnitude with the infinite lights contrasted against the ink-black night sky. Even I'm impressed whenever I take time to stare out.

However, I'm more intrigued by my Petite Seductress' ass in her dress as it swishes from side to side. My dick lengthens at the memory of the pounding that I gave her in the lounge. I follow her and stand flush against her body as she places her small hands on the glass as if she could touch the lights beyond. I bend down and nuzzle my nose against her neck, breathing in her seductive perfume and the maddening smell of our sex. I grind against her, pushing her body into the glass and placing my big hands on top of hers, holding her in place.

The vixen ignores my advances and peppers me with

questions about the view, the decor, the fucking construction—shit, I just want her. So in response, I unzip her dress and slide it down her body. My fingers skim along her soft skin, sending shivers across her body and goosebumps to rise. Then unclasp her sheer, nude-colored lace bra. Two of my fingers push into her exposed core, not surprised to find her sopping wet—her thong still in my pocket.

"Is all of this for me, my Little Pet?" I demand as I slip my fingers in and out of her channel, delighted that she's still so tight even after repeatedly taking the girth of my ten inches.

"Yes, Sir," she mewls, arching her back and pressing her mound into my hand, seeking even the slightest bit of relief.

"Who do you belong to?" I demand, pinching her sensitive gem between my thumb and forefinger with one hand and alternating pinching her hard nipples with the other.

"Aah... You, Sir... Only you," she moans greedily grinding her mound against my palm.

I swat her pussy quickly three times.

"Whose is it?" I demand.

"Ooohhh... You, Sir... Only you!"

I slip my fingers wet with her arousal to her virgin ass and apply pressure to the puckered hole with the tips. Her gasp makes my cock twitch and my balls fill with my seed.

"What did I tell you earlier, Little Pet?"

"Th— That you will take my last hole, Siiir?" She pants, wiggling her hips to extricate my probing digits from her snug hole.

"Correct. Tonight, I fully claim you. Undress me, Little Pet," I command.

With no hesitation, Lola faces me and quickly removes my jacket, tie, and shirt, trailing her fingertips along my chiseled chest, six-pack abs, and the v-cuts of my Adonis belt. She drops to her knees gracefully, unbuckles my leather belt, opens my trousers, and pulls them down with my boxer briefs. My heavy cock falls free, nearly striking her in the face. With a moan, she takes me into her mouth and twirls her tongue around my tip, massaging my balls.

"Oh no, Pet," I reprimand her. "Did I tell you to suck me?"

As she pulls back with a disappointed sigh, Lola lifts her hazel eyes darkened by her desire and shakes her head.

"Words, Pet," I remind her.

"No, Sir, I just want to give you pleasure since I know how much you like my wet, warm mouth on your delicious cock. Am I wrong?" The minx asks with a sly smirk.

I respond by lifting her to her feet and putting her across my bent knee, foot braced against the window, spanking her ass in rapid succession. She will not sass me tonight. Her lustful cries drive me crazy and I can't wait any longer to make her dark hole mine. I pick her up and effortlessly carry her to the sofa, positioning her on her knees facing away from me with her hands braced on the back. She looks at me over her shoulder, her long hair partially covering her face, her eyes wide with trepidation and desire. I rub down her spine to her reddened globes to gentle her before I kneel behind her and lave her sweet pussy with my flattened tongue. As though I were starving, I eat her like she's a plate at Per Se. I lick her seam, suck and bite her pussy lips, then nibble on her clit before I plunge my tongue into her core. Orgasm after orgasm drawn from her until she collapses against the sofa, sweat glistening on her damp skin.

I rise to my full height to rub my dick along her pussy lips, covering it with her juices—a natural lubricant—before I press my tip to her puckered hole. Lola stiffens and I swat her ass to get her out of her head. I lean into her body as I press against her hole, putting only the tip of my cock inside of her ass. I grip her hips when she pulls away and lean over to growl into her ear.

"Be still, Little Pet. Open up and let me in. I need to feel your tight, virgin ass wrapped around my big dick. Your last hole is mine!" I growl as I fully seat my member deep inside of Lola's ass, not stopping at the resistance.

"Oh... Fuck... Baz... Ooohh..." Lola cries as I move in and out of her ass, the snug fit gripping my dick and suctioning it back in.

Fuck, she feels so good. I won't be able to hold out much longer. So I play with her clit, tweaking and pinching it until she thrusts back against me, pummeling her ass. Her passionate cries have me on the edge.

"Come undone for me, Lola! Give it to me. Give me everything!"

I roar as I feel that tingle start at the base of my spine and shoot to my expanding cock. I unleash my full load deep in Lola's well-used ass. Just as I come, she screams her release shaking and swearing as her body responds to mine giving me what I commanded.

* * *

"Who is she, Sebastian?"

Damn, leave it to my Lola to not forget about my earlier unintentional indiscretion with Bridget. I know better than to lie to her, so I tell her the truth.

I pull her onto my lap also knowing that I need to keep my hands on her to prevent Lola from spiraling out of control before I can finish.

"Her name is Bridget Heimonen, a Finnish model that I played with at Peepshow," I start and Lola squirms to get out of my grasp.

I hold her in place, then continue, "Despite what you may believe, I don't fuck every woman I see and I didn't fuck her. What you saw was Bridget attempting to persuade me to have sex with her. I was telling her I'm not interested and I'm involved with someone. So, you were angry with me and ignored me for no reason."

I finish with smacks to her butt cheeks.

"Then, why did you take so long to get to the room?" She questions with a frown, still doubting me.

"Melody forwarded a business call to my mobile I had to take. I wasn't with Bridget. I had stepped out to the vestibule to speak freely."

I give her a moment to absorb what I said and unconsciously hold my breath, hoping that she'll believe me and won't get angry again.

"Oh," she says, still thinking too much and not letting go.

"Listen, Lola, I've never been in a relationship before and I'm sure that I'll get things wrong like tonight proved, but I'm trying. I get that we haven't known each other for long. Our initial plan was for me to teach you about D/s. But to me, it feels like more and I'd like to explore it. I can't make any promises. But I'd like to see where things take us."

I hold up my hand to stop her from interrupting me and continue.

"I know how important your company and its success is to you. So, you have my word that I won't let this interfere nor harm the business partnership that Lola's Coterie has with STEELE International. We can even include an addendum to the contract if that will ease your mind."

I stop to give her a chance to respond.

Lola is quiet for so long. I pull back to get a better view of her face. She's staring out the window with a pensive and sad expression on her lovely face—my heart drops.

With a sigh, she turns her gaze to me. I brace myself for a no, made worse by me opening myself up to a woman for the first time in my thirty-five years.

"Baz, I'm scared, too. I shut myself off from love since my parents died thirteen years ago. The only people that I've allowed to get close to my heart are Luc and Leonie."

I struggle to maintain a neutral face when she mentions

Luc being in her heart—a place that I now realize I wish to be.

"This past week with you has been amazing…"

I tune Lola out when I realize that she's trying to let me down nicely. I just nod when I think I should, but I don't hear a word she's saying to me. The distance in her eyes tells me enough. It's not until she smacks my chest I tune back in.

"You weren't even listening to me!" She yells.

Feeling stupid for getting caught not paying attention and wallowing in self-pity, I can only shake my head in acknowledgment with a glum expression.

"Oh, I get it. You thought I was rejecting you so you tuned me out, huh?" Lola asks with an eye roll.

Again, I go with the truth. "Yes," I admit.

She shakes her head and mumbles something about unbelievable and how she opened her heart to a big baby.

I grasp her face and demand that she repeats herself.

"I agree with you, loser! I want to see where this goes, too!" My Petite Seductress exclaims, her eyes glowing.

"Oh, well… Damn… Okay… Let's do this!" I laugh and wrestle her beneath me as she squeals in delight. For once, my brain and my dick are in agreement.

* * *

I STRETCH in my king-size bed as I awaken at my usual 5 a.m. The warmth of a soft body presses against my side and a small hand rests on my hard dick. With a start, I sit up and glance down to see Lola squinting up at me in with a startled expression on her sleepy face.

Shit, I forgot.

Smiling at her, I lean down. This morning, I learn the benefits of being in a relationship as Lola and I make good use of my hard dick and her warm, soft body.

AS WE FINISH EATING a hearty breakfast that Lola made for us—the benefits keep rolling in—I take a deep breath and dive off the deep end.

"Now that we completed the expansion deal, you must be in the city more. What are you going to do about your living arrangements?"

Lola pauses, sipping her green tea and eyes me over the brim of her cup. I maintain a nonchalant air and take the last bite of my omelet before turning in the kitchen banquette to face her. Like a pro negotiator, Lola just as nonchalantly completes her sip and carefully places her cup back on the saucer before she speaks.

"I will meet with the realtor that Luc recommended finding an apartment."

That damn Luc, again. I barely hold back a growl. But I know that I can't push her too much on him or she'll balk.

"Sounds good. What will you do until you find a place? We have meetings scheduled over the next few weeks that will require your presence," I say, blowing on my coffee and taking a sip from the mug.

"The suite is still available for a few more days, so I'll

stay there," Lola hedges aware of where I'm going with this line of questioning.

"Yeah, I can see where that could be appealing. The St. Regis is near to STEELE and you're already settled. Too bad you must move to another hotel once the next guest's arrival date comes."

"True. Or, I can just stay at Luc's Fifth Avenue penthouse until I find a suitable place of my own. If not, he's already told me I can just live there when—"

I cut her off with a growl, yank her from the banquette, and swipe the surface clear with my forearm before depositing her on top, wedging myself between her thighs.

"No... You will check out of the hotel today and move in here with me! You will not stay with any other man. I don't give a damn if he's old enough to be your father as you so told me the other night. You are mine and I will take care of you!"

I dictate, all cool negotiator behavior thrown right off one of the balconies of the fifty-fifth floor.

The vixen laughs at me so hard that she snorts and falls back onto the tabletop clutching her stomach. Tears pop out of her eyes, squeezed shut in her glee. Yeah, she got me to lose my cool, again. This woman will be the death of me. I know. With only one of my t-shirts on, her natural D-cup tits shake and the hem rides up past her waxed mound. My dick comes to attention and I lean over her to whisper in her ear.

"Laugh all you want now. But soon, you will cry and beg me to let you cum. But, I will not, Naughty Pet."

Instantly, Lola stops laughing and looks at me with her head slanted to the side trying to assess the situation. I hold a straight face until she hiccups, a laugh caught in her throat from the whiplash change in my mood.

Yes, Pet, the Dom is never far. Now, it's my turn to laugh as the vixen shivers in anticipation and her nipples harden.

SEBASTIAN

A few hours after I punish my Pet to her satisfaction, we take a much-deserved soak in my en suite bathroom's sunken tub. Afterwards Lola and I leave my duplex to drive over to the St. Regis New York. We'll gather her things and check her out of the hotel.

The elevator doors open at the fifty-second floor and I smile in anticipation of seeing my younger brother leaving his penthouse. My jaw drops when Leonie and Roger fall through the doors too engrossed in a passionate kiss with their arms wrapped around the other, to notice that they're not alone.

Lola and I exchange shocked looks—me because he's *Roger The Responsible* and not prone to one-night stands nor to overt public displays of affection. As he hikes Leonie's long, shapely leg around his hip, thrusting at her pussy I cough.

"Good morning!" Lola singsongs delightedly, her eyes twinkling in merriment.

Roger nearly drops Leonie in his haste to find the source of the unexpected greeting. She in turn squawks flailing her arms out to find purchase on the wall. Equally surprised, it's Roger's turn to pick his jaw up from the floor at seeing me with a woman coming from my apartment. I'm able to suppress my laugh until Lola bursts out laughing. Leonie joins in, her amber eyes dance in delight. She and Lola giggle and converse in French about how funny the whole situation is and how they can't believe they're so busted. Meanwhile, I peer over their heads at Roger who's trying his best to remain stoic while studying the floor indicator to avoid my eyes.

"So, what's up, man? Good night?" I rib him.

A flush creeps up his neck from beneath his shirt collar as he ignores me.

Pressing on, I add, "I take it the dessert was more than satisfying? A bit of sweet passion fruit filled with lots of seeds? *Succulente, n'est pas?*"

At that, Lola and Leonie's laughter increases, filling the elevator with their unrestrained guffaws and snorts. Fortunately for Roger, the doors open and he grabs a still laughing Leonie by the hand to drag her out of the elevator. I put my arm around Lola and follow them through the lobby to the sidewalk where our cars and drivers await.

"Seriously, where are you headed?" I ask, looking from Roger to Leonie. "Lola and I plan to get her things from the hotel and bring them back here."

Leonie bugs her eyes out at Lola and starts speaking rapidly to her in French, gesturing animatedly with her hands. With a glance at me, Lola pulls Leonie to the side, murmuring a response. Leonie's eyes filled with concern dart to mine, then back to Lola before speaking rapidly, again. I hear Luc's name mentioned with not going to be happy and too fast. As the Dom in me is about to charge over and relieve my sub of Leonie's haranguing, Roger finally speaks.

"Better question, what's up with you? I've never seen you bring a woman to your home before and definitely never move them in if that's what you meant by bringing Lola's things back here."

I run my hands through my hair and turn to glance back at Lola, whose attempts to calm Leonie are proving difficult. For a moment, I consider whether we are rushing by moving in together after only a week. But my heart seizes when I think of her in Luc's penthouse or anywhere besides with me. Fuck it. I follow my instincts in business and have been successful. So with matters of the heart, I'll do the same.

With true confidence, I respond, "You're right, I've never had a woman over to visit nor lived with one. But Lola is not just anyone. She's the one who I want to build a relationship with. Not just fuck for the night—"

"Whoa, brother, The One?" Roger's eyebrows shoot to his hairline and he looks stunned.

I'm as stunned when he repeats my words back to me. I tip my head to the side and consider my statement. Is Lola

The One? Or was that a mistake? I shrug and shake my head as Lola puts her arm around my waist and leans into my side. I peer down at her and my heart skips a beat when I take in her gorgeous face smiling at me so full of trust and security. I smile back, slip my arm around her shoulders, and kiss the tip of her nose before turning back to Roger to respond.

"Yes."

Roger gives me his intense stare for almost a full minute before he nods.

"I'm taking Leonie back to the hotel for her to pack while I do some work at the office before we fly back to Paris this afternoon. I'm giving her a lift since Lola and Luc are staying for the meetings."

I eye Roger. But let it go as he let what I told him go—for now at least.

"Superb idea. We'll see you soon," I clap him on the shoulder and nod at my driver Edgar to open the Maybach's door. Lola and I slip inside and settle in for the quick ride to the St. Regis.

"Everything okay with you and Leonie?" I ask, hoping that her best friend hasn't dissuaded her from moving in with me since she's quietly looking out of the sedan's window.

Lola turns to face me and nods her head, "We're good. She's worried, that's all."

I study her face and ask for confirmation to allay my fear, "Are you worried?"

Lola's eyes brighten and her face lights up as she takes

my hand and squeezes it before answering, "Not even for a minute!"

I tug her onto my lap and nuzzle my nose against her slim neck. Holding her close, I inhale her sweet, natural aroma under the scent of my bodywash. She giggles as my warm breath tickles her skin and tangles her fingers in my hair, holding me close to her before tugging to pull my lips to hers. We share a soul-stirring kiss that solidifies our new relationship.

We arrive at the hotel and stride to the elevators, barely noticing the other guests bustling in the lobby. I put my arms around Lola's waist to hold her back against my front as the elevator fills. The proximity combined with her wiggling her plump globes on my once flaccid dick turns it into a battering ram. I nip her neck with my teeth to still her before I throw her against the wall and fuck the shit out of her—damn the other guests. This woman drives me wild.

Once the elevator clears, I take control and flip us to press her against the wall bending my knees to push my pelvis up and into her ass. Lola moans as she wantonly thrusts back against me, urging me on. My hand slips under her dress and cups her mons, pushing two fingers roughly inside of her tight channel, her ever-ready cream easing the way for my probing digits.

"Ooh, baby... Fuck!" Lola groans, widening her legs to give me more access when I repeatedly stroke the textured area of her sensitive G-spot.

I grind my thick staff into her bountiful bottom. As I

inch her dress up to her hips with my other hand and add a third finger. Lola turns into a screaming banshee as she comes, shaking and panting, gripping my fingers with her pussy walls.

"Who do you belong to, Little Pet?" I demand my fingers continuing to thrust in and out of her spasming, dripping pussy.

"Uh... Uh... Uh... Uh," is all that Lola can say as another orgasm rips through her core, her trembling body leaning heavily on mine.

I pinch her nipple with my other hand and she squeals.

"Who do you belong to, Pet?" I repeat.

"Ooohhh... You, Sir... Only you!" Lola pants.

She comes undone, gripping my fingers as she cums for the third time as the ping sounds announcing that we've reached the Presidential Suite's floor.

I gently withdraw my fingers from her pussy rippling with aftershocks and pat Lola's mound while softly kissing her neck, the skin damp with sweat. A groan falls from my mouth as her dress slides back down, covering her lush curves. I extend my other arm to prevent the elevator doors from closing while I lap her sweet honey from my fingers and hand. When Lola turns, her eyes shine with satiety as she bites her fleshy, lower lip. I pat her ass when she passes me to exit the elevator, a smirk on my face knowing that I gave her such pleasure capable of making her swoon.

"Everything good?" Comes the deep rumble of Roger's voice edged with laughter.

I snatch my fingers from my mouth and whip around. My brother and Leonie emerge from the other elevator having witnessed me sucking my digits and patting Lola's ass. Now, it's our turn to experience embarrassment. The four of us laugh and Leonie links arms with Lola sashaying to the suite's double doors. Roger gives me a shove and follows them. I trail behind, enjoying the last remnants of Lola's delicious essence.

* * *

"You have more clothes than I do! Are you sure this is for two?"

Lola calls out from my bedroom's oversized dressing room and walk-in closets—equivalent to two New York studio apartments combined. She's adding her clothes, shoes, and handbags to the custom racks, drawers, and shelves.

"Whatever. Am I supposed to walk around nak—" I start.

But the words get stuck in my throat. Before me is a dick hardening sight. Lola bent at the waist—a red lace thong disappearing between her mouthwatering ass cheeks uncovered from my T-shirt she's wearing—placing shoes on the lower shelf. My bollocks go crazy.

Lola glances over her shoulder at me with a puzzled expression in her eyes since I stopped mid-word. She laughs when she sees my mouth hanging open and my eyes fixed on her enticing bottom. She shimmies her hips and the T-shirt slips further to reveal her voluminous breasts bouncing free. With a low growl, I loosen the string on my sweatpants to free my dick, too. I advance, lining my rapidly hardening shaft with her seam and impaling her instantly. Both of us groan in mutual satisfaction as we join as one in absolute carnal rapture.

Since I entered Lola with no preparation—yes, she definitely drives me mad—I spank her ass to give her pussy time to grow accustomed to my girth and length. I move at a slow, rhythmic pace. Lola's juices coat my cock as her arousal catches up to mine. The feeling of being bare inside of Lola is indescribable. My cock feels every surface of her pussy walls, including the texture of her G-spot that I brush my tip against each time I re-enter her channel. The increased movement of her ass hitting back against my groin pushes my dick deeper within her drenched folds, my tip touching her womb.

Again, my inner caveman surfaces and grunts as I mount Lola and increase my pace plundering faster and harder wanting to plant my seed deep into her fertile womb. I adjust my grip, placing one hand on the top of her shoulder to hold Lola in place. The other hand I place under her opposite thigh to lift it, changing the angle to go even deeper. The sounds of our mating reverberate around the room.

I feel Lola's walls tremble, milking up and down my shaft as I squeeze her clit with the fingers under her thigh. She tosses her head back and wails my name as she convulses with her orgasm. I lift her off of the floor to drive up into her pulsating pussy. Mad in my desire to fuck her raw, I chase the orgasm brewing at the base of my spine.

"Fuck yes, baby... Take it... Take all of it... YES!" I shout my voice gruff with desire.

My movements become disjointed as I feel Lola cum for the fourth time and my dick swells deep within her sopping wet pussy. I shift to face the wall and brace Lola against it as I ram into her again and again until I can't hold back any longer. I grip her hips tightly and possessively bite the sensitive area where Lola's shoulder meets her neck as my orgasm rips through my body. My cock jerks deep inside of her, erupting with seed that coats her womb. I can't stop thrusting like a feral animal claiming its mate until every drop of my jizz spews from my tip.

My knees weaken and I lower us to the floor, pulling a boneless Lola into my lap. My spent dick falls from her pussy that's dripping with our combined essence. I stare at the puddle forming beneath our entwined legs, transfixed by our coupling. Lola sighs and lays her head against my chest where my heart beats helter-skelter.

If the last twenty-four hours are any proof of how we'll interact in my private space, then we'll be more than fine.

The past week has been a blur of meetings at STEELE's New York headquarters where Baz arranged for Blair and me to use one of the office suites on the executive floor. Close, but not distractingly so as he stated. Apartment hunting with the realtor Baz insisted that I use. He didn't want me working with Luc's recommendation. Then there's the passionate sex every evening after which we soak in the large, sunken tub in his en suite bathroom. It's a ritual we instilled from our first night together. A girl could get used to this life. Demanding work and just as rigorous sex. Both satisfying.

Speak of the devils. Right on time for our next meeting, Baz and Luc stride into my office with Blair close behind them, eyes firmly fixed on Luc like a lovesick puppy. It makes me wonder if they're spending time together outside of business hours. If they are good for them since it'll be a distraction from Luc questioning my move into

Baz's duplex. I roll my eyes thinking about his overly dramatic reaction when I told him I wouldn't need to stay at his penthouse. Oh, well, I'm a big girl, I shrug to myself. Both men briefly greet me as they continue to debate some topic on their way to the conference table next to the wall of windows. I take a deep breath. Here we go.

"Hello, gentlemen. What rousing topic are you discussing?" I ask as I join them at the table, eyeing one and then the other with my brow raised questioningly.

"He thinks—"

"You should—"

They start at the same time.

"What I was say—"

"Anyway, the best—"

My shrill whistle rings through the space ending all conversation and they stare at me stupefied. I remove my fingers from my mouth and put my hands on my hips.

"Enough, already," I admonish them. "I have a lingerie business to run, not an MMA match to referee. Again, what are you talking about?"

Luc looks chastened, and Sebastian clamps down on his lips, champing at the bit to speak. So, I turn to Luc and gesture for him to speak.

"Pardon, Lola," Luc begins sincerely. "I am concerned that the..."

We finish that meeting and a few others with Sebastian's team before we break for lunch delivered by Mangia that Blair and Tina arranged in one of the conference rooms. I rise and stretch my arms overhead to ease some tension from the compression of my spine caused by sitting for hours. When I open my eyes, I see Sebastian glaring at Luc and Luc staring at me. Oh, boy.

"Well, those went well," I state, as I walk to my desk while discreetly adjusting the neckline of my navy silk wrap dress. "I have an appointment with the realtor after lunch, so I won't be back until tomorrow."

"Lunch is ready," Blair announces from the door.

Luc's eyes leave mine and glance over at Blair who smiles at him tentatively.

"*Tres bien,*" Luc responds with a nod as he stands and buttons his suit jacket. "Shall we?" He asks, gesturing to the door with a sweep of his right hand.

"Actually, I need a word with Lola. We'll join everyone shortly," Sebastian answers in a domineering tone, keeping his steady gaze on me.

Luc hesitates, protectively looking between Sebastian and me. Then nods again as if surmising that I'm safe before he follows Blair out of the office who also hesitates to assess the situation. I give Blair a confident smile to ease her mind and she turns to follow Luc. Sebastian goes to the door and locks it, then comes to my desk to press the button to darken the glass walls. Double oh, boy.

Sebastian leans his rear against my desk and crosses his arms over his massive chest and his long, muscular legs at the ankle, his eyes never leave mine. I shiver from the dominant stare like a rabbit caught in the predatory sight of a gray-eyed wolf on the hunt. My nipples bead and my pussy drips in response. He's so close that I can detect his sexy cologne that I now know is Creed Aventus. The iconic name derived from ventus—the wind—illustrating the Aventus man as destined to live a driven life, ever galloping with the wind at his back toward success. How apropos. I'm in the office, where I'm an independent, successful businesswoman and not in our bedroom or at LEVELS New York. I refuse to submit to him. I won't be the first to give in and speak and I won't turn away from his eyes.

Sensing I'm not about to back down, Sebastian ends the standoff. Judging by the flare of his nostrils, he can scent my arousal just as much as I can feel it.

"So, you do not think Luc wants you?" Sebastian questions with a tilt to his head and that blasted unwavering stare.

I steel my shoulders to draw on my resolve to not submit before I respond.

"Luc is like a father to me and—" I answer, but Sebastian abruptly raises his hand to stop me.

"What father acts like a jealous lover when his daughter moves in with the man that she is seeing?" He questions.

I try to respond, but Sebastian is on a roll and continues as though I didn't even open my mouth to speak.

"What father marks his territory by pissing around his daughter? Most importantly and worse... What father ogles his daughter's tits as they strain against her dress???"

Sebastian's voice rises with every word until he's hissing the esses in dress and he's towering over me.

I swallow, but hold his gaze thinking he's not so far off,

but I can't let him get even more upset. So, I try to diffuse the situation with a deflection.

"Oh, Baz, don't you see how Luc and Blair act when they're together?" I rush on before he can interrupt. "She's mad for him. It's been for some time. He's spending a lot of non-business hours with her going to dinner and to the ballet."

I slide my palms up Sebastian's biceps to clasp my fingers behind his neck, leaning my body into his until he drops his arms to his sides. I brush my breasts against his hard chest and gaze warmly into his eyes as they darken with lust.

"Blair just asked me this morning if I mind her leaving early today to go with Luc to an event in Greenwich, Connecticut. I figured you could skip out early, too, so we can go to Peepshow at LEVELS since we haven't been in over a week. What do you think, Sir?" I purr in his ear as I lick then nip the outer shell.

His body jerks in response, and he wraps his arms around me as he growls in my ear.

"I know what you are doing, Naughty Pet. You cannot manipulate me by pressing your bountiful breasts and sultry pussy against me."

I yowl when he bites and tugs on my ear with his teeth and try to pull back only for him to crush me to his unyielding body.

"We will go to Peepshow, and we will perform a punishment demonstration for your bewitching behavior, Naughty Pet."

My pussy clenches and I whimper as he quickly spanks my right butt cheek, left, crease of my ass and thigh, right, left. I dance on my tiptoes and whine against his neck.

As he halts, Sebastian stands and I sway in his arms. Disappointment courses through my body that he ended his reprimand. My pussy continues to pulsate to the beat of his spanks, aching for his massive cock to fill it completely.

"A sample of what will occur tonight. Now, let us eat lunch."

* * *

THE VIEW across the East River is spectacular where I stand on the terrace of the Sutton Place penthouse I have to make mine. It reminds me of the one I had from my family's apartment further north of Fifty-seventh Street. I smile at Robin Sanchez-Waghorn, the realtor that Baz recommended to me. She's very knowledgeable and has shown me six apartments that are exactly what I'm looking for in my new home. But this sunny, spacious penthouse in a magnificent, Rosario Candela designed building is by far my favorite.

"I'll pay full price and want to close in a week," I tell Robin with a smile excited that I've found the perfect home.

"Fantastic!" Robin exclaims. "This is the most distinguished Sutton Place building. I'm confident that the board will approve your application as you'll be an impressive addition to the residents. Would you like to take another walkthrough before we leave?"

I slowly spin in a circle to take another glimpse, then head back to Baz's penthouse to get ready for our date tonight. I pause at the thought I consider going to Peepshow to serve as a punishment demonstration as a date, but nothing Baz and I have done is conventional. So, with a shrug to myself, I follow Robin through the penthouse and out of my soon-to-be front door.

TONIGHT, I want to be brazen. I chose a lingerie set from my new Las Vegas collection: the bra creates a flesh-tone barely there illusion with its sheer stretch-tulle cups; it's framed with delicate eyelash-trimmed lace and has black crossover straps and binding that highlight my curvy shape; I also made the briefs of sheer stretch-tulle outlined with contrasting black binding; added detail of panels trimmed along the waistband with more eyelash lace to highlight the deep cutout front and back. The overall appearance is my naked body crisscrossed by black lace and straps as a play on being tied up.

I hear a sharp intake of breath behind me as I stand in front of the full-length mirror in the dressing room. Startled, I peek over my shoulder to see Baz standing in the doorway staring at me with his mouth agape. My outfit struck him speechless—mission accomplished.

"Oh, hi," I say nonchalantly as I adjust my boob in the tiny cup watching his reflection in the mirror. "I'm almost ready," I add as I slip my feet into the nude-colored five-inch mules.

I sense his presence close behind me. My gaze returns to his reflection where he stands holding a wide, black leather choker with a silver ring attached to it. Baz lifts it in front of me and puts it around my neck. I dab it lightly with my finger, just realizing its purpose.

"From now on when we go to LEVELS, you will wear this collar. It shows that you are a sub who is the partner of a Dom and not available to anyone else." He tells me, gazing into my eyes. The closure locks in place and he reaches into his pants pocket to remove a delicate silver chain that he clips to the collar's ring.

My eyes follow the length of the chain as it dangles between my overflowing cleavage. It trails down my stomach to end in a leather loop Baz holds in his right hand. Now, my mouth hangs open as I peer back up at Baz who has an unreadable expression on his face.

"I... I..." I stutter not able to form a coherent sentence as alarm bells go off in my head sounded by my independent-woman self. I clear my throat to try again, "You expect me to wear a collar with a chain on it like I'm a dog on a leash?" I end on a shout, my face reddened in anger and embarrassment. What was I thinking getting involved in this Dom/sub shit? I ask myself angrily.

Sebastian raises his eyebrow and cocks his head before he braces my hands against the mirror and issues a barrage of spanks on my exposed ass as he responds.

"When will you learn to not question your Dom,

disobedient girl? How many times do I have to remind you who's the sub and who's the Dominant? You asked to learn the ways of D/s. Yet you question my putting a collar on you in a haughty tone. For that you will receive ten more lashes during our demonstration."

I'm forced to watch myself get spanked. To stand witness to the flashes of emotions that flit across my face as Sebastian continues his tirade as he watches my reactions in the mirror. From my initial anger to shock to pain to acquiescence, at which point he stops since after that blistering punishment, I'm submissive.

He stands and dabs my tearstain face with his handkerchief, "You must trust me if this will work. It does not mean the collar degrades you. It signifies that you are mine just as this gold bracelet that I wear signifies that I am yours."

My eyes quickly jump to his at the mention of mine and open wide at yours. Sebastian's eyes widen with mine when he realizes how I interpreted what he said to me. He hesitates a moment as if deciding whether to clarify his statement or leave it to hang between us like the chain between my breasts. Does it mean more than what's on the surface?

He leaves it alone when he tells me to freshen up so we can leave. Then strides out of the dressing room. Leaving me to wonder.

. . .

NOW THAT THE spanking Baz gave me in the dressing room has my head back in sub mode, I can just let go and feel. But that doesn't stop the nerves from happening. They flutter below the surface as Sir leads me by the delicate chain attached to the collar around my neck through the crowd at Peepshow. His destination, one of the mini stages that serve as spur-of-the-moment demonstration areas for members to show off their BDSM skills to those that gather to watch. Thankfully, he didn't book the primary stage—my heart would have definitely jumped out of my chest. The only reason that I gave in so easily to the mini stage is tonight's Masquerade Night. A time where everyone wears masks and can really enjoy the freedom of anonymity as they amp up their hedonistic deeds.

To keep my mind off of what's about to occur, I focus on Baz as he walks in front of me. He looks even more commanding and sexy than usual. Tonight's attire an all black outfit: heavy, leather boots; leather pants that fit oh so right front and back on his firm ass and massive bulge; an untucked, loose-fitted, long-sleeve shirt with laces instead of buttons; topped off with bed-head tousled hair and slight stubble on his gorgeous face. Yum.

All too soon, we step up onto a mini stage that I realize is in the middle of the crowded room. It has a vamp red leather spanking bench and various implements. Leave it to Baz to want to be the center of attention. Great. I give myself a mental pep talk and square my shoulders as I peer around at the people who have already turned in our direction in anticipation of a show. Again, I'm thankful for the gold mask with a black feather plume. Baz turns me to face him—his face half covered with a simple black mask like Zorro—and bends to place his lips to my ear.

"Now, Little Pet, I want you to relax and trust me. I will not embarrass you nor allow anyone else to make you feel poorly about your choice. Remember this is your decision and we will stop if you use your safeword. Do you understand?"

"Yes, Sir," I muster up in a strong, confident tone even though my stomach just flipped and I'm glad that I skipped dinner.

Sir addresses the group to inform them we will exhibit a punishment due me for putting another man ahead of him. He announces twenty lashes plus ten extra because of my flippant response to the collar with a flogger. I'm not sure if fear or arousal or even a combination reddens my face. But I shiver and my pussy clenches, eager for what Sir is about to do to me.

I slip out of my mules. Sir makes quick work of placing me on my belly across the bench with my wrists and ankles in matching vamp red suede cuffs. He adjusts the legs of the bench and my thighs open wide. If not for the scrap of material my barely there briefs offer as coverage, everyone would have an unobstructed view of my pussy and puckered bottom hole. Fortunately, the black material of the crotch hides the wet stain made by my sopping pussy. It doesn't go amiss by Sir I learn when he runs his fingers across the silk and slips two of his thick digits inside of my channel. I moan piteously when he removes them after three languid thrusts and steps away from me.

I tremble as rampant thoughts run through my mind. Then stop instantly when I feel the leather fringes of the flogger drag along the sole of my right foot, along my calf, up my thigh, across my right cheek. The hit to my left butt cheek resonates with a thwack before the fringes continue along the path of my left leg. I bleat out one. I fist my hands and try to stay still. A lesson I learned over the weeks that I must do or I risk receiving additional spanks. Sometimes that's a pleasurable thing. But tonight, I'm not so keen to stay on the stage for longer than necessary.

Sir continues his ministrations with the flogger and adds my pussy into the mix causing me to yelp instead of bleat. By the twentieth lashing, I'm fighting to stay still. Not to avoid the leather fringes on my hot, sore globes and thighs, rather to get relief for my core that's vibrating from trying to hold back my orgasm. Another sub lesson in control taught to me oh so well by Sir. At somewhere around twenty-three, I can't keep up with the count and become incoherent, even drunk-like. I reach subspace where pain morphs into pleasure. I can let go by putting my trust in Baz to take care of me. Since I can't utter my safeword, I can only rely on him to stop if he senses that I'm in distress. I float blissfully.

A second of pressure at my channel entrance follows a full-on thrust as Baz enters me with his massive cock. The force so strong that I shift along the bench, my wrists and ankles sliding in the cuffs saved from abrasion by the soft suede linings. From a distance I hear grunts and cries of lust as Baz chases his release while my body responds with wave after wave of orgasms. The erotic energy that surrounds us causes the group watching to join in seeking their own pleasure. A bacchanal-like atmosphere reaches a frenzied peak and we come as one with Baz's dominant roar heard above all.

I LANGUIDLY WAKE to warm water dripping on my breasts and the sound of humming. I peek around and realize that we're no longer on a mini stage in the middle of Peepshow. Rather, we're in the oversize bathtub of Baz's suite upstairs surrounded by fragrant bubbles instead of lust-driven revelers. With a contented sigh, I lean back against Baz and let him tend to me as my eyes drift close, again.

SEBASTIAN

*T*hree weeks in and I'm not disappointed or ready to call it quits with Lola. In fact, I'm settling into our routine with some minor adjustments to my usual schedule. That includes changing the time for my training sessions with Borya to 11:00 a.m. since I'd rather roll around with Lola in our bed satisfying my morning wood than sparring with the giant Russian. Especially now as I block his deadly kicks with my forearms.

"*Da, mal'chik!*" He says with a satisfied grunt since I survived his latest onslaught. "Your focus is back and you seem much more relaxed, less uptight, *da?* Is the time better? Or are you getting some *sladkaya kiska?*" He taunts, hoping to piss me off and I'll lose concentration as we start round five on the mat.

"*Otvali*, Alexeyev!" I growl as I go at him with a series of strategically placed punches and kicks that send him reeling backwards. No one disrespects my girl.

After the grueling hour and a brisk shower, I call Lola in her office. It's on the opposite end of the executive floor where I situated her into a suite of rooms initially as her temporary headquarters. However, I'm sure that I can persuade her to make it permanent.

"Hey, babe, do you have a minute to talk shop?" I ask her.

I laugh to myself about one of our scenes. Lola pretends she's a newly hired shop girl in one of her boutiques. While I'm a buyer who forces her to model the lingerie for me before I ravage her delectable, curvy body.

"Sure, what's up?" She asks, although she sounds distracted.

Lola's tone of voice gives me pause. So I ask her what's wrong. She tells me that the Sutton Place penthouse she bid on didn't pass inspection and that they can't sell it. This happens after they couldn't close within seven days as was part of her original offer. Instead, the sellers requested thirty days. I didn't mind the delay since I look forward to coming home to her every night. She sounds so disappointed, her voice thick like she's on the verge of tears. Good thing I can cheer her up.

"I'm sorry to hear that, darling. Robin will find an even better penthouse for you, don't worry. Okay? Besides, you get to stay with me longer. You know you'll miss waking up with my tongue deep in your sweet, little pussy, licking your cream for my breakfast."

We talk some more and then I spring the excellent news on her.

"Remember how we wanted Lola's Coterie in the west wing of the Vegas mall closer to the entrance from the casino? Well... As it turns out, we had to end the lease for one of the anchor stores early because of the owner's impending divorce and can offer it to you—"

I have to pull the headset from my ear as Lola's shrieks of joy threaten to deafen me. I put our call on speaker and sit back in my chair as I hear her yelling the wonderful news to Blair. Then silence. As I'm checking the connection to figure out what happened, I look up to see Lola running at top speed despite the high heels across the floor towards my office. With a laugh, I get up and open the door for her just as she jumps into my arms, wraps her legs around my waist, and smothers me with kisses. My dick hardens and lengthens from her warm core pressed against me. I carry her inside and kick the door shut before striding to my desk to darken the glass walls for some much-needed privacy.

Yeah... not... disappointed... at... all.

***

THE VIEW of the world-famous Las Vegas Strip sparkles like rare and exceptionally beautiful, fancy color diamonds as my G650 private jet flies into McCarran International Airport. I never tire of seeing the bright lights flashing in the middle of the bleak desert. I squeeze Lola's hand as we touch down and kiss her soft, fragrant cheek. Her spirits are much higher now that we've checked off the Mile High Club for her in the bedroom at the back of the jet.

"The view is phenomenal, Baz!" She exclaims leaning closer to the window, her excitement like that of a child staring into the windows at FAO Schwarz during the holidays. "I love Vegas! The shows, the shopping, the atmosphere! I can't wait to see the space!"

As soon as the pilot gives the all clear, we gather our things and walk to the cabin's exterior door. I can't wait to start the surprise that I have in store for Lola. I hate to see her sad. Although secretly, I'm glad that the penthouse fell through. Perhaps it's a sign that she's meant to stay with me indefinitely.

I have my Vegas driver Dario take us along the entire Strip so that Lola can oh and ah. Then we double back to the driveway for one of the two STEELE five-diamond resort and casino properties in the middle of the action. We'll stay in my penthouse that's on one of the top six floors. The penthouses act as a bridge to connect the two properties with the mall between them from the ground level to the third floor.

The valet opens the door of my Black Badge Rolls-Royce Cullinan for Lola while Dario opens my door. I stride around the back to reach Lola and take her hand in mine. We walk through the ornate, but tasteful main lobby towards the private reception foyer for the twelve Bridge Penthouses designed to attract high rollers and the über-wealthy clientele. Various staff members greet me by name.

A few of the woman give Lola the once over. They can't compete with my girl's beauty, so I don't even bother to acknowledge their lust-filled stares. The center of my attention is practically skipping beside me. She's so happy about the retail space for Lola's Coterie. At least she's able to get her first choice in the boutique if not in her penthouse.

We pause at the etched-glass, double doors for the doorman to allow us entry to the separate foyer. Beyond are three reception and two concierge desks, four sitting areas, and a bank of three private elevators, each accesses two of the Bridge Penthouses in this tower. Lola looks up at the two intimidating security guards who flank the entrance, then at me. I shrug like it comes with the territory and she smiles, her hazel eyes more dazzling than the lights on the Strip. So, entranced by Lola, I barely hear the greeting from one of the two concierges as we pass their desks on our way to the elevators.

"Good evening, Mr. Steele!"

I reluctantly pull my gaze from Lola and look towards the voice to see the female concierge walking towards me with an envelope on the properties' signature stationery.

"I have a message for you, Sir." She tells me in a seductive tone and emphasis on the Sir.

"Thank you," I respond, taking the envelope. She brushes her fingers against mine and smiles flirtatiously.

I have to hold back from rolling my eyes and I feel Lola stiffen next to me. "That will be all, Margaret," I finish brusquely, noting her name so I can tell Roger to have human resources correct her behavior or replace her. STEELE has a reputation to uphold. We will not tolerate staff wooing us, nor our guests. This is not a brothel, nor are our employees anything but professional and respectable.

We get on the elevator, and I quickly send a text to Malcolm. As my fingers fly across the screen, I hear Lola huff. I glance up to see that she has her back to me and is staring at the floor indicator with an annoyed expression on her pretty face. I finish my text before I slip my arms around Lola's waist to pull her back to my front and nuzzle the side of her neck. I take a deep inhale of her sultry perfume and close my eyes when my cock grows against her round bottom—damn, this woman drives me wild. Sadly, we don't have time to christen my suite, so I only hold her until the doors ping open.

"Come on, babe, we have to get ready for dinner," I tell her as I take her hand and lead her into the entryway. I know it's bad when Lola doesn't react to the breathtaking views of the Strip and the desert beyond.

"Hey," I start as I lift her chin to bring her eyes to mine. "I just sent Malcolm a text to report that concierge's inappropriate behavior."

Lola twists her mouth to the side and raises her perfectly sculpted eyebrow with another huff. So, I continue.

"Despite what you may think, I have not nor will I ever have sex of any sort with an employee. As a rule, I do not mix business with pleasure."

To that, she jerks back and widens her eyes at me—damn. I take her hands in mine and bend my knees to bring our eyes on the same level.

"Lola, let me be very clear, you and I are not in that category. You made me break my rule... Only you have ever made me want to set it aside. Understand?"

Lola pins me with a stare, then exhales and nods her head in acceptance.

"Words, Little Pet. I will have your words," I correct her.

"Okay... Okay!" She replies all sass with an eye roll. When she spins on her heels to head towards the wall of windows, I give her ass a sufficient swat. I enjoy watching it jiggle under her pants as she yelps in surprise.

After a quick tour, we go into my bedroom to get ready. Lola emerges from the dressing room in a black sexy as fuck cutout, fringed stretch-cotton and mesh, sleeveless maxi dress. The plunging neckline enhances her ample D-cups. I want to yank on the wispy fringe and delicate ties that crisscross the open back to feast on her mouthwatering, curvy body. Her luscious globes in matching black briefs peek out from under the sheer skirt. It falls to a billowy, ruffled, asymmetric hem where her legs are on display in high strappy heels. I let out a low wolf whistle in appreciation.

"You like?" Lola asks coyly as she spins and the dress lifts and falls around her beautifully.

"More than like," I start as I put my hands under the vee of the neckline to knead her more-than-a-handful breasts.

"I love it," I finish as I pinch her pebbled nipple between my fingers and nip her neck.

The vibration of my mobile in my trousers pocket bumping against my thick dick reminds me we don't have time for carousing. Instead, I step back from my Petite Seductress to answer the call from Malcolm.

"Yeah… Great, thanks for taking care of that for me."

I end the call quickly and take Lola by the hand to leave the penthouse before we sidetrack my surprise plans.

Lola glides through the Bridge Penthouses foyer with her head held high. Purposefully ignoring a much-subdued Margaret who stands behind the concierge desk and doesn't even dare to look in our direction. I chuckle to myself and kiss Lola's hand to prove that she's it for me. She turns her head and beams a beatific smile at me, and my heart soars.

I lead her through the bustling main lobby and action-packed casino to the high-end mall. My excitement builds with each step in anticipation of her elated response to my spectacular surprise. She never questions where we're going or why we're headed away from the restaurants. She trusts me to take care of her—the Dom in me is pleased.

When we arrive in front of the large retail space recently vacated by the former anchor tenant, I punch in the code for the door lock. As I step back, I gesture for Lola to enter ahead of me. The interior is black since the lights are off and they covered the windows and doors with paper to block the inside from passersby's view. So she sidesteps to the left to let me guide the way and claps her hands in delight.

"Is this it? Is this the space for Lola's Coterie?" She asks bouncing on the balls of her feet, holding her beaded clutch to her chest.

"Maybe," I tease her with a Cheshire Cat grin.

"Don't tease me."—THWACK—"My heart can't take it." She says as she hits me on the chest with her clutch.

"Okay... Okay. Wait there while I turn on the lights," I tell her and walk into the darkness.

I get a few feet when the lights flash on and loud screams of surprise echo throughout the vast space. Lola screeches and jumps back as Leonie, Roger, Luc, Blair, Tina, Walter, Malcolm, Lydie Jackson, and the servers wave, clap, and stomp their feet. I join in and swoop Lola up in the air, then carry her over to the table set for dinner. As I put her down, she fists my hair and brings my face to hers for a passionate kiss. It almost makes me want to kick everyone out so I can have my way with her. Reluctantly, I let her go when Leonie grabs her arm to pull Lola in for a hug.

"*Félicitations!*" Leonie exclaims, beaming with her amber eyes aglow.

Luc comes over next and kisses her cheeks before pulling Lola into an embrace. "*C'est une excellente nouvelle pour* Lola's Coterie, *petite chérie!*" He extols, hugging my Lola, again. *Le bâtard.*

"Let me introduce you to my brother Malcolm and

Lydie," I interrupt hurriedly taking her from Luc's embrace.

"Lola, this is my brother Malcolm, and this is Lydie Jackson an old family friend and the overall vice president of Jackson Corporation," I introduce Lola when we reach them.

"Not so old and not only a friend!" Lydie laughs as she hits me playfully on the chest leaning into me as she shakes Lola's hand. "So, you're Lola." Lydie adds giving Lola the once over in the direct way Lydie has with people.

"Yes, I am. Can't say that you're familiar," Lola says haughtily before turning her back to Lydie and shaking Malcolm's hand.

I'm just about to smack my younger brother in the back of his head for daring to let his eyes dip to Lola's breasts, when Lydie takes my arm. She announces that she needs to speak with me. As she turns us away, I see an emotion that's a combination of irritation and disappointment flit across Lola's face. Then she pastes on a pleasant smile and nods at us without meeting my eyes.

As Lydie drones on about some joint business idea that she and her brother Lucien want to present to STEELE, I can't take my eyes off of Lola. She's laughing with Luc and Malcolm, both of whom she has enthralled. She's so beautiful, charming, and smart that she's a magnet for men like Luc, Rockett, Malcolm—but Lola is mine. So, I tell Lydie to set the date in a couple of months when she and Lucien have more details. Lydie mumbles something about not seeing me as much recently and now has to wait two months for a meeting. But I barely listen as I make my way back to my Petite Seductress.

"—I'd love to go dancing! What a marvelous way to continue the celebration!" Lola gushes to Malcolm as she squeezes his hands between hers. "Let me tell Leonie. She'll love it, too."

Lola goes to pass without acknowledging my presence, so I grab her by the waist and pull her close to press my lips to her ear.

"I have plans for us after dinner," I growl and nip her delicate lobe.

Her only response is to flick at her ear like I'm a pesky gnat as she pushes me in the chest to move pass, again not meeting my eyes. I let her go to avoid a scene and watch as she hurries to Leonie and they wiggle their hips mimicking dance moves. Out of my periphery, Luc approaches me and I brace myself for dealing with his shit.

"This is an excellent space for the boutique. We will do well so near to the high traffic of people entering and exiting the casino," Luc says as he holds his hand out for a shake.

I can't let this man get under my skin with his reference to we as Lola and him. So I shake his hand and hold a civil conversation with him until the servers announce that dinner is ready.

The night is less of the original idea that I had of us laughing and celebrating the boutique. Correction, Lola is thoroughly enjoying herself first throughout the meal, engaging with everyone but me. Now in one of the resort's nightclubs, dancing with Leonie. The two of them attracting the attention of every man in the damn universe. I notice that Roger looks as glum as I feel. I haven't spoken with him about his deal with Leonie, but I can tell he has feelings for her.

Fuck it. I will not sit here sipping glass after glass of the Jackson Special Blend Scotch, moping for the rest of the night. Nor do I want to take Lydie up on her many requests to dance despite her pouting. So, I slap Roger on the shoulder and we stalk over to our dancing queens.

I stake my claim by coming up behind Lola. Entwining our fingers and raising our joined hands above her head to wrap them around the back of my neck, I dip my knees to grind my pelvis into her ass. I make sure she feels how much I miss her attention. At first she stiffens, but then loosens up when she realizes that it's me and not one of the lame dudes salivating around them. We dance like we have sex—hot, heavy, sweaty, long.

A few hours later, we stumble off of the penthouse elevator kissing while wrapped in each other's arms. I bend down and toss her over my shoulder in a fireman's carry. She squeals and slaps her palms against my back.

"Let me down, Captain Caveman!" A tipsy Lola yells, laughing and snorting. "You're a beast! Grrrr!"

I smack her ass a few times as I stride over to the wall of windows, then stand her facing the exterior where the sun is just beginning to rise. I lace my fingers with hers and press our palms to the glass, bending down to rest my chin on her shoulder. At first she squirms, but then settles as we quietly watch the natural blazing colors of the sky outshine the artificial lights of the Strip.

Our bodies speak to one another without words, stoking the fire of our burgeoning relationship. Lola turns to me, cupping my face in her hands as she stares longingly into my eyes. I tilt my head to nuzzle my cheek into her palm, then shift to place a gentle kiss on it. With a sigh, Lola leans into me and wraps her arms around my neck. I scoop her up into my arms and carry her to the bedroom where I revere her body until neither of us can stay awake any longer.

"*Non*, I don't want to talk about it!"

Leonie exclaims slicing her hand through the air to cut off my questions regarding Roger and her and why she's sexting with Giovanni Mattei.

Only three weeks ago Leonie and Roger were dancing it up at the nightclub in Vegas. Now as we sit eating pastries and sipping tea in Angelina Paris, the legendary 1903 tearoom near *le Jardin des Tuileries*, Leonie is going at it with Giovanni. I'm surprised that my best friend isn't sharing with me whatever happened between Roger and her.

"Are you not telling me because Roger is Baz's brother and you think I'll say something to him he'll tell Roger?" I guess putting my hand over the screen of her mobile and pushing it to the tabletop.

Leonie dramatically blows out a pfft of air and rolls her eyes, tossing her long mane of wavy, mahogany hair over her shoulder. She sits back and regards me silently, her amber eyes drilling into my hazel ones. I mimic her position, prepared to wear her out until I get answers. I miss her and want the time that I'm here for the week to catch up. Hence, the afternoon tea with her and why I'm not at the office taking care of some business that I can't handle via teleconference or video conference from New York.

"No, that's not it. I know you wouldn't tell anything to Sebastian," Leonie twirls a section of her silky hair around her finger while she stares into the distance. "I just don't know what to make of him. I thought it could have been *un coup de foudre*. You know, a stroke of lightning or love at first sight..."

She trails off and looks aware sadly, twirling and untwirling the same lock of her hair. I realize that she's serious and the bolt of lightning must have hit at the initial expansion meeting when I noticed them staring at each other strangely.

"Well, what happened? You were definitely close in the elevator at their residences in The STEELE Tower and Vegas..." I prod her to keep talking about what happened next.

"Yes, but he's so serious and uptight. If I didn't study when I said that I would, he would chastise me for not being focused... I'm not a child!" She slaps her hand on the table and the dishes clatter, but fortunately don't break.

I can tell she's really distraught and get up from my chair to hug her, offering words of understanding and comfort. It's rare that Leonie gets upset and I hate it when she does. After a moment, she pulls herself together and gives me a squeeze before shooing me back towards my seat.

"Anyway, I'm going to the Grand Prix—"

I cut her off by waving my hand in the air, "I'm going with you! I will not let you get caught up with *God's Gift*, especially when you're feeling down and are vulnerable. No rebound sex!"

I hold up my hand to stop her from interrupting me, "No! It's next week and I'm here anyway, so I'll just leave when the race is over. We'll be a part of the glamorous crowd." I add using air quotes reminding her of what she told me a couple of months ago.

"*Fantastique!*" Leonie exclaims clapping and jumping up to hug me.

Of course, the surrounding guys gawk at *The Lion*.

It does not thrill Sebastian at all that I've extended my stay in Europe to include a few days in Monte Carlo for the Grand Prix. He growled his disappointment and attempted to command me with his Dom-mind control back to New York. My best friend needs me and that's final.

Sebastian lost it when he wanted to scene over the mobile video view and I told him I couldn't because I was getting ready for dinner with Luc. He ended our call abruptly saying that he had a meeting that he had to get to and he'll talk to me later. The man is maddening, grrr!

* * *

THE SUITE that Baz arranged for me at the STEELE Monte Carlo is palatial with a beautiful view of the sparkling azure water of the Mediterranean Sea. But the many vases filled with gorgeous, delicious scented flowers are all that matter to me. Each card has an original message from Baz from the sentimental—I miss you; The bed's too big without you—to the raunchy—My dick will fall off; I can't taste your pussy on my lips anymore. I take pictures of them and send them to Baz via text.

I add a message of my own—a photo of me naked, lying on a chaise on the terrace overlooking the Med. The sun is glistening on my skin, shiny from the suntan oil I slathered all over my body. I'm caught in the throes of ecstasy. My long, wavy black hair fans around my head as it's thrown back with my mouth open in an O. I cup my large, heavy breasts and pinch my nipples into tight buds while I widen my thighs to put my slick pussy on full view. Before I can sit back up, my mobile is ringing with a call from Baz.

"What the hell, Lola!" He shouts when I answer. "Who the fuck took that picture!"

He's so loud that I have to hold the mobile away from my ear. I can still hear him yelling without being on speaker. Once his tirade is over and it's quiet except for his heavy breathing, I respond.

"Why hello, darling. The flowers are gorgeous, tha—"

"Don't give me that shit, Lola! Answer me!" He shouts, cutting me off as he lets loose a string of curses that would give a sailor lessons.

Oh dear, he's really pissed and I need to calm him down pronto.

"Baz, I took the picture," I start.

But he interrupts me demanding to know how I got the angle, what's or rather who's around me, can they see me, on and on. Oh boy, my Caveman is definitely losing his shit.

"No one is around me. I put my mobile on the ledge and used the timer. And no, I wasn't naked when I set up the shot. I had on a robe. Only for your eyes, baby, only you," I purr into the phone.

Now, Baz's breathing is heavy for other reasons. We continue the call with a scene where I'm on a deserted island and he washes ashore naked, the survivor of a shipwreck…

* * *

"This is the life," I sigh contentedly as I sip a refreshing Sea Breeze cocktail in a tall, frosty glass.

"*Oui, Chérie. Nous sommes très heureux d'être ici, sur Plage du Larvotto,*" a radiant Leonie agrees sipping her champagne.

I think how happy I am that I came with Leonie to Monte Carlo. Yesterday and today have been amazing, especially since Giovanni is busy with his pre-race activities.

At the moment, we have on bright colored, skimpy, string bikinis with the tops on since the paparazzi are always near for the Grand Prix festivities happening around the clock. God help me if Baz sees a topless photo of me online.

Leonie and I took a break today to relax on the beach with some of our friends here for the race or who live near. It's one of the few sandy spots on the Monaco coast. Sure we could have spent time at pools at the hotel or at their luxurious villas. Instead, we want to feel the sand between our toes and splash in the warm waves of the Med.

Tonight we're going to a party on a royal's yacht with more of the glitterati. Then, the race is tomorrow and the after parties begin. It's a whirlwind of fun in the sun with my best friend. So worth it.

SEBASTIAN

$\mathcal{I}$ stand here with steam coming out of my ears. I still haven't stopped fuming since I saw those photos all over the internet, social media... fucking space. Lola prancing around town in a pair of short booty shorts. Wearing some tiny ass bikini that didn't do much to cover her big tits. Gamboling in the surf on the shoulders of some motherfucker. A tight ass dress that hugged her curvy body on a yacht. I nearly had a stroke.

I barely kept my sanity enough to tell one of my assistants to arrange my flight plan ASAP. Then, in the air, more photos surface of Lola at the race, this time in a simple, halter dress. It's not what she's wearing, rather what she's doing—being swung around by some asshole after the race in the pit because their team won. Yeah, I was okay with her hanging with her best friend, but not okay with all the attention she attracts. Damn!

Little does she know that I'm at the Grand Prix after

party being held at one of Roger's new specs. It's a hillside villa used as the venue to showcase the property and to encourage buyers. When she called me earlier, I pretended that I was in a meeting and couldn't talk. Actually, I was over the Atlantic Ocean mentally pushing my G650 to go faster. When I landed, I went to Roger's personal villa so Lola wouldn't know that I was in Monte Carlo ready to pounce on her.

"Hello, sexy."

I glance down to see a buxom redhead in a designer dress stroking my biceps and running her tongue over her pink, glossy lips. I know that she's not one of the high-end call girls that spend their time in locations where the rich and famous congregate. The invitation list is for a certain caliber of attendee and the security is airtight. So as not to offend a potential owner, I flash her a charming smile and ask her to excuse me. I pull my mobile from my pants pocket to answer a pretend call. She nods and reluctantly releases my arm. Gracing her with an award-winning smile, I stride away and don't look back.

Loud cheers erupt from the lower terrace and the deejay stops the music to announce the winning team. I weave through the guests as I rush over to the wall, fully expecting to see Lola with them as she told me she was going to the post-race party. Yup, there she is laughing with Leonie who's in the arms of the driver whose tongue is down her throat. I search around, but don't see Roger, who probably won't be happy to see Leonie with some other guy. I know I'm pissed with Lola.

"Mattei! Mattei! Mattei!" The crowd chants. He grins, keeping his arm around Leonie as they pose for the cameras. Lola is opposite them with her arm looped through the same ass from earlier. Fuck... that.

As if by kismet, Lola's gaze sweeps around the villa and lands on the terrace where I stand glowering down at her. She does a double take when she recognizes me. I merely stare at her and can sense even from this distance her astonishment at seeing me here. I refuse to move—the Dom in me is on overdrive. She whispers something in Leonie's ear, who promptly lifts her shocked gaze to me on the terrace, before hurriedly making her way through the crowd.

Just as she nears another woman stands in front of me and puts her hand on my chest, babbling in French something or the other about the race. Lola pauses for only a moment before stepping to us and forcibly putting herself between me and the woman while telling her in French to back off. The woman startles. Then rapidly disappears into the crowd, the scent of her perfume wafting behind her. My eyes never left Lola's face. I wait for her to make the first move.

"Baz! What are you doing here? Why didn't you tell me you were coming when we spoke earlier? I've missed you so much!" She exclaims, reaching her arms around my neck to pull my face to hers for a hungry kiss.

Once in her arms, my angry mind can't deny my aching soul's need for her. So I lift Lola into an embrace, kissing her like she's the air that I need to breathe. Suddenly, all is right in my world. No longer agitated or feeling that something is absent from my life. In this moment, I realize Lola is a vital part of me I can't be without. Even for little more than a week.

"Oh, Baz. I'm so glad that you're here," Lola sighs as I lower her to the ground, sliding her body against mine, relishing the feel of her so close to me at last.

I take in the sight of her in a long-sleeve, antique gold metallic wrap, mini dress and sandals. I want to unwrap her curvy, little body and drive my hard cock deep inside each of her three holes to remind her she belongs to me and me only.

"I missed you too, babe," I tell her sincerely, stroking my thumb on her soft cheek flushed a pretty pink from her excitement. "You look beautiful."

Lola giggles and twirls making the hem of her dress rise showing the tops of her shapely thighs. I have an urge to sit Lola on the wall and have my way with her despite the other people around us. Sure that she wouldn't agree, I settle for another embrace, resting my chin on the top of her head.

That's when I catch sight of Roger staring from a distance at Leonie with that guy Mattei. Roger's facial expression is indecipherable to a stranger. However, I'm his brother so I can tell by the stiffness around his mouth that he's struggling to keep a straight face and his emotions under control.

The couple he was speaking with is oblivious as his eyes dart from them to Leonie who's the center of attention sipping champagne amongst the jubilant racers. When the peals of her laughter rise above the music and other voices, Roger visibly vibrates with white heat. I can't just witness my younger brother's turmoil and not try to fix it.

"What's up with Leonie?" I ask Lola pointedly.

Lola shifts uncomfortably before asking, "What do you mean?"

I cock my head and give her my Dom stare to compel her to tell me what's going on. When she ignores my look, I pivot and walk towards the stairs to ask Leonie for myself.

"Sebastian! What are you doing?" Lola shrieks as she attempts to catch up to me in her fuck-me heels, careful not to misstep. "Don't you dare say anything to Leonie! It's Roger you need to speak to not—"

Lola halts and I turn to see her standing wide-eyed with her hand over her mouth. Aha! I knew there was something going on.

"What do you mean it's Roger I need to speak to?" I frown, stalking back towards her.

"I promised Leonie that I wouldn't say anything and I'm not. If you want answers, then speak to Roger," she replies with a lift to her chin and hazel eyes blazing in pure pertinacity.

Lola's loyalty is admirable, if not annoying. I nod and make a note to ask Roger tomorrow. I will not ruin Lola's and my evening after we've been apart for a long nine and a half days.

"Sebastian, what are you doing here!"

I turn to see an anxious Leonie looking around the

bustling terrace, more than likely seeking Roger. I can tell the moment that she sees him when Leonie's cat-like eyes flash wide with hurt, then narrow to angry slits. Meanwhile, he's whispering in the ear of another stunningly beautiful, well-known supermodel.

Leonie continues to glare at the couple until Roger raises his head as though sensing her presence and pins her with his signature intense stare. They continue to glower at each other until Mattei glides up behind Leonie and slips his arms around her waist, burying his face in her neck, lustily whispering in Italian. The scornful eye that Roger throws at Leonie is strong enough to make me flinch. In response, she lifts her chin defiantly and takes Mattei by the hand, only stopping briefly to ask Lola if she minds if Leonie leaves. With a wistful smile, Lola shakes her head, then pins Roger with a scathing glare.

"Nice to see you, Leonie," I tell her more determined than ever to find out what's happening between her and my younger brother. On the surface it appears as though he's at fault given Leonie's reactions.

"*Bon soir*, Sebastian," she replies attempting to keep her smile in place. "Take care of my girl. She's missed you," Leonie tells me softly.

Before they walk away, I give Mattei the once over to let him know that he better not fuck with her. My investigator will do a full background check. I'll prevent anything that has the potential to impact Lola negatively, including some hotshot hurting her best friend.

Then, I turn to face Roger. He pretends the conversation with the model captivates him. Yet, the set of his shoulders belie his genuine emotions—he's agitated. Yeah, there's more to this story. I'll get it out of somebody, just not tonight. The only significant mystery I'm solving is how quickly I can get Lola out of here and back to the hotel.

"Babe, let's leave too so you can show me how you set up that scandalous photo," I growl against the shell of Lola's ear.

At first she's rigid, still thinking about Leonie and Roger. When I discreetly slip my hand inside her dress to cup her mound artfully playing her clit, she loosens right up and moans her agreement. I bring my finger to her mouth for her to suck it clean while I nibble on her lobe and grind my erection into her back.

"Mmm mmm," Lola hums, sucking my digit and sending a zing to my throbbing cock.

"Let's go... Right... Now," I grab Lola's hand and part the crowd, suppressing the urge to bulldoze through them. Lola's laughter at my eagerness fills my ears.

We get into Roger's convertible Aston Martin Vanquish and zip to the hotel. If I were racing in the Grand Prix, I would beat Mattei by miles. When we arrive, I toss the keys to the valet. I take Lola by the waist to keep her steady on those sky-high heels as we rush through the lobby to the elevators. I walk as though I have blinders on to avoid interacting with the staff—no delays, no opportunities for flirtatious concierges.

Unfortunately, we share the elevator with two other

couples. So I can't get my hands on Lola until we arrive at the top floor that only has four suites the size of four-bedroom apartments. The hotel only reserves this floor for royalty and the über-wealthy. Lola barely gets to swipe the keypad before I'm untying the bow on her dress. The alluring floral scent of her perfume increases my desire for her as I bury my face in the side of her neck for a whiff.

"Baz, I want to taste you on my tongue. Feel you stretch my throat," Lola says in a low and sultry voice.

She gracefully lowers to her knees in front of me, unbuckling my belt and unzipping my pants. My achingly hard cock is finally free from the tightened confines of my trousers and right where it has wanted to be all this time.

"Hmmm... So big... So thick. Ooh, are you crying for me, baby?" She asks, putting the tip of her little pink tongue on the bead of pre-cum dripping from my dick. "Yummm!" Lola hums around my pulsating dick sending vibrations shooting through me, her full lips wrapped around my girth and her hooded, hazel eyes staring up at me.

The sight of my enormous cock filling her small mouth makes me growl and I grip her silky hair tightly in my fists to guide her movements.

She works my shaft like her favorite lollipop. Down, suck, up, swirl, suck. Her salacious eyes stay on mine. I've never had a woman experience as much pleasure from giving me head as Lola. Her body quivers with excitement as she takes me to the back of her throat, then down until I can see the outline of my cock in her neck. She reaches into her open dress and strokes her clit making my dick jump and her gag. I cup her big, pillowy tits and knead them before I sharply pinch her pert nipples, eliciting a strangled groan from her mouth.

She continues with her pattern—down, suck, up, swirl, suck. On her next down stroke, I pull her hair to get her attention and hold her steady with her lips pressed to my groin until she gags. Then, I fuck her fast, pumping my hips and fisting her hair until her eyes water. She ineffectively pushes against my thighs, taut with the power I'm using to fuck Lola's throat.

When I can't hold back any longer, I thrust deep one last time and throw my head back roaring my release as my seed pours down her throat. Lola swallows every single drop. The universe explodes behind my closed eyelids. I can't hear any sound except for the thrumming of my blood rushing in my ears. Then I pant as I slowly return to Earth. I gaze down at Lola, who's still beautiful despite the trails of mascara, smudged lipstick, and messy hair. Her pride in bringing me to my knees clear in the satisfied smirk on her face.

"So good baby," I praise Lola, rubbing my thumb over her lips swollen from my unrestrained fucking of her face.

I lift my girl up into my arms and carry her through the suite to the moonlit terrace, the warm breeze drifting over from the Med. I want to make her come undone for me on the same chaise she posed on for that photo she sent two days ago.

SEBASTIAN

*M*y meeting lasted longer than expected, so I rush into the penthouse. Instead of going upstairs to change, I detour to the kitchen to apologize to Lola for keeping her waiting for me. She left work early to go grocery shopping, then to cook dinner for us—her specialty Bouillabaisse in homage to our time spent on the Mediterranean coast two weeks ago. I kiss her where she's sitting at the breakfast bar sipping a glass of white wine, my favorite Jackson Scotch sits in a Waterford crystal snifter beside her. My mobile chimes an incoming text, so I lean my hip against the bar to respond and chuckle when I read Lydie's message.

"What's so funny?" Lola asks, peering at me over the rim of her glass.

"Huh?" I respond distracted by returning the text and laugh some more.

Lola nudges me and repeats her question. To which I

answer nothing, then place my mobile on the counter. I give her a quick kiss on the forehead and head to the bedroom to put on a pair of sweats and a long-sleeve T-shirt. When I return to the kitchen, Lola looks pissed.

"What's the matter?" I ask, curious what changed her mood so abruptly.

She just glares at me, her nostrils flaring from her heavy breathing for a full minute before she responds.

"What the fuck, Sebastian? You told me in Vegas that Lydie is just an old family friend even though she was flirting with you and rubbing all over you all damn night!"

That's when I notice that Lola is holding my mobile in her hand, shaking it at me accusatorially. I make the mistake of getting defensive.

"Why are you going through my mobile, Lola!" I stalk over to her and reach to take the device from her.

Incensed, she takes a deep breath and rips me an extra one, then throws my mobile at me which I easily catch. Her eyes are like sharp daggers, her face is bright red, and she's breathing heavily, again. I know that I should back down, but I don't appreciate her invading my privacy. Lydie is only a friend and I should repeat that fact but I won't on principle.

"I wasn't going through your mobile, you pompous ass! It was unlocked, and I saw a name that started with an ell and thought it was Leonie! I'm not the girlfriend who snoops!" She snarls at me, even more pissed than before.

Without thinking of the consequences, I let my temper get the better of me.

"Who said you're my girlfriend, huh?" I retort.

Instantly, Lola recoils as though I slapped her in the face and she blanches, then blinks rapidly before spinning on her heels and rushing from the kitchen. I throw my head back and shout in frustration. I refuse to run after her and wait a few minutes hoping that she'll calm down and I won't have to deal with this shit. It's been an interminable day and I'm not in the mood to coddle her when she's in the wrong. Despite a niggling in my mind telling me to apologize and make this right.

After I finish my drink, I go out into the hallway and call her name. When I don't get an answer, I check every room and don't see her. I dial her mobile number and it just rings until her voicemail picks up. Next, I call the concierge to ask if he saw her leave. He confirms that Lola left the building fifteen minutes ago.

Fuck!

LOLA

I cannot believe that Sebastian spoke to me that way and accused me of invading his privacy. Most of all, I'm beyond hurt he said I wasn't his girlfriend after three solid months together. In fact, the dinner tonight was for our anniversary—I just hadn't told him that was the reason I cooked. I knew it was too good to be true.

The crosswalk light turns red and I bring my attention to my surroundings. When I walked as quickly as I could without running through the lobby, I didn't pay attention to the direction I took. I just had to put as much distance between me and him. The pain was so intense that I got an instant headache. I rub my temples, then I see that I'm still on Fifth Avenue, only a few blocks south of Luc's penthouse. My subconscious taking me where I'll find comfort, I wonder.

Fortunately, I had the sense of mind to snatch my handbag when I left our—I mean—Sebastian's duplex. So, I take my mobile out and notice several missed calls and text messages from him. Too bad.

Instead of calling him back, I send a brief text to Luc to let him know that I will spend the night at his place. He'll see it in the morning when he wakes given that it's after one in the morning Paris time. The doormen know me, so I have no trouble getting in his building and use the code to call for the private elevator. Once inside, I take a shower and crash in one of the guest rooms.

Sebastian

I can't sleep. I pace and drink Scotch all night until the sun rises. My voicemails and text messages to Lola range from angry to conciliatory to blaming her to begging her to come home. I'm worried sick.

The shrill ring of a telephone startles me as I must have fallen asleep. I jump up at the sound and realize that I'm on the couch in my home office and the landline is ringing. I rub my hand over my bleary eyes and cradle my pounding head in my hands. Damn, I'm hungover. I don't make it to the telephone and wonder why they didn't call my mobile. Not seeing it anywhere, I get up and head to the desk to call the number.

A crunch under my foot and a sharp pain causes me to look down. I see shattered pieces of my mobile on the floor. Fuck! I must have thrown it, and that's why they're calling the telephone. Cursing, I fall into my desk chair and pick a piece of glass out of the sole of my foot. The house intercom rings and I answer it with the hand not staunching the flow of blood from my foot.

"What!" I growl.

"Mr. Steele, sir, I apologize for disturbing you, but your office called asking me to ring you. Your assistants have been trying to reach you. But didn't get an answer and they're concerned," the concierge quickly tells me.

"Shit. What time is it?" I ask, wondering why I don't have a clock in here.

"It's eleven-thirty, Mr. Steele," he replies.

"Fuuuck!" I yell. Then add a thanks before hanging up to call Tina.

"Sebastian Steele's office, Tina speaking."

I give Tina some instructions: cancel my appointments for the day; deliver a new mobile to me at home immediately; let my cleaner know there's broken glass in my home office that needs removal. I'm taking the day off and do not disturb me. Once I finish my call with Tina, I wrap my t-shirt around my foot and drag my sorry ass to my bathroom to get my shit together.

* * *

It took me four excruciating days to find Lola. Now, I stand here on a private beach watching her sit at the shoreline as she stares out at the Caribbean Sea. Those days taught me I should have listened to her and put my ego to the side. The accusations I made of her and not admitting that I was wrong as soon as she clarified she wasn't snooping didn't help the situation. Our first fight and it's all my fault—dummy.

Lola's movement to stand draws me back to the present. Hungrily, I watch her rise wearing a black string bikini bottom and a white cropped tank top. Sand clings to her luscious butt and her long hair blows in the breeze, covering her eyes so she doesn't see me standing a few yards away from her. She tosses her hair over her shoulder and looks up. She pauses in the middle of her step and shields her eyes with her hand since the sun is obscuring my features. So she doesn't get frightened, I walk towards her and call her name praying that she will forgive me and come home. I can tell it will not be easy when I notice she squares her shoulders, folds her arms under her braless breasts and quickens her pace, ignoring me. I refuse to give up.

"Lola, I'm sorry, I shouldn't have said those terrible things, and you didn't deserve that cruel treatment, especially not by me." I raise my voice to tell her as I walk closer to her.

She only hesitates for a moment, then shakes her head.

When she nears me, Lola gives me a wide berth to reach the villa's seawall gate. I follow her. But she turns and puts her hand up to stop me.

"I can't right now," Lola says before opening the gate.

"Please, Lola. Please let's talk. I was wrong. Won't you listen to me? Please?" I urge, knowing that if she closes that gate I'll beg her to give me a chance.

Lola pauses again with her back to me. This time she raises her hand to wipe at her face. Fuck... She's crying. I'm such a miserable asshole.

Without thinking twice, I rush over and pull Lola to my chest, wrapping my body around hers. I refuse to let go when she squirms to loosen her arms I have pinned to her sides. I bury my face in her hair and clutch her even tighter.

"Baby, please forgive me. I fucked up and I want to make it right. Please let me make it up to you. Please," I beg huskily in her ear, dragging my lips down to her neck and nuzzling her sensitive spot. "I don't want us to be apart. It's hurting both of us, please."

Her body trembles with her emotions. I turn her around to face me, bending my knees so we're eye level, holding her by the shoulders.

"I warned you at the beginning that I've never been in a relationship and would undoubtedly fuck up," I pause staring intently into her hazel eyes red from her tears. "And I did... superbly. I apologize. What can I do to earn your forgiveness?" I ask sincerely.

One tear falls from her eye as she stares into my soul,

weighing the veracity of my words. I can read the emotions rolling across her tearstained face. I can tell that Lola is fighting an internal struggle. So I lean in slowly, giving her the opportunity to pull away. Then I brush my lips along the tracks from her tears, tasting the salt, placing my lips softly against hers.

She whimpers and I press my tongue past her lips and against her teeth, demanding that she open for me. When she denies me entrance, I bite her plump, lower lip and push my tongue between them as they part with her moan.

A deep passionate growl rumbles through me. I sweep her mouth with my probing tongue to capture her taste again and to conquer her resistance. I end the searing kiss by nipping, licking, and sucking down her throat as she offers it to me, acknowledging my dominance. Then lower my head to latch onto the tightened buds of her nipples through the cotton of her tank top. Suckling strongly, pulling hard enough to draw pants and gasps from her slack mouth.

Immediately, Lola's response to my demands is to arch her back. She twists the fingers of one of her hands in my hair at the back of my head to anchor my mouth to her breasts. The other hand grips my shoulder to anchor her to me.

As I keep one arm around her waist, I place the fingers of my other hand inside of her bikini bottom and dive into her sopping wet channel. I need to stretch her tight pussy to prepare her for me to reclaim her. I swat her wet pussy lips a few times to punish her for leaving me. My palm smacks her engorged clit, and she mewls in pain and pleasure, grinding her mound into my hand.

I can't wait any longer as the crude sounds of my hand spanking Lola's soaking pussy combined with her thrashing drives me mad. I lift her up, slamming her back into the seawall while I unzip my jeans. I drive my aching, weeping cock to the hilt deep inside of her in one unyielding thrust.

Lola cries out in pain and ecstasy at my brutal invasion of her tight pussy. She wraps her legs around me, digging her heels into my ass to push me deeper. We both groan, feeling every one of my ten inches graze her G-spot and stroke inner walls. Lola meets each of my frantic thrusts with one of her own, her body bowing to ease my way inside of her. Suddenly, the dam breaks. Lola screams curses at me for hurting her so badly, for not trusting her like I tell her to trust me, and for being a big asshole. I can't help but to agree with her.

The rhythmic sound of skin on skin mixed with the squelching of her soaking pussy drive me into a frenzy. I grab under her thigh and lift her calf to my shoulder, changing the angle to drive up deeper into her. Each thrust sending my tip to graze her cervix. Each time that I withdraw, her greedy pussy grips my cock, refusing to let me go. She feels so good, so tight and wet, that I lose control and pound into her pussy with guttural grunts.

Once again, I lower my head and suckle and bite her pebbled nipples until she squeals and her pussy clamps down on my thickening cock. Lola cries out in wild abandon with her eyes squeezed shut, tossing her head side-to-side, babbling in the throes of ecstasy as she cums over and over and over. Now that she's peaked, I ram into her like a feral beast chasing my orgasm. I don't stop until I feel my dick pulsate and shoot rope after rope after rope of my essence deep into her core. Unable to remain standing, I sag to the sand with Lola limp in my lap.

"HOW DID YOU FIND ME?" Lola asks as we soak in the outdoor sunken tub, the air fragrant from the fresh, tropical flowers in the surrounding garden.

"I tried asking Leonie and Luc, but they refused to tell me," I answer annoyed, still pissed with them. "So, I had my investigator do the search." I hedge, not wanting to divulge the methods he used, including hacking her mobile and laptop.

"Hhhmmm... I see," Lola says, more than likely envisioning the lengths to which I went to get the information.

I run my sudsy hands over her full breasts and cup their weight in my large hands as I knead them to distract her from this line of questioning.

"What is Lydie to you, Sebast—"

I cut her off, but she raises her hand and turns in the tub to face me, putting herself out of my reach.

"Don't... Tell me the truth. We both know that I saw her text where she calls you Sebbie, reminds you she'll be in town soon, and to be ready for her with no distractions.

What does she plan to do with you? Am I a distraction, Sebastian?"

Lola is trying hard to keep a straight face. But I can see the hurt in her eyes and hear the tears in her voice. I go to comfort her. Once more she stops me. I sigh and lean back against the tub lifting my face to the sky wishing that I could erase the whole encounter. But, I remind myself to listen to her and to set my ego aside.

"Lydie is a childhood friend... Period. She calls me Sebbie because she couldn't pronounce Sebastian when she was little. It's not a term of endearment. At... all." I stop to gauge Lola's reaction. Then, continue since she nods in understanding. "In Vegas at your celebration dinner, she told me about a business idea that she and her brother Lucien want to present to STEELE. So, I told her to book the meeting when they had it fleshed out. Our families are close because our mothers were best friends before they married and had us. So we do lots of partnerships as I explained to you a few weeks ago. The meeting is in two weeks."

I won't allow her to stay out of my arms a second longer. Instead, I move to her and lift her onto my lap, sloshing water out of the tub and onto the stones.

"You are not a distraction in any way. You know what you are?" I ask her, cupping her small face in my hand.

She shakes her head, and I raise my eyebrow.

"No, Sir," she whispers.

I smile at her correction to use her words and not a shake of her head.

"You are my girlfriend, Lola Lewis. And I am your boyfriend. Exclusive... Period," I tell her unconsciously, holding my breath in hopes she doesn't disagree.

Her silence makes me nervous as she looks pensively out at the Caribbean, but I hold out on saying more. I leave it to her to respond. After a while, she slowly returns her gaze to mine.

"I understand that you're new to relationships and I haven't had but two. So, yes, we'll both make mistakes. And I too apologize for yelling instead of asking you about the text. I just felt that the way she behaved in Vegas insinuating that she's more than only a family friend. The flirtatious tone of her text combined with you laughing while reading her messages. Then your harsh defensive reaction... It just appeared she was more to you and I was less."

Lola ends quietly with a little shrug and her eyes downcast, glistening with unshed tears.

Her raw pain hits me in the chest like a sledgehammer and I flinch. It's visceral. I lift Lola's face to meet my gaze and kiss her deeply. Desperate to put all of my unspoken emotions into it, to prove to her how much she means to me—more than I can express with mere words.

Lola senses the depth of my feelings for her. She wraps one of her arms around my neck, burrowing into my body. With her other hand, she guides my hardening shaft into her warm sheath to meld us into one.

LOLA

The words I love you bang behind my teeth, demanding I speak them out loud. But I swallow those three words back, afraid to open myself to hurt more. Rather, I connect with him in the only way that a woman and a man can. I cover his body with mine and put him inside of me like a key in a lock. I clamp down on him, holding his member in place. Then lower myself until he's fully seated in my core.

Slowly, I circle my hips and rock back and forth as his girth stretches me. I plant my feet on the bottom of the tub to give me better leverage. Lifting myself up and down, I ride Baz as my passion builds and increases my pace. I grip his strong shoulders never taking my loving gaze from his eyes black with ardency matching my fervor.

He must sense that at this moment I need to control our carnal union—not his dominance. Baz places his firm hands on my flanks keeping me balanced as I use my body to pound onto his, impaling my tight pussy on his massive dick unceasingly.

As my passion peaks, my inner walls quiver signaling my impending orgasm. Suddenly, Baz's fingers pinch my clit. I spiral out of control, screaming his name as my muscles ripple with wave after wave of contractions from the rapid, pleasurable release of my orgasm.

While I'm still amid my mind-blowing release, Baz effortlessly lifts me off of his lap—it's his turn. He flips me around onto my hands and knees, tightly grips my hips, and slams his engorged cock inside of my still spasming sheath. A possessive, feral growl rips past his clenched teeth.

Baz bucks and pumps into me, his fingers digging into my slippery flesh so firmly that he's bound to leave marks. His guttural groans make my inner walls grip his length as he drives deeper and deeper within me. Baz continues to jackhammer into my hole until his enormous dick expands impossibly further before he lodges himself in my core and roars his release. My name a prayer falling from his lips.

The sound is so loud that it resonates all around us and makes my body shiver in response to his triumphant outcry. I collapse into the water as he drops his heaving chest onto my back and cradles my head in his arm—we're completely spent by our erotic exertion.

My BODY THRUMS from two days of nonstop coupling as we lie on the exclusive beach for STEELE St. Barth's. Baz risked my ire, but refused to stay at Luc's private villa after we recovered from the tub. Once again, Baz insisted that I belong to him and that only he will see to my needs, including shelter. He also told me I could forget moving out of our penthouse when I admitted I stayed that first night at Luc's penthouse. Baz's possessive Captain Caveman really turns me on and I can't deny him anything when he's all testosterone.

Despite Lola's Coterie New York and Las Vegas boutique openings in a month, I don't regret taking a break after working long hours every day to meet the deadlines. It's worth it to relax here with Baz.

"Hey, the sun is scorching. I'm going in for a dip. Do you want to join me?" He asks putting his aviators on the bed of the cabana.

"Not right now, I can barely walk... Remember?" I smirk.

Baz busses his lips against my stomach above my string bikini bottoms and I giggle, ruffling my fingers through his thick, black hair. He lifts his gray eyes to mine and trails his tongue along the edge of bikini. I massage his scalp and stare back at him. He buries his face on my mound and inhales deeply of my instant arousal. A sharp nip makes me yelp and jump away from his mouth.

"Are you denying me, Pet?" Baz croons as he kisses the painful spot.

My nipples pucker and I suck in a breath when his

finger slips beneath the material and slide inside of my pussy. I clench on his digit and close my eyes, raising my hips from the bed.

Baz adds another thick finger and thrusts both of them in and out as my walls vibrate. He continues his assault until I clench on his fingers mere seconds from my climax. I arch my back, welcoming the pleasure barreling towards me.

Abruptly, Baz removes his fingers and towers over me sucking the digits into his mouth watching me intently with hooded eyes. I drop onto the bed with a frustrated growl, then rise onto my elbows to see him walking away from me to the surf. Damn, he's built like a god. His powerful body's well-defined muscles are magnificent beneath his olive-toned skin deepened by the few days in the sun. I lie back closing my eyes reliving the divine pleasure that Baz's body gives to mine.

Flirtatious peals of laughter and the sounds of splashing wake me from my daydream. I rise back up onto my elbows to find the source of the interruption. Some topless trollops are splashing Baz and giggling like hyenas when he rises from the water, the sun glistening on his wet skin, looking like Adonis Rising from the Waves. He pushes his hair back out of his eyes, then says something to the two women that I can't hear from this distance. But his gestures are obvious as he points in my direction and nods his head. They just laugh and move closer to him without ceasing their childish deluge.

To hell with that nonsense! With a menacing growl, I

leap off of the cabana's bed and stalk over to the giggling groupies. I'm on fire by the time I get to them. So, I let them have a piece of my mind—the uncensored version. I call them every name that I can think of except for the one their mothers gave to them.

Meanwhile, I can tell that Baz is attempting to hold in his laughter by keeping his Dom face in place and his arms folded across his sculpted chest. I almost forget what I'm snarling at the two hussies when he flexes and makes his pecs and biceps bulge.

I swivel my glare back to the bimbos, scared and not sure how to handle a petite firecracker seconds from exploding. So, they turn on their heels and scamper away, their fake asses implanted on the tops of their thighs. I watch them with smoke curling from my flared nostrils. No longer will I idly stand by and allow anyone to take my man!

SEBASTIAN

*J*t's been just over two weeks since Lola and I returned from what felt like a honeymoon or at least the start of a new chapter in our relationship. She really put it in perspective when she told me to envision Luc as Lydie and me as her. Just imagining reading a text from Luc to Lola that I interpreted as flirtatious makes my blood boil. So, I get an idea of her reality. We've moved on and promised each other that we would talk things out, not yell or accuse. All is good in our world. I muse as I wait for Lola in my office so we can go to dinner at Le Bernardin with my roommate from Harvard and his newlywed wife.

My thoughts as I stare at the Manhattan skyline standing behind the desk in my office.

"Sebbie!"

I'm surprised to hear Lydie calling out to me since she and Lucien are not due in until tomorrow afternoon for our meeting. Turning to face her, I realize Lucien is here, too. Lydie is a tall, gorgeous woman with waist-length dark brown hair that flows down her back and intelligent green eyes—the signature Jackson family trait. She's only six inches shorter than me in high heels. Her long, shapely legs easily close the distance between the door and my desk. Lydie wraps her arms around my neck and kisses my cheek, the edge of her lips close to the corner of mine.

Just at that moment, Lola walks into my office and starts when she sees Lydie in my arms, her hazel eyes darkening. I quickly step away, removing my hands from Lydie's back and attempt to convey with my eyes that nothing bad is happening. To Lola's credit, she visibly shakes off her triggered ire and replaces her frown with a smile.

Lucien who caught my reaction and followed my gaze quickly surmises the situation and defuses it by extending his hand to Lola with a charming smile.

"Hello, I'm Lucien Jackson and this is Lydie my sister. We're close friends of Sebastian and his family," he adds to dispel any thoughts of romantic involvement between Lydie and me.

Obviously, Lola appreciates Lucien's gesture and her tepid smile warms tenfold, making her hazel eyes glow.

"Nice to meet you, Lucien. Sebastian speaks highly of you"—she responds shaking his hand—"Lydie and I met."

She looks beyond Lucien to Lydie, who still stands beside me.

"How lovely to see you, again, Lydie," she continues as

she saunters over to me and lifts her lips for a kiss I eagerly provide slipping my arms around her.

"You're early. Isn't your meeting tomorrow afternoon?" She sweetly asks Lydie as Lola turns in my arms to lean her back against my front, blocking Lydie from me. My dick jumps at Lola staking her claim on me.

"Well—" Lydie scowls, folding her arms across her full breasts, but Lucien cuts in to respond to Lola.

"Yes, I flew in from Paris earlier than expected. So, we thought it would be nice to have dinner tonight. Are you free?"

Lola tilts her head back to look at me over her shoulder since she knows we already have plans and she'll defer to me to answer Lucien's question. My dick lengthens at her submissive behavior outside of sex and play.

"We have dinner plans already with my roommate from Harvard—" I start.

"Oh, do you mean Scott or Alan?" Lydie interjects.

I have to restrain myself to keep from rolling my eyes at her attempt to show her familiarity with my life to one-up Lola. I can tell that she picked up on Lydie's ploy when Lola's shoulders stiffen.

I pointedly ignore Lydie's question and continue my sentence, "and his newlywed wife at Le Bernardin in thirty minutes. So we must pass. However, we're all on for the opening of Lola's Coterie New York tomorrow night, including Malcolm."

Lola relaxes against me again and I inwardly sign in relief.

For the second time, Lucien prevents Lydie from speaking by bidding us good night and taking her by the arm to escort her out of my office. He turns and winks at Lola and me as he shuts the door.

THE NEXT MORNING, I wake as usual before Lola. Since our connection in St. Barth's, I take time to watch her sleep so peacefully before I fill my mouth with her sweet juices, then ravage her waking body. As I lie on my side resting my head on my forearm, I reach out gently to swipe a lock of raven hair blocking her face so I can see. Lola is so beautiful.

I'm glad that we didn't derail after the encounter with Lydie—I owe Lucien one. Lola and I had a fantastic time with Scott and Lauren. It was the first time that Lola met a close friend of mine. Not because I didn't want her to meet anyone, rather we've been busy and I don't have many friends outside of my family including the Jacksons.

It was also interesting to observe Scott fall head over heels in love with Lauren and marry her so quickly. Scott, who like me was a self-professed bachelor and dedicated to his family's business. I remember teasing him about it being a shotgun wedding. With a far-off look in his eyes, he told me he can't wait to settle down and to one day have children with Lauren. Then, he looked back at me and told me when the right woman comes along, the one who's worth it, she'll change my mind like Lauren changed his. I thought he was nuts and declared that wouldn't be me.

Now, I run my fingertip along Lola's silky cheek, and she murmurs my name. Even in her sleep she responds to my touch. She satisfies my Dom plus she's smart, funny, gorgeous, and not a gold digger. I brush my thumb over her full lower lip and she opens her mouth with a sigh. Is Lola beginning to make me rethink my life? Perhaps Scott isn't so crazy.

As if sensing my thoughts and growing desire for her, Lola opens her eyes and stares at me, then pulls my face to hers and kisses me passionately. All thoughts, questions, answers, fade away. I roll on top of her soft yielding body and settle myself between her welcoming thighs. My inner caveman grasps her butt in my hands to hold her steady as I plow my cock to the very end of her wet sheath, possessing her fully.

"Mine!" I growl into her ear as she mewls.

* * *

LYDIE AND LUCIEN want STEELE International to partner with Jackson Corporation's new members-only, high-end, jet-set hot spots. The concept is a combination of beach bar, restaurant, and dance club with the first location at our hotel and marina in Monte Carlo followed by our St. Barth's resort. They want to roll the spots out at key STEELE properties worldwide over the course of five years.

The name as expected is typical Lucien—Jackson Hole a play on a watering hole for drinking liquor and accessible body areas. Their brands of liquors and cigars would be the exclusives and Lucien would create the menus and signature cocktails. The three areas would be the bar, the restaurant, and the beachfront that offers cabanas, beds, and chaise lounges. Sexy hosts, bartenders, and servers plus dancers and live bands and deejays would round out the staff and entertainment. Basically, Jackson Hole would be LEVELS on the beach minus the BDSM.

I think back to Lola and me on the STEELE Resorts beaches in Monte Carlo and St. Barth's and can visualize the attraction and the benefit. However, the main and the only relevant requirement: will Jackson Hole at STEELE add to our bottom line?

We continue talks for a few hours with our teams weighing in, making recommendations, switching properties, expectations, and so forth. It's easy to make a speedy decision since our companies have partnered on so many successful endeavors over the years. The rehashed idea satisfies all parties.

"That ran smoothly," Lydie pushes her chair back from the conference room table and stretches her long legs.

I can't help but admire their sinuous lines as her skirt rises to reveal her bare thighs. Still, she's not Lola and I've never felt a sexual attraction to Lydie. I'm her confidante and close friend since we're the eldest of our siblings. She's working to take over the helm at Jackson Corporation from her father just as I am with STEELE from mine.

Over the years, she's turned to me for advice, especially since she craves approval from her father Connor. Lydie will do anything to prove she's as good as a son to lead. The son in question is Lachlan, my best friend and the second oldest of the Jackson clan. He's two years younger than me and one year younger than Lydie. Lachlan being the eldest son—Lucien is the third child and Laurent is the fourth—is the President of Liquor and their father's preferred heir. But Lachlan is a reluctant heir apparent because he loves his older sister more than he wants to please Connor. He refuses to hurt Lydie, knowing how much she wants to run their company.

For now, Uncle Connor is holding out on making an ultimate decision since he's not retiring for at least two years. He's also hoping in that time, Lydie will marry and turn to her family life and Lachlan can step up to the helm.

"Yes, I'm thrilled with the outcome and eager to get in touch with the Los Angeles-based architecture firm Hawkins, Brown, Dennis LLP that specializes in high-end bars, restaurants, and clubs. A business acquaintance worked with them recently. She recommends them and says that one of their associate architects is extra creative and forward thinking—"

As Lucien goes on excitedly about the plans, my mobile vibrates with a text. I pull it from my trousers pocket and discover it's a message from Lola. I smile to myself and open it immediately.

Hi! Melody said your meeting is over. Hope it went well ;)

I text her back: *Hi, babe. We're all set, thanks. Just wrapping up.*

Okay. I'm looking forward to the opening tonight! TTYL

"Earth to Sebastian..." Lydie says tapping her Montbanc, gold, fountain pen on the table to get my attention.

"Yeah, just a second," I tell an impatient Lydie while I shoot a quick response that I can't wait to see which dress I'll rip off of her later.

"This girl has you—" Lydie starts.

But Tina interrupts as she comes into the conference room to tell me I have an urgent call from one of my project managers that needs my immediate attention. I tell Lydie and Lucien that I'll catch them later at Lola's opening as I leave the conference room.

LOLA

J've been so busy since Sebastian and I returned from St. Barth's. It's been a whirlwind of activities to prepare for Lola's Coterie New York's opening: print and television interviews with various fashion, beauty, and business editors and correspondents; model selections and alterations for the fashion show; fix last minute glitches; complete the staff; confirm the attendee list; so on and so on.

Not to mention the Las Vegas boutique's opening two weeks later and all that entails—just in another city. I've flown out a few days to take care of some details and even hired a second assistant Billie Chandler who's based in Vegas to handle that office. Sebastian's director of their West Coast retail properties recommended her to me.

Billie is a Southern belle originally from Savannah, Georgia. But the contractors and anyone else who's tried to take advantage of the petite, brown-skinned beauty have learned beneath her sweet accent and big green eyes is a feisty woman. She's like me—can charm the best of them, but can turn into a spitfire when necessary. Billie is an absolute godsend, I smile to myself.

When I'm in Vegas, I stay at Baz's suite. However, I'm keeping New York as my base. Not just because I made myself the promise to buy a place here if the company's expansion deal went through, but also because I enjoy being with him. It's been so good recently. I'm afraid to jinx it or scared something will happen. I try to shake the fear that haunts the edges of my mind and tell myself to just live and not worry about unexpectedly losing what I love. Do I love Sebastian? I definitely feel deeply for him and almost told him those three words when we were in the bathtub in St. Barth's. Once these two boutique openings happen, I think I may tell him anyway and just let whatever happens unfold.

I woke this morning to Baz touching my face and looking at me tenderly, then taking me forcefully with his punishing and possessive ravishing of my body. My nerves have been on edge all this time, so it helped to reassure my feelings for him and to calm my agita.

It was the first time that we had sex in a few days because I've come home late, exhausted from my busy schedule. Baz has been patient especially for a man who's used to fucking for hours each day. But he gets why I'm driven and determined to make my company a success— another reason that I'm falling for him. I'm still on track for my expansion plan by my thirtieth birthday that's right after the Vegas opening. I haven't even planned what I will do, yet. I've been all over the place.

The morning flew by and it's already time for lunch. Blair called for delivery of salads—I don't want to be a bloated balloon in my sexy, revealing dress tonight. I send a text to Baz to check in on his meeting with Lucien and Lydie. Ugh!

Baz tells me she's only a childhood friend and they're not romantically interested in each other, only confidantes. But somehow, I perceive Lydie wants more. Until me, she may have only held back because Sebastian hadn't made a move and has been a serial playboy who fucks different women without commitments. I think she was just biding her time until he was over that phase, but now he's seriously involved with me and it's bothering her. I can handle Lydie secretly lusting after Sebastian. But if he betrays me, our relationship ends. I put those disturbing thoughts aside and send him a quick text.

Hi! Melody said your meeting is over. Hope it went well ;)

He texts back: *Hi, babe. We're all set, thanks. Just wrapping up.*

Okay. I'm looking forward to the opening tonight! TTYL

There's a longer pause than before, so I scroll through my email. My mobile dings with a new text from Baz.

I can't wait to see which dress I'll rip off of you later...

I giggle, but don't respond because I just received an email from Billie that I need to handle and Luc walked into my office. Work now, party later.

"Hi, is everything okay?" I ask Luc who has a frown on his face.

It's good to see him since we usually spend time together regularly when I was in Paris full time. I'm thankful that he's been here for the past few days helping me to tie up loose ends and just being the rock that I've depended on for so long. Now that I think about it, I've spent more time with him than I have with Baz over this week. A reversal from the first time we were in New York. Despite the frown, Luc is as dashingly handsome as ever in his bespoke three-piece charcoal gray suit, white dress shirt, cobalt blue tie, and black Oxfords.

"*Oui, tout est bien,*" he says waving his hand with a half smile that doesn't reach his stunning, dark blue eyes enhanced by the color of his tie.

I don't believe him for a minute, but I don't press him for the truth. As if on cue, Blair comes in with the food delivery bags, but pauses when she sees Luc. Then her eyes fly to mine with a worried expression. She stands there frozen in place with the bags dangling from her hands as though she's not sure how to proceed.

I glance between the two of them and surmise that something is amiss with the pair, confirmed when Luc avoids my gaze. To break the tension and to act normal, I ask Blair to set up the conference table by the windows with lunch. I talk to Luc about Billie's email that shares some of her concerns about the Las Vegas boutique. Luc looks relieved and grateful for the subtle distraction.

"Tell me, what's happening?" He asks as he leans

forward, elbows on his knees, eager to move beyond the tension in the office.

We discuss the details over lunch. Luc has the best advice and puts my mind at ease. It's decided that we won't delay the boutique's opening and instead I will stay in Vegas afterwards to settle the issues and to monitor the outcome. I call Billie to fill her in so she can take care of the next steps. She's on her way to the airport for tonight's opening, but can handle it before her flight takes off. That crisis averted, we move on to other business for the next couple of hours.

A SHARP WOLF whistle pierces the air as I stand in front of the dressing room's center island putting my earrings on. I peer over my shoulder to see Baz standing in the door looking every inch the powerful Alpha billionaire in his custom black tuxedo and patent leather dress shoes. He's leaning against the doorframe with his hands in his pockets, smirking at me. Sexy devil!

"My... My... My... look what we have here..." he says as he stalks towards me with a glint in his predatory, gray eyes.

I shiver in anticipation as his eyes rake my body from head to toe. I can tell he sees my nipples pucker against the pewter chain mail, floor-length, vee-neck, backless gown that clings to my body. The sheer detailing under my bust and zigzagging along the sides add to its sexy appeal. The glam squad worked their magic with my hair split down the middle and brushing against the sides of my breasts and sultry makeup. I slowly turn in a circle with my hand on my hip to give him the complete view. The five-inch metallic sandals give my ass a lift and elongate my legs. I'm proud of the dress since it's my novel idea to debut an evening gown collection based on lingerie soon.

"Hot damn, Little Pet. Who are you trying to impress tonight?" He croons as he steps into my personal space.

With a coy shrug, I respond, "My Dom, Sir."

Baz hisses in a breath and bites his lower lip as if trying to control himself. With a shake of his head, he refocuses and pulls a red box from the breast pocket of his jacket. The click of the closure reveals an extraordinary pair of giant diamond drop earrings that glitter in the light. My mouth falls open and instinctively, I reach out to gingerly touch them.

"For you, Little Pet. Allow me," Baz says as he hands the box to me and removes the diamond studs that I had just put on, then replaces them with his gift.

I turn to stare in the mirror on the island and grin broadly at the sight of the exquisite diamonds dangling from my ears—they're so big. I glance at his reflection and beam.

"Thank you, Sir"—I turn to slip my arms around his neck and press my body into him—"They're incredible."

THE RED CARPET is bustling with photographers, television crews, and international glitterati. My heart pounds in my chest as I step out of the Maybach and take Baz's hand. Feeling my nerves, he squeezes my hand and puts it into the crook of his elbow, pressing it close to his side as he bends down and softly kisses me. The paparazzi go wild and scream our names. I seem like a movie star!

We make our way down the carpet, posing for pictures and chatting with reporters. Leonie and Giovanni are just ahead of us. When Leonie hears them calling my name, she turns and makes her way back down the carpet towards Baz and me. Giovanni holds her hand possessively.

"*Chérie*, this is your night!" She gushes.

The supermodel looks fantastic in a sexy outfit: a white, silk satin, elbow-length shirt that only reaches above her navel with the top buttons open to show off her cleavage; a low-slung miniskirt made of Swarovski crystals with a slit up to the belt buckle at her waist; clear strappy sandals with double buckles above her ankles. Her long legs and flat tummy are amazing. Her smile is as dazzling as the crystals. Leonie tosses her back-length hair and twinkles her amber eyes as she hugs me close. The paparazzi reach a frenzied peak and thousands of flashbulbs pop.

Luc appears in a classic tuxedo cut perfectly to emphasize his height and muscular frame. He, too, hugs me and congratulates me on my success—ours I correct him with a smile. I swear that there are tears in his eyes, but he blinks and the moment passes. All of us pose for the cameras before we walk through the doors of Lola's Coterie New York.

The boutique is breathtaking and resembles my other

locations, but with a nod to New York with the Manhattan skyline featured in the hand-painted wallpaper instead of Parisian street vignettes. It's the largest of my boutiques with three floors and includes a section for custom design requests. It was Baz's idea to make this location different and do the same for the others. Not cookie-cutter replicas, each distinct. I've already commissioned redesigns for the London space to continue the concept.

The night is like a dream. The boutique impresses everyone. A few hours later, the party winds down. I slip away to have a moment to myself as my emotions hit. I find a spot near a corner that's slightly obscured by an étagère and watch the scene in front of me with a wistful smile.

"Oh, no, that's nothing. Our families expect Sebbie and I will marry. He's just sowing his wild oats as they say—"

"Well, he seems pretty involved with the designer—"

"No, Sebbie is just getting her out of his system before we settle down next..."

The voices trail off as they pass, not realizing that I'm standing here. I recognize Lydie's voice, but not the other woman. I'm stunned. My stomach knots and bile rises in my throat. With a slight cry, I rush to the staff area clutching my arms to my chest.

Somehow, I'm able to regain my composure. More like I hear my father's words in my mind, "Lola, are you a wolf or a super wolf? Because there are no sheep in this family." I make my way back to the main salon. Even the sight of Lydie's hand on Sebastian's forearm doesn't make me lose my shit. I also remember that we promised to talk things through, so I'll wait until I speak with him. However, I can't bring myself to go over to Sebastian. Instead, I walk over to the temporary bar, finish a glass of champagne, and take another as I turn to decide where to stand.

As I scan the clusters of people who remain, I catch Sebastian's eye. He smiles and bids me over. But I shake my head and sip the bubbly. He frowns and walks over, Lydie's eyes follow him like a hawk tracking its prey. I have to take a deep breath to hold on to my calm.

"I was looking for you," Sebastian says as he puts his hands on my hips and draws me in for a kiss.

I avert my face and ask softly, "Were you?"

Sebastian leans back and squints his eyes, trying to gauge my mood. It's a struggle, but I keep a neutral face. He can tell something is off. So, he pulls his mobile from his trousers pocket, sends a text, then takes the flute from my hand and places it on the bar.

"Let's go," he commands and grabs my hand striding through the crowd ignoring people attempting to engage us in conversation. Once we get outside, he doesn't hesitate at the calls of the remaining paparazzi and puts me in the sedan. He doesn't say a word until we're in the penthouse.

"What's wrong?" He asks.

I open my mouth, then close it.

Sebastian flares his nostrils and pins me with his Dom stare.

I inhale a deep breath and square my shoulders, "Are you sowing your wild oats with me before you marry

Lydie?" The words rush from my mouth and my stomach churns just hearing them.

Sebastian visibly flinches and takes a step back, frowning as he runs his hands through his hair.

"What the fuck are you talking about?" He asks, barely containing his fury.

I cross my arms over my breasts and plant my feet, bracing myself for a fight. "Do not curse at me!" I retort. "That's what I overheard your 'family friend' telling some woman twenty-five minutes ago!"

"Whaaat???" Sebastian yells and stops pacing to stare at me, his mouth set in a line.

A throw my hands up and repeat myself, then add that he told me she's just a confidante in air quotes. My snarky response sends Sebastian in a tizzy and he stalks towards me. I back up until I bump into the wall. I raise my hands and push on his chest as he pins me in place with his enormous body.

"And you believe her?" He seethes in my ear.

Fuck if my body doesn't react to his dominance and my pussy throbs and gushes.

"I'm asking you aren't I?" I boldly quip, glaring up at him with my eyebrows lifted.

"Are you asking me or are you accusing me, Lola?" He continues in a low rumble glaring right back at me.

"I'm asking you, dammit!" I yell and hit his hard chest with my small fists, trying to hold my angry tears back and ignore his massive bulge poking my stomach.

Sebastian searches my eyes for what seems like an eternity. Then his features relax and he lifts my hands above my head placing his palms against mine twining our fingers pressing the backs of my arms against the wall. I whimper and squirm to move away. He's too much, too big, and I can't think with him so close and so dominant.

"No, I am not sowing my wild oats with you nor am I marrying Lydie. I do not understand why she said those lies. But, I will find out," he ends ominously, breathing it in my ear as he brushes his lips and nips along my jawline.

My body shudders and I arch my back, baring my neck to him in submission. Fuck! It's a love-hate situation that makes me so angry with myself. I love the way I feel with Baz, but I hate that I submit so easily to him. It messes with my mind. The question if it's worth it falls aside. Baz bends his knees and rocks his erection against my mound as he whispers words of desire and need along my skin, amping up my arousal. I moan and pull against his powerful hands, aching to touch him and hold him buried within me, soothing the pain in my heart.

"I'm yours, Lola... Only you... I promise," he croons.

Baz takes off his bow tie to knot it securely around my wrists, pressing my arms back against the wall. When he's done, I maintain the position like a good sub.

The telltale sound of his zipper reaches my ears as Baz frees his cock and I shudder, my nipples hardening. He lifts my gown up to my waist and pulls my thigh around his flank as he thrusts his throbbing cock deep inside of my dripping pussy.

"So good, baby... Fuck," Baz's voice is rough with male

desire as he rocks his hips pushing his bulbous head further inside as my channel adjusts to his size. "So tight and wet. All for me, Lola? Are you mine?" He groans when he's fully seated within my welcoming depths and my inner walls tighten around his girth.

I hiss in a breath as he nudges my cervix. Fuck, he's so long and thick. I sense every inch and texture of his gigantic dick as it stretches my channel. I lift my other leg around his waist and dig my heels into his sculpted ass.

"Move, dammit... Fuck me!" I yell, pushing my arms against the wall and arching my back, my heavy breasts rising to his face.

I hear Baz growl and he widens his stance as he pummels me with his colossal cock, slamming my back against the wall with each painful thrust.

"Are you mine, Lola?"

He demands an answer I'm hesitant to give. Although my body already said yes when my juices gushed more to coat his dick easing its passage in and out of me.

"Harder!" I yell, writhing wantonly.

"Are you mine, Lola!"

Baz shouts as he rises onto his toes and uses his thigh muscles to pin me in place while he pulls my dress off of me. Then cages me in with his hands against the wall under my shoulders.

The sub is bare, and the Dom fully clothed, only his dick exposed for the brief moments when he pulls back before driving deeper back inside.

I lower my arms around his neck and hold on, trembling as he forces orgasm after orgasm from me, my body drenched in sweat.

"Are... you... mine... Lola!" He punctuates each word with a savage thrust that repeatedly bangs me back into the wall.

Baz won't stop until I answer, he's like a machine using his power and strength to tear down my defenses. I sense another round of orgasms threaten to undo me and I clamp down on his punishing cock to force his release so I can avoid the answer.

Baz howls in response. He lets my pussy have it as he pistons in and out before he withdraws completely, pushes me to kneel before him with my hands clasped behind my head, and jerks his shaft as he unleashes a torrent of his hot cum at my open mouth eager to have his seed. It's so much that it rushes down my neck, covers my breasts, and drips to my thighs. I watch enthralled as he coats my body, then reaches down and rubs his seed into my skin, marking me as his. The smell of our sex permeates the air.

"You are mine, Lola, whether or not you want to admit it," he says, his voice hoarse from his yelling.

I bow my head.

"*O*h, look!" Lydie exclaims nodding her head in the direction beyond where I sit at our table at Eleven Madison Park.

We're meeting for dinner so I can ask her about the comments she made at the boutique opening two weeks ago. Since Lydie has been out of the country on business, we couldn't meet in person. Other than texting with her to set the date, I've avoided all contact. The timing is good because Lola's not here since she and Luc left for Las Vegas three days ago. Unfortunately, I couldn't rearrange meetings, so I'll fly out in the morning—the opening is tomorrow night.

I turn in my chair to glance over my shoulder. A man in his mid-thirties across the restaurant on one knee proposing to the stunned woman at his table. I continue to watch in fascination as the woman covers her mouth and tears fall from her eyes. Even at this distance, I can see the enormous diamond nestled in a blue jeweler's box sparkle as the stone catches the lights.

As I watch the scene unfold before me, a vision of Lola and me in a similar situation pops into my head. I wonder how Lola would react. Would surprise overwhelm her? Or have a nonplussed attitude? Would she clap her hands and dance like she does when she's excited? Hell, how would I feel... Am I even ready to get married now or...

A light touch on my hand displaces the daydream. I turn back around to Lydie who has now curled her fingers around mine, smiling softly at me. I stare at her and wonder at what she said about us expected to marry. Has she always felt that way? She's never mentioned it to me, nor has my family. Could I marry Lydie and be happy? Was she even serious when she said it? Or just saying it to avoid an arranged date like the ones her father forces on her for a potential business merger between powerful families?

As I study more closely the way her green eyes shine and how she's leaning towards me while rubbing her thumb across my palm confirms she's definitely not pretending. She's in love with me. Fuck!

How the hell did I miss it all this time? Or is it only recently since I started dating Lola? Now that I think about it, Lydie has complained about not seeing me as much as during my pre-Lola days. Even then, Lydie and I only saw each other every few weeks because I was busting my ass trying to salvage that wreck of a deal I lost to Rockett.

Sure, Lydie and I have been close from birth. Since we are only a year apart and being that the Jacksons are an extended family of ours, we've spent much of our lives together. Yet, it never occurred to me to view her romantically—at all. Lydie has teased me relentlessly about being a playboy, but never hinted at wanting me for herself. I just assumed that she just wanted me to be careful or to slow down. Now, I doubt it. This is some crazy shit.

Lydie has always been a grounded woman. She's not an airy ingenue. She's driven like me and focused on proving herself as the most able of the Jackson children to run their company when their father retires in two years. So, I'm, perplexed by this 180-degree turn in her behavior.

"How romantic!" Lydie enthuses squeezing my hand and smiling. "We should send them a bottle of champagne! I'll be so excit—"

I yank my hand from hers and abruptly cut her off.

"What are you going on about, Lydie?" I demand, scowling at her.

"Wh... What do you mean, Sebbie?" She asks clutching her hand to her breasts as though I stabbed her with a knife from my place setting.

"Why did you tell some woman that our families expect you and me to marry and that I'm just sowing my wild oats with Lola? What the fuck is that about?" I ask, my voice rising as I nearly lose control.

Lydie shifts uncomfortably in her chair and looks around to check if anyone overheard what I said to her. She looks down and adjusts the napkin in her lap, stalling for time before she faces me.

"What makes you think I said those things?" She asks in a gloomy voice.

"Lola overheard you and asked me about it," I retort, not giving a damn who hears me. I'm pissed.

At the mention of Lola's name, Lydie drops the coy manner and her green eyes pierce me as her face contorts in anger. She leans over the table to whisper-yell at me.

"How dare that gold digger whine to you about me! She's just another one of your bed warmers! You can't be serious about her? We're the more likely pair, Sebastian..."

As she continues her rant, I sit back stunned speechless staring at someone I do not recognize. I would have never imagined this venomous harpy in front of me as Lydie. I can only give her the excuse of snapping under the pressure that she puts on herself to please her father. Perhaps she feels that I could be the business merger Connor seeks.

I take time to get my thoughts in order and allow her to finish. After a few minutes, she stops, red-faced, chest heaving, and nostrils flared. Her eyes flit across my face to judge my reaction. I keep a neutral expression and regain control.

"Lydie, I apologize if at any point in the years we have known each other, I gave you the impression that we could be more than friends"—I raise my hand when she opens her mouth to speak—"Our families are close and you and I have shared more than I have with other women. But that does not equate to a romantic relationship, nor a potential one. I will forgive your comments about Lola and will not discuss them with her as it is best that the three of us remain cordial for our families' relationship."

I lean forward for emphasis, "However, do not for one minute believe that you can continue to slander Lola's name. Nor insinuate that you and I have a rapport beyond friendship. Do you understand, Lydie?"

The Dom in me takes control.

She sits back in her chair and studies my face. I can see the emotions play across hers as she decides what to do next. I hope that she understands and we can move forward without a blight on our friendship, but I mean what I said.

Once again, Lydie looks down at her lap and adjusts the napkin before she brings her gaze to mine. Her face set in an expression that I've seen her use in board rooms—cool and detached. Good, she's settled down.

"Sebastian, I did not realize how serious you are with her. I must admit the thought occurred to me you and I would make a brilliant team as we are so alike and close. But I can admit that I was wrong and understand you. Accept my apology," she replies humbly, but still an Alpha female.

"I accept your apology and appreciate your understanding," I respond with a nod.

She places her napkin on the table and rises as she tells me she has an early meeting and needs to get home. I stride around the table and help her from the chair. With a dismissive wave of her hand, she refuses my offer to walk her to her car and leaves the restaurant poised and dignified.

I watch her walk away and wonder if this will negatively impact our families and our business partnerships. But the Lydie I know is gracious. She would never cause a disruption. I can only hope that Lydie is in control, again.

* * *

"Hi, babe, I just landed. Where are you?" I ask Lola as I settle in the back of my Cullinan at eight o'clock the next morning. I'm eager to see her and flew out at six New York time.

"Baz... Hi..." Lola responds distractedly.

I can hear a male's voice whispering in the background. What... the... fuck!

"Who are you with, Lola?" I demand sitting up and gesturing to Dario to drive faster.

"What?" Lola's voice rises and I can hear a door shut.

"Who... are... you... with?" I seethe envisioning her lush body damp and sated from fucking some asshole in Vegas for a business convention. Fuck, it better not be Luc!

"Listen, Sebastian, I don't have time for your Captain Caveman shit right now! I'm in the middle of a crisis!" She screams.

Fuck, there I go, again...

"Sorry, darling. I didn't mean to accuse you of anything. It's early morning, and I just heard a man's voice in the background. Forgive me?" I ask in a conciliatory tone.

A beat passes, then Lola tells me to meet her at the boutique because there was a water leak that caused damage. I tell Dario where to drive and immediately make calls. The first to my younger brother Malcolm, who's already at STEELE Las Vegas. Heads will roll if they don't get shit fixed before Noon. My girl will not worry about a thing, just enjoy her boutique opening as planned.

I merely nod at staff who greet me as I rush through the lobby and casino to reach the mall entrance where Lola's Coterie Las Vegas sits. There are curtains in the windows and on the door to prevent passersby from seeing inside until the opening party. A security guard dressed in the STEELE Las Vegas uniform stands beside the door. When he sees me, he immediately opens the door and I stride in, scanning the group of workers and people for Lola.

"Sebastian!" I hear her cry out.

Lola is running towards me, her face red and swollen with tears. I hold her close when she throws herself into my arms and buries her wet face in my chest. I rub her back and kiss the top of her head, inhaling her intoxicating perfume. I can't help my dick from reacting to her curvy body, but ignore it so I can focus on the situation.

There's water tricking down from the HVAC unit on the second floor. The contractor told me it was worse before and that they expect to have it repaired in an hour. The actual damage is to the lingerie, furniture, and flooring. Malcolm called his associates at film studios and I called house staging designers I work with regularly for their inventory that Lola could use until she replaces the original pieces. Jets are on standby to bring lingerie from her Paris, London, and New York boutiques. I relay this information to Lola and she looks at me like her hero. My dick jumps and she smiles coyly at me when she feels it bump against her belly.

"So, it'll be fine, darling," I murmur as I brush my lips across hers. Damn, I miss her and she smells so good.

"Lola, Mr. Steele… Excuse me."

We turn to the voice and Billie stands there holding her hand over her mobile needing to speak with Lola.

"I will talk to Malcolm and the workers. Don't worry," I tell Lola as I kiss her forehead. "Nice to see you, Billie," I smile at the pretty assistant who nods, flashing a charming smile.

"Sebastian."

I turn to my right and see Luc walking towards me. I realize that it probably was him whispering in the background. I know that I trust Lola, I just don't trust him despite Lola saying he's her mentor and maybe involved with Blair. I take a deep breath to stave off my irritation.

"Luc," I nod and firmly shake his extended hand.

"I'll update you on the situation…"

Once again, Lola takes my breath away. This time in a sleeveless, deep-vee neckline, silver, intricately patterned mini dress with garnets sewn onto the delicate sheer material. Silver metal sandals add five inches to her height. Her raven hair is up in a messy bun and her makeup is a dewy natural except for the smoky garnet eyeshadow. She looks like a classy showgirl from Moulin Rouge. This time, I gift her with rare, red diamond earrings and matching bangles, two on each arm. Lola teared up when I put the set on her and thanked me with a kiss full of promises. She never asks for anything and it makes me want to give her the world. Gold digger, my ass.

I never leave her side as she mesmerizes everyone around her. Lola glows with pride and confidence, graciously accepting the well wishes and congratulatory remarks from the guests. When she and Leonie pose for photos, the flashes are blinding. Leonie looks just as ravishing in a floor-skimming, sheer gown embellished with tiny crystals that molds to her voluptuous body, only a flesh-tone thong beneath it. I'm still no closer to finding out what happened between her and Roger—everyone is mum. Mattei can't seem to stay away from her. I investigated his background and nothing stands out as dangerous. He's a billionaire from a prominent noble family. So, I'll just monitor things. I smile as Lola saunters over to me and wraps her arms around my waist, holding me close. I whisper how I will make her strip for me later and her face flushes as her laughter rings out.

"OKAY, brother, give it to me straight," Malcolm says to me as we eat breakfast at one of the resort's restaurants the next morning.

I kept Lola up all night as promised, now she's passed out in our suite upstairs. So, I'm catching up with him. It's been a while since we spoke in depth about anything besides business. Undoubtedly, he wants to pry into my private life.

"What?" I ask nonchalantly, sipping my coffee.

"Don't hedge with me, Baz. What's up with you and Lola? You've gotten close fairly quickly..." he responds, cocking his head to the side.

They're not used to me being with a woman longer than a few hours. I've been too busy to spend time with everyone like normal. Only Roger has seen me with Lola. So, I know that my family has loads of questions. When we get back to New York, I'll invite everyone over for dinner and formally introduce them to her. I'm sure that Lola will like to get to know my family, especially since she doesn't have a lot of friends who live there permanently. Her fashion crowd travels all over the world. A regular set of people may help her acclimate and not think so much about her parents. She and Haley are less than a year apart and besides my mother the only women. Perhaps they'll get along well.

"Yes, we have and I'm thrilled. I never thought I would be in a long-term relationship at this point in my career. But Lola... Lola just does it for me."

I can't explain it any more than that and Malcolm understands.

"When we get back, we'll have everyone over and introduce her formally. Is that all right with you, Dad?" I tease him.

"Whatever, fucker." Malcolm eyes me, then nods to himself. "Mr. Playboy is pussy whipped!" He guffaws loudly and the patrons turn to stare, including the two women who have been giving us the come-hither expression that we've chosen to ignore.

"Your time will come, bro, don't think for a minute it won't happen to you," I laugh along with him.

"I thought I told you?" Lola responds.

"No, you didn't tell me you were staying for a week after the opening," I grouse. "I hoped that we could spend a few days in Cabo San Lucas to relax."

Lola stops rifling through the files on the living room coffee table to peek up at me.

"Oh, I'm so sorry, baby," she says as she opens her arms for me. "I must have completely forgotten with all that was going on. Forgive me?"

I grudgingly go to her, and she pulls me in for a kiss. I try to convey my need to be with her alone on the beach, but she doesn't get the message.

Pulling away, Lola turns back to the files mumbling that she promises to make it up to me when she gets back. I almost reply with a snide comment when the elevator dings and Luc steps out. Great.

LOLA

*B*az left two days ago after staying with me for two extra days. I had to make up for bolloxing his plans to surprise me with a trip to Cabo San Lucas. So, I surprised him with a day at the spa where I played the masseuse and gave him a very, very happy ending. We had a delicious dinner at the resort's three Michelin star Italian restaurant with Leonie, Giovanni, Luc, Blair, Billie, and Malcolm—who flirted shamelessly with Billie. It appears as though things are back on with Luc and Blair. They spent the evening whispering to each other. Everyone has the hots for my beautiful, smart, and sassy assistants. I hope that I don't lose them soon; I laugh to myself. Baz and I spent the second day at my office on the third floor of the boutique, each doing our work. Afterwards we had an early dinner. Then retired to the suite where I worshipped my Adonis for the rest of the night and early morning before he had to go to the airport. I miss him already.

That's why I'm hustling through my work to leave a day earlier than scheduled. Luc had to return to Paris for a board meeting yesterday. But thankfully he already put in his time helping me with some heavy lifting. I had Blair stay so she can pitch in with Billie to get through some issues I don't have to address personally. So far, we've gotten through most of the pressing matters and I'm on target to fly out on a redeye flight.

Baz arranged for Blair and me to use one of the STEELE corporate jets. I already asked them to adjust the flight plan, but to keep it secret so I can surprise Baz. I can't wait to see his expression. I'm sure that he'll be super excited. I without a doubt will be, I think gleefully.

"THANK YOU, Stan. I know it's late or rather early morning!" I smile as I hop into the back of my Bentayga.

Just as I hoped, I finished my work and some additional interviews Malcolm arranged for me at the last minute with some prominent Vegas magazines and news shows. He's nice and told me that everyone is looking forward to meeting me. I smile, not sure what he means, so I'll ask Baz after I jump his bones.

I'm literally bouncing on the seat as we make our way from the West 30th Street Heliport to The STEELE Tower. I look out of the window thinking about all that I've accomplished in these past four months. I remember the first day when Stan picked us up from the same place.

Then, I shiver when I remember how I felt when Baz grabbed my arms to keep me from falling when I bumped into him at LEVELS New York. What did Leonie call it? *Un coup de foudre.* Indeed, love at first sight, I sigh.

The penthouse is quiet as I walk in on the bedrooms level, but my skin tingles as if in warning. As I put my bags down, I look around trying to pinpoint what's bothering me. A sound from the direction of the guest suites makes me head in that direction. My sneakers are silent on the tile floors.

As I get closer to the partially open door of the first guest suite, I head into the outer lounge to reach the bedroom. I hear a woman sobbing softly and a male murmuring. My heart skips a beat and my stomach flips. Who is in there? I don't remember Sebastian mentioning a couple staying with us. I brace myself as I walk closer to the door and peak inside.

"—your happiness is a top priority for me and I will do anything to make it happen."

Sebastian is shirtless, only wearing sweatpants sitting on the rumpled bed stroking Lydie's face, wiping tears from her eyes as she gazes at him lovingly. Her mussed hair from his fingers running through it. She's in one of his t-shirts.

I have to cover my mouth with both hands to keep the gasp from escaping my lips. Tears form in my eyes, and I back away from the door. Without looking where I'm going, I bump into a table and a low squeak pops out of my mouth. My hands move behind me to catch my balance.

Not wanting them to spot me, I quickly slip out of the lounge and into another guest suite. I press my ear to the door to listen for either of them coming to check on the sound.

"I see nothing. We must have misheard a noise... Let's get back to the bedroom."

My heart shatters as I listen to Sebastian. Before I physically break down, I crack the door open to check if I can make it back to the elevator undetected. Sure enough, I witness them returning together to the guest suite. Sebastian has his hand on Lydie's waist holding her tightly and she's leaning heavily into him. Once they're inside, I run to the foyer, grab my bags, and leave.

Once again, I find myself walking from Sebastian's duplex to Luc's penthouse in the middle of the night. This time, I'm not going back.

Sebastian & Lola's Story Continues: *Heighten My Desires*

Turn the page for the Steele Family, Author's Note, and a Preview of Part II

THE STEELE FAMILY

STEELE INTERNATIONAL, INC

Multigenerational, multibillion-dollar business luxury real estate development and management corporation

Headquarters & Family's Primary Residences:

The STEELE Tower, New York City

A modern, gray-tinted glass fifty-seven story mixed-use skyscraper on southwest corner of Fifty-Seventh Street and Fifth Avenue within Billionaires' Row

Global Offices:

- The United States of America (New York City, New Jersey, Chicago, California, Miami, Las Vegas)
- The Caribbean (St. Maarten, St. Barth's, St. Lucia)
- The French & Italian Rivieras (Nice, Cannes, Positano, Capri)
- Monaco (Monte Carlo)
- The United Arab Emirates (Abu Dhabi, Dubai)

STEELE FOUNDATION: A STRONG AND SUPPORTIVE HOUSE

Builds and manages attractive, affordable housing for urban, lower-income families

Available for download at **bit.ly/STEELEFamily**

Author's Note

Thank you for reading Sebastian and Lola's sexy, sizzling romance! I hope that you enjoyed the start of their passionate love affair. If so, I'd love to hear your thoughts, please share a review at **bit.ly/CLBooksSI1Review** and tell your friends.

Here's a hint at what's up next for this darling duo. Click below or flip the page for a preview.

Heighten My Desires Sebastian & Lola Part II

Did you catch on to the dynamism of Roger *The Responsible* and Leonie *The Lion*?
Well, you'll have your questions answered! Click below or visit https://amzn.to/3jbKoar.

Ignite My Desires Roger & Leonie Part I

At **CharmaineLouise.com** take the *Four types of lovers. Which are you?* **Quiz** to match your Sexy Fantasy: sub, Voyeur, Dominatrix, or Dominatrix sub Switch.

Follow me on social media including my CLBooks Coterie Fan Club below or on your favorite channels below and subscribe to my newsletter at **bit.ly/ CLBooksNewsletter** for a **Free Book**.

Ready to take it to the next level? Well do not hesitate, Pet… **Click here for Bedroom Kandi by Kandi Burruss Luxury Intimate Toys & Bedroom Accessories and Sensuous Bath & Body Products.** Now.

Fulfill Your Desires.

xoxo

Charmaine Louise

facebook.com/CharmaineLouiseBooks

instagram.com/charmainelouisebooks

twitter.com/CharLouBooks

pinterest.com/charlouny

amazon.com/Charmaine-Louise-Shelton

goodreads.com/charmainelouisebooks

bookbub.com/authors/charmaine-louise-shelton

STEELE International, Inc.
A Billionaires Romance Series Book 2

Heighten My Desires Sebastian & Lola Part II

Click on the link below or visit amzn.to/321M9RA to get
your copy.
Keep reading for a sneak peek!

Heighten My Desires Sebastian & Lola Part II

Books in the Series:

Discover My Desires Sebastian & Lola Prequel

(Available Exclusively to Subscribers)

Fulfill My Desires Sebastian & Lola Part I

Heighten My Desires Sebastian & Lola Part II

Ignite My Desires Roger & Leonie Part I

Stoke My Desires Roger & Leonie Part II

Justify My Desires Roger & Leonie Part III

Deepen My Desires Sebastian & Lola Part III

Capture My Desires Malcolm & Starr Part I

Embrace My Desires Malcolm & Starr Part II

Cherish My Desires Malcolm & Starr Part III

A Trilogy of Desires Sebastian & Lola Parts I-III

A Trilogy of Desires Roger & Leonie Parts I-III

Series Extras

Series Playlist

LOLA

"Oh... Oh... Oh... Fuck... Yeesss... Sssir!"

The sounds coming from my mouth reverberate around the Cellar as my Master rains an onslaught of ruthless blows to my bare ass and thighs. I lie naked face down, cuffed to the red leather spanking bench atop the main stage in the middle of the room. My poor bottom and puckered hole are on full display for all the members—the crème de la crème of society—at LEVELS New York to witness. His chosen punishment for me since I had the absolute audacity to scene with another Dom. Yes, it was revenge for my Master denying me pleasure when I wanted it and needed it the most. Do I regret it? Absolutely not I affirm as I relish the pleasure in the pain.

"Tell me, Naughty Girl. Why did you choose to disobey

me and scene with another Dom although you belong to me only and I expressly told you your climax will wait until you earned it?"

He demands in a clear voice that resonates throughout the Cellar for everyone to hear my greedy sins.

Thankful for the break in my spanking, I try to draw out the much-needed reprieve. With a voice hoarse from my cries, I tearfully reply to my Master.

"Ppp... Please—Hiccup—Please... Sir, I do not know what came over me—"

WHAP... WHAP... WHAP

I yowl from the punishing blows. Then attempt to twist my bruised bottom from his hard hand. The pain more intense since I'm mortified by the already large crowd gathered and growing quickly upon hearing my pitiful cries.

"Wrong answer, Naughty Girl. Let us try it again, shall we?"

He continues with a snarl, "Tell me, Naughty Girl. Why did you disobey me and scene with that Dom despite being told that you will have to wait until you earned your climax?"

WHAP... WHAP... WHAP... WHAP

I take a moment to clear my throat enough to squeak out my response, now chastened by his reprimand.

"Sssir... I was a naughty girl... And I was desperate for relief after you took me to the edge for over two hours this morning... I couldn't concentrate at work... Sssoo... I sought a Dom who would scene with me just until I reached my release nothing further… And… And… I did not expect you would ever find out…"

I end on a pitiful whisper, praying that my Master doesn't punish me further for admitting the full truth. I purposefully came to LEVELS tonight seeking my unsanctioned pleasure behind his back.

WHAP… WHAP… WHAP… WHAP… WHAP

"Is this where you sought your pleasure with a Dom behind my back, Naughty Girl? On this soaking wet pussy that is dripping your juices down your thighs in a puddle on the floor?"

I cringe and scream as my Master repeatedly spanks my swollen, throbbing pussy with his unforgiving fingers. My arousal almost peaks and I pant to catch my breath so I can answer him.

"Yeesss… Ssir!"

I keep my answer brief as my Master has taught me and because I hope to assuage him quickly so that this embarrassing punishment will end.

"Well, Naughty Girl, I can tell by the sweet smell of your arousal and by your engorged clit that you are enjoying this spanking. Which leads me to believe that you need another form of correction to ensure that you understand your mistakes and will avoid such erroneous behavior."

With that, my Master squats behind me to remove the red, suede-lined cuffs that anchor my ankles to the spanking bench. I watch him from over my shoulder admiring his devilishly handsome face scowling, his eyebrows scrunched above his piercing, gray eyes that lift to meet mine. I nearly swoon at the sight of him and feel my pussy clench in need of his ten-inch, thick member.

"Do you like what you see, Naughty Girl?"

He asks as he gently ghosts his fingertips along my calf, up my thigh, and up to my—

"Ooowwweeee!" I screech when his large palm slaps my sore butt cheek. Fuck, that was unexpected. Smiling faces tell lies is the truth.

My Master chuckles darkly to himself as he strides to the front of the spanking bench where his bulging cock strains against his trousers on level with my hooded eyes. I lick my glossy lips and seductively look up at him through my eyelashes.

"Ah, ah, ah Naughty Girl, I know how much you enjoy sucking me off, but no pleasure for you tonight. You will only have my ten inches in your tight little ass," he admonishes me. "Come."

My heart sinks.

He finishes unbuckling the cuffs at my wrists and helps me from the bench. Then takes my small hand in his large one as he leads me to the wicked St. Andrew's Cross. A cane leans against the well-worn wood polished from so many uses by Doms and their subs. Tonight, it's my turn. I shudder at the thought, not sure if it's in fear or desire.

Without words, my Master cuffs me once again, this time spread-eagle to the cross, my back to the awe-struck audience. I close my eyes when I realize more members have gathered on the other side. High-profile faces peer at me with rapt attention. They can fully see my naked body, my heavy, D-cup breasts with pebbled nipples, and swollen pussy lips fully exposed. My face is as red as I imagine my burning ass must be.

"Now, Naughty Girl, you will count out loud the ten lashes of the cane. If you miscount, we will start from the beginning. Do you understand?" He asks loudly, playing to the infatuated crowd who oh and ah in response.

I take a deep breath and open my eyes to look at him before I reply in a resigned sigh, "Yes, Sir, as you wish."

The whistling sound of the cane zipping through the air is my only warning. At first impact, I feel no pain. Then the sensation hits me like a shot and I scream out the first stroke.

"Ooowwww... One..."

My Master unrelentingly canes my ass and thighs, already reddened and marked with his large palm prints from the spanking that he gave me only moments before. I wantonly writhe against the St. Andrew's Cross, counting each of the savage hits until I can no longer think coherently and the sounds of the Cellar fade away.

My last image before I enter subspace is that of my climax galloping towards me. It's so intense I won't be able to rein it in. My only prayer is that my Master doesn't stop my punishment and allows me to cum. If he decides to bring me back from the edge, that would be pure torture. Fortunately, all thought ends as the welcoming darkness of floating freely consumes me.

. . .

"No... other... Dom... is... to... ever... touch... you... Pet!"

I wake to my Master growling in my ear as he savagely emphasizes each word with a harsh thrust of his massive dick in my tight ass. Just the sound of his voice sends me spiraling towards another climax. His authoritative power makes my pussy walls clench down hard on nothing in my empty channel and takes my breath away. I pant and push back meeting every thrust with one of my own—my sore, bruised ass slapping against his groin sending shock waves through my body. Damn, he feels so, so good! This is what I needed, I resolve, secretly pleased with my punishment.

Now, as the muscles of my pussy and ass tighten from my impending orgasm, I keen and ball up my hands. My fists pound the cross I'm now braced against with my feet on the floor, my Master having removed the four cuffs. He holds me with one arm hooked around my waist and the other hand clasping my throat to keep me in a submissive position. I feel his cock swell and he speeds up his movements. My Master becomes frantic, chasing his orgasm before he throws his head back and bellows my name with his release. His dick spews copious amounts of cum, some sliding down to coat my pussy and thighs. With a final upward thrust that lifts me onto the tips of my toes, he pumps the last of his jizz deep inside of me. I scream his name as I cum with him.

"Sebaaasstiaan!"

The sound of my hoarse voice screaming aloud rips me from my dream. I bolt upright in the bed sweating, breathing heavily, wildly looking around for the LEVELS members, the Cellar, and my Dom... Sebastian.

I flop back down against the pillows, noticing that the sheets are in disarray tangled around my body. Not the arms of my former lover holding me in his warm embrace as I hoped. The realization sinks in my brain past the haze of my sexy fantasy that I'm not in New York at all. Rather, I'm at the resort in Fiji for the eight-day fitness retreat as my birthday gift to myself.

A much-deserved getaway after the last four months of expanding my luxury lingerie company, Lola's Coterie to New York City and Las Vegas. Plus the short-lived, sizzling relationship that I had with Sebastian Steele, the Alpha billionaire whose company STEELE International, Inc. owns the retail spaces that my new boutiques are in. The third and fourth after my flagship in Paris and second location in London.

I made a vow to myself I won't go into my birthday dependent on any man. So I chose to end things with Sebastian upon returning home from Vegas early to find him with Lydie Jackson in the penthouse duplex that we shared on the fifty-fifth and fifty-fourth floors. Conveniently in located The STEELE Tower above my boutique. The Tower is a modern, gray-tinted glass fifty-seven story mixed-use skyscraper on Fifty-Seventh Street and Fifth Avenue on Billionaires' Row in New York City.

Better to be alone, than with someone who tells me one thing but does another. For the third and final time, I will not allow Sebastian Steele to dupe me into believing Lydie is only an old family friend and confidante. Especially when I saw them with my own eyes on the bed in one of the guest suites at the penthouse. Sebastian in only sweatpants, soothing Lydie who was in one of his T-shirts with mussed hair smiling lovingly at him. No, my thirtieth birthday marks a whole new decade for me and the continuation of my plan to expand Lola's Coterie globally. That's my sole focus once again.

I roll over with a groan and leave the stifling confines of the empty bed. I rip the damp, silk, babydoll nightie off of my hot, drenched body that's still reeling from a sleep-induced orgasm. Then head to the en suite bathroom of my cliffside villa on the private Fijian Laucala Island to shower before my first session begins. The retreat is hosted by Starr Knight, the owner of the Beverly Hills-based fitness studio and wellness center Starr Light Fitness & Wellness. I pray that she can help me get my head back in the game with her mediation, yoga, Pilates, and whatever else she recommends for an aching heart. I'll need the works, I reflect with a resigned sigh.

* * *

Available Now
Click the Link Below for Your Copy

Heighten My Desires Sebastian & Lola Part II

I dedicate my first contemporary romance novel to all who like me have Sexy Fantasies floating in their heads.

Fulfill Your Desires.

xoxo
Charmaine Louise

WELCOME TO CHARMAINELOUISE — THE SENSUAL LIFESTYLE

GLITZY. GLAMOROUS. STEAMY.

CharmaineLouise New York, Inc. invites you to indulge in *The Sensual Lifestyle* through **CharmaineLouise Books** and **CharmaineLouise Intimates**. CLBrands immerse you in *Sexy Fantasies* with CLBooks contemporary romance novels and give you *Sexy Under Things & Loungewear* with CLIntimates.

Ready to take it to the next level? Well do not hesitate, Gorgeous... Click here for Bedroom Kandi by Kandi Burruss Luxury Intimate Toys & Bedroom Accessories and Sensuous Bath & Body Products.

Charmaine Louise Shelton the Founder, CEO & Author of CLNY loves all things classic, elegant, feminine, and of course with an erotic edge! Favorite outfit of choice is a cashmere cardigan, leather pencil skirt, and seamed silk stockings with stiletto heels. Sexy Fantasy Type: sub with a dash of Voyeur. When not writing and designing, Charmaine Louise travels and spends time with her Maltese buddies, ZIGGY and Jynger.

CharmaineLouise — *The Sensual Lifestyle*

~ Visit online at **CharmaineLouise.com**

~ Subscribe to **CharmaineLouise Newsletter**

~ Find us on Facebook **@CharmaineLouiseNewYork**

~ Instagram **@CharLouNY**

~ Twitter **@CharLouNY**

~ Pinterest **@CharLouNY**
   #CLNY

CharmaineLouise Books *Sexy Fantasies* launched summer 2020. Sizzling, contemporary romance with your soon-to-be favorite Alpha Doms, Powerful Billionaires, and the women they lust after and love for second chances, insta-love, enemies-to-lovers, and more.

Want to chat it up and share your thoughts with other CLBooks Lovers? Read our blog, join our Charmaine-

Louise Books Coterie Fan Club and follow us on my author pages and social media to be in the know about the book release dates, exclusive content, giveaways, contests, and more!

~ **Purchase your eBook and paperback novels from my Author Page by clicking here!**

~ Read and subscribe to our blog *The World of Sex*

~ Connect on **Amazon Author Page**

~ **Goodreads Author Profile**

~ **BookBub Author Profile**

#CLBooks#CLBooksCoterie

CharmaineLouise Intimates *Sexy Under Things & Loungewear* debuted in 2003. Inspired by the sensuous sirens and sylph swans of the past and present, the hand crochet cashmere and silk collections are for the sexy: hence, the line names Ginger — Bombshell; Diana — Showstopper; Jackie — Timeless; Lena — Classic. Also known as The Movie-Star from Gilligan's Island; Ms. Ross The Boss; Mrs. Kennedy Onassis; Ms. Horne.

Do you thrive on seduction and being sexy lounging at home? Read our blog and follow us on social media to receive the tips, the latest additions to the collections, private sales, and more!

~ Read and subscribe to our blog *The Art of Seduction*

~ Find us on Facebook **@CharmaineLousieIntimates**

~ Instagram **@CharmaineLouiseIntimates**

~ Twitter **@CharLouIntimate**

~ Pinterest **@CharLouNY**

#CLIntimates

Fulfill Your Desires.